A QUEEN'S PRIDE

FELINE NATION - BOOK ONE

N. D. Jones

KUUMBA
PUBLISHING

Baltimore, Maryland

Kuumba Publishing
1325 Bedford Avenue
#32374
Pikesville, MD
kuumbapublishing.com

Publisher's Note: This is a work of fiction. Names, characters, places, and incidents are a product of the author's imagination. Locales and public names are sometimes used for atmospheric purposes. Any resemblance to actual people, living or dead, or to busi-nesses, companies, events, institutions, or locales is completely coincidental.

Book Layout & Design ©2017 - BookDesignTemplates.com

Editor: Chris at Hidden Gems
Cover Design: Ravenborn Covers
Original Character Concept Design: Shinji

A Queen's Pride/ N.D. Jones. -- 1st ed.
ISBN: 978-1-7352998-0-8

Dedication

Najja Akinwole
Baltimore City College High School Graduate (June 2020)
International Baccalaureate Diploma

Proud Momma

BLACK LIVES MATTER

Prologue: The Source

Refusal of the Panthera Tigris and Puma Concolor to Cede Their Lands North of SaltCross Mountains
1789

[Contains a proposed Treaty with the Panthera Tigris of 1788]

Communicated to the Fatherland Party Chief, January 13, 1790

Department of War, January 13, 1790

Sir:

The commissioners of the Chief of the Fatherland Party have received the answer of your Panthera Tigris and Puma Concolor children to our talk. We are saddened to share that the negotiations did not conclude to our satisfaction. Despite our best efforts to address the objections of our feline brethren to the policy of our government, we have no choice but to move forward without their agreement. Already have your neighbors, Panthera Pardus, Panthera Onca, and Acinonyx Jubatus, secured in themselves land south of SaltCross Mountains.

The objections of Tigris and Concolor are of nominal concern. Their lack of vision and civility will not halt our expansion efforts. The Fatherland Party will grow our nation . . .

SaltCross Mountains Treaty
1799

ARTICLES OF A TREATY MADE AND CONCLUDED BY AND BE-TWEEN

Generals David R. Murray, Benjamin H. Wilson, P. L. Albright, and Jacob S. Sawyer, duly appointed commissioners on the part of the Republic of Vumaris, and Unica Waddi of the Panthera Tigris Nation and Hubrax Cherla of the Puma Concolor Nation.

Article I.

From this day forward, war between the parties to this agreement will cease. The government of the Republic of Vumaris desires peace, as do the Tigris and Concolor Nations . . .

Article II.

The Republic of Vumaris agrees that the following lands will be the reserved territory of the Panthera Tigris and Puma Concolor Nations: AutumnRun, DimRock, and EarthBorough. The nations of Panthera Tigris and Puma Concolor henceforth relinquish all claims or right to any portion of the Republic of Vumaris, except in aforementioned territories . . .

Article III.

The Panthera Tigris and Puma Concolor Nations expressly agree:

1st That they will withdraw all opposition to current and future political parties.

2nd That they will not attack any human.

3rd That they will not engage in transmutation spasm beyond their reserved territories . . .

Article IV.

The Republic of Vumaris hereby agrees and stipulates that the country west of SaltCross Mountains and north of MistBreach Mountains shall be held and considered to be unceded. No human or person without the felidae gene shall be permitted to settle upon or occupy any portion of the land without the consent of the Nations of Panthera Tigris and Puma Concolor . . .

Treaty with the Kingdom of Shona (Feline Nation)
1902

ARTICLES OF A TREATY MADE AND CONCLUDED BY AND BE-TWEEN

Chief Thaddeus Rupert of the Republic of Vumaris, Progressive Action League, and Khalid Bambara Leothos and Sekhem Zarina Leothos of the Kingdom of Shona, viz., Panthera Leo, Panthera Pardus, Panthera Onca, and Acinonyx Jubatus.

Article I.

It is agreed that a boundary line between the Republic of Vumaris and the Kingdom of Shona should be fixed between the lands. The boundary line is as follows: beginning at the Osa Forest and ending at the Ocean of Samgi . . .

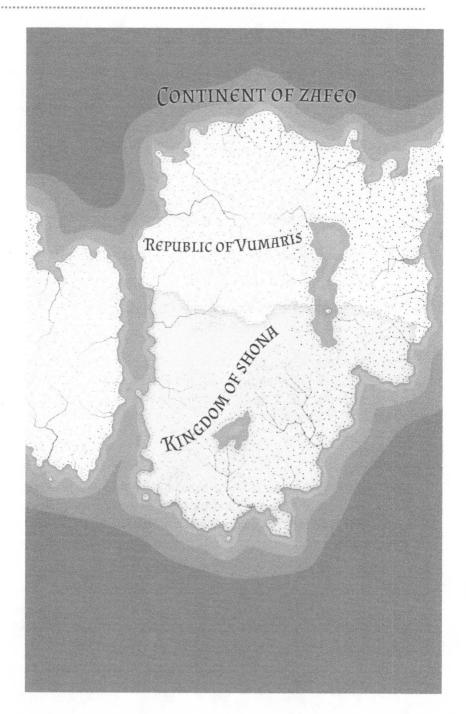

Chapter 1: Ruler of Lions

1985
The Republic of Vumaris
Historic District of Minra City
First Evolution Union Headquarters

"This is an insult."

Asha's father's words mirrored her own sentiments. She sat between her parents—Bambara and Zarina Leothos, the khalid and sekhem of the Kingdom of Shona.

The man seated directly across the conference room table from Bambara, Chief Silas Royster of the First Evolution Union Party, paled at her father's barely contained growl. Fingers laced in front of him and on the table, Chief Royster inclined his head at Bambara.

"I can understand how, from your perspective, you could view the addendum to the 1902 treaty as an insult to your kingdom. I assure you, Khalid Bambara, we do not intend it that way."

"Your intention changes nothing." Bambara crumpled the paper he held in his hand.

A copy of the same document had been given to Zarina and Asha. Upon reading it, Zarina had turned it over, the only sign of her displeasure with the document's contents. For Asha, she'd had to read the addendum a second and third time to make sure her interpretation had been correct. She wished it hadn't been, but she'd read enough treaties between the various nations of felidae and humans to comprehend the legal language.

Next to Chief Royster sat his second-in-command, Deputy Chief Frank London, a short, slender man with eyes too large for his slim face and a nose so narrow Asha wondered how he managed to breathe. But breathe he did, adding to the conversation in a nasal voice that grated.

"We haven't changed the treaty in eight decades."

Zarina lifted Asha's paper from in front of her, placed it atop her own, and then folded the documents into quadrants—a sekhem's subtler response than a khalid's. "You say that as if we should be grateful for your country's continued adherence to a treaty we signed in good faith. You were neither alive back then nor was your party in power." Zarina glanced over Asha's head to Bambara. "Did the First Evolution Union exist at the turn of the century?"

"Fledgling. Inconsequential. But yes, they existed."

Satisfied, Zarina returned her focus to the humans, the only other people in the conference room with the royal Shona family. The leaders' respective bodyguards were on the other side of the door. No one in either negotiating party felt threatened by the other. This meeting was but a formality her parents engaged in every time a new party came to power. A first for Asha but far from her last. By the time she ascended to the rank of sekhem, however, these men would likely be retired and another party in power. They meant nothing to her. Once she returned home, she wouldn't have to lay eyes on them again or their country for another fifteen years.

She refrained from sighing of boredom and slumping in her chair. Her parents wouldn't appreciate either action. But Asha would give anything to have been allowed to remain in her suite. Perhaps, if she had, she would've been able to coax Ekon from his duty as her Second Shieldmane and into spending time with her while her parents were preoccupied.

"We are in power now." Chief Royster's voice didn't betray him, but his scent did—a mix of anxiety and impatience. "My party's fifteen-year tenure has only begun. We are confident, at the conclusion of our term, the good people of this republic will see we are the best party and will reelect us for another term of office."

"Fifteen years," Bambara scoffed. "That is but a single grain in the hourglass of time. The treaty you wish to renegotiate is not even eight of those grains. But the Shona, the felidae, we were here from the beginning of time. You did not birth us." Bambara nodded to Zarina and Asha. "We birthed you. If you've forgotten, humans are the genetic anomalies, not us."

"Yet the humans of this republic have treated us as if we have no more right to this land and to exist than birds occupying a tree you want to use for your child's treehouse," Zarina added.

Her parents had an amazing knack for completing each other's thoughts with seamless effort.

Chief Royster's laced fingers tightened, but his face remained neutral. Deputy Chief London, however, glared at Zarina, his big eyes expressive in a way that delivered his silent anger over the reminder of their genetic inferiority to those with an active felidae gene.

"There are more humans than feline shifters." Chief Royster inclined his head again as if his statement of fact should matter to Bambara and Zarina. "We need more land to accommodate our growing populace."

"Hence the reason for the addendum to the 1902 treaty," Deputy Chief London added. "Surely you understand our predicament."

"Your predicament doesn't concern us, although humans have forced them upon us time and again." Bambara slid his chair back from the table. Zarina and Asha did the same. "There hasn't been a single treaty engaged in between a felidae nation and this country that has stood the test of time. Each one has been broken." Bambara stood and raised a finger, dark like his lion's mane—a sign of his strength and good health. "The government of your republic, regardless of the sitting party, have shown that you have no honor, that your word, including those written on paper, mean little."

"No," Zarina said and stood, "not little. They mean a lot, but none of what is actually said or written. We came all the way to your home, paying our respects to people who, no matter our genetic connection, think themselves superior."

Following her parents' lead, as she always did, Asha pushed to her feet. She hadn't liked the turn the meeting had taken, but she was relieved to have the negotiations end sooner than expected. If they hurried, Asha would have time to watch Vumarian television. There wasn't much she enjoyed about the country, especially the people, but their television shows and music were fantastic.

Chief Royster also got to his feet. "The talks have only begun, please sit. We haven't had an opportunity to fully explain our plan. We're not asking for much. One or two of your cities on the border of Vumaris and Shona. CloudFrost or FlameRock, perhaps. The addendum doesn't stipulate which Shona region would be annexed to Vumaris. That's what the negotiations are for."

Her father's low rumble of a growl was all the warning he would offer Chief Royster. The human would do well to proceed with caution.

Zarina slid the folded documents toward Chief Royster, whose wide eyes and red face were evidence enough that he wasn't a stupid man. Lucky for his party, since he would lead them for the foreseeable future.

Asha stood at attention, waiting for what would come next. Her father's warning growl hadn't surprised her, no more than her mother's regal forthrightness.

"For longer than I like to recall, humans have expanded into our territory, with no care to the felidae already in residence. You came, took, and killed, all in the name of your belief in your manifest destiny to spread your ideas and people from one end of the continent to the other." Palms going to the dark wood conference table, Zarina leaned forward, her stare taking in the men across from her. "You have no God-given right to our land. You never have."

"We've never encroached on the lands of your kingdom." Deputy Chief London, still seated, glanced from Zarina to Bambara then back to Zarina. "We've never been anything but respectful of the Panthera Leo's borders."

"That's because," Bambara said, his hand grasping Asha's and holding it with a father's protective touch, "Shona is so far south of the continent, with hot, uncomfortable climes for humans, that your people didn't think it worth their effort to wage war with our kingdom."

"Are you threatening war?" Sweat broke out on Chief Royster's forehead. "We have a peace treaty with—"

"Felidae not protected by your peace treaties now call Shona home. Shona is their refuge, the only land left to our kind on this continent. We will not cede a single plot of land to Vumaris."

Zarina placed her hand at the small of Asha's back. None of her parents' gestures were meant to treat Asha as a child but were intended to include her in their stance as protectors of their kingdom—people and land. "We do not wish war, Chief Royster." Zarina stepped around her chair. The hand on Asha's back subtly pushed her toward Bambara. "Indeed, we have even respected your laws against transmutation spasm while in your republic, despite our desire to run and roam. No, it is rarely the felidae who've brought war to humans. We've come in peace, and we'll leave the same way. Thank you for your time."

Deputy Chief London surged to his feet, his pronounced laryngeal prominence bobbing. "You can't leave. You haven't signed the addendum."

"Did you not hear my mate?" Bambara, who'd begun to move away from the table, his hand still holding Asha's, stopped.

"Yes, yes, of course, but we aren't done here."

"You may not be, but we are."

Deputy Chief London opened his mouth to respond, but Chief Royster cut him off with, "Frank, that's enough."

"What do you mean? B-but the party . . ."

With a firm shake of his head, blond hair cut short, blue eyes intelligent and with a hint of shrewdness, Chief Royster silenced his second-in-command. "Thank you for your visit. You're welcome to stay until your party is ready to return south. Minra is one of the oldest cities in the republic. There's much to see here and to experience. There's plenty in our country's capital that would appeal to a girl your daughter's age. I also have an eighteen-year-old and, I swear, she knows more about the city than I do." Chief Royster shrugged—his nonchalance almost believable. "The girls would have fun together, I'm sure."

She'd never had a human friend, and she doubted she would gain one this visit.

Leaning down, Bambara kissed Asha's cheek, his full beard scratchy in a way she both loved and hated. Asha couldn't imagine her father's human face any other way, but his beard had a coarseness to it that invariably left short-lived red marks wherever they touched her soft skin.

"Being unable to transmutate makes my insides itch," he whispered. "I want to run and play." Bambara kissed her other cheek. "Are you ready to go home, my hafsa?"

Hafsa, young lioness. When combined with sekhem, as in Hafsa Sekhem, the endearment became part of her title. A weighty expectation, that of the future sekhem of her people. To Asha's eternal happiness, her mother would hold the title for years to come, giving her time to mature into the role before the full weight of leading a country of millions of felidae resided on her shoulders.

"From our kingdom to your republic, we thank you for your hospitality." Her mother had such a melodic voice, even when the sound was of her polite but deadly dismissal.

Led by Bambara, with Asha in the middle, they exited the conference room, negotiations ended and the treaty's addendum unsigned. Asha couldn't care less about the addendum. Her parents' decision was final. They would not relinquish any part of their kingdom to Vumaris. War wouldn't come. There hadn't been a war between Zafeo's felidae and humans in over a century.

She wondered if there were more sitcoms to watch and if she could convince Ekon to watch them with her. If she did, they'd likely kiss. Asha did enjoy Ekon's kisses. The young lion had the softest lips and a tongue made for more than boasting.

Asha couldn't wait to put this trip to Vumaris behind her. It had been a colossal waste of time.

"Another race when we get home, Dad?"

Asha wouldn't win, but that never stopped her from challenging herself to be better, to be more than she was the day before. That had been the first lesson she recalled learning from her parents, and she'd taken it to heart.

Frank London cursed foully. Well, Silas thought, dropping back into his leather chair, at least his second-in-command had waited until after the door closed behind their Shona guests before launching into a bout of vile curses. Silas considered interrupting, especially when Frank referred to Sekhem Zarina by names no man should say about a woman—human or felidae.

"I thought lions were the king of the jungle. Apparently not in Shona." Frank rounded on him, as feral as any wild felidae. "You're just going to sit there?"

"You're upset enough for the both of us." With the tip of his shoe, Silas slid Frank's chair toward him. "Calm yourself and have a seat."

"They didn't sign. You know the platform we ran on, the promises we made. Of course I'm not calm."

"Sit anyway. We need to discuss next steps."

Ignoring Silas, Frank stalked to the line of windows behind him. There wasn't much to see beyond other restored buildings lining Imperial Street. Their headquarters was set in the historic district of Minra. A mile down the road, humans had once marched off to wage battle at Autumn Run. Two thousand soldiers had left the city, defeat of the Panthera Tigris their mission during the war. Only two hundred or so had returned—a devastating defeat—but the soldiers had come back with tiger heads, pelts, and teeth as proof that the felidae could be killed like any other animal. The young nation had used the loss at Autumn Run as a nationalist's battle cry. When they had returned to Autumn Run the next year, with triple the soldiers and weaponry, they had claimed every acre of land the felidae tigers and cougars had dared to deny them.

Humans weren't inferior to the felidae. The tigers and cougars had learned that lesson well, as had other felidae nations. Apparently, the Shona lions needed reminding of their place in Zafeo.

Silas didn't like his party's contingency plan, though. The felidae were the beasts, not civilized humans like himself and members of his political party. But, as Frank reminded him, the First Evolution Union had made promises to their supporters. If they failed to keep them, another party, likely the Fatherland Party, with their long history of dealing with and controlling felidae, would rout them from their hard-won political and social gains.

He'd worked too hard, kissed too many asses, and told too many lies to lose it all because two lions possessed more pride than common sense.

His back to Silas, Frank continued to stare out the window. The man had defected from the National Science Union Party, bringing with him a more conservative, anti-felidae element that didn't exist in Silas's party. The conservatives weren't Silas's base of supporters, but they were Frank's. Until this round of elections, neither of their parties had possessed enough political clout and deep pockets to oust the long-standing Fatherland Party.

Together, though, Silas Royster and Frank London were a winning combination—a force no one, not even the Fatherland Party, could stop. That included Bambara and Zarina Leothos of the Kingdom of Shona.

Finally, Frank rejoined Silas at the conference table, his too-large eyes reminiscent of an owl's, though the man pretended as though he didn't require glasses for reading small print. "We promised them land."

"I know." Silas reached for his full glass of water.

The meeting had been so short, the ice had barely melted. The three glasses on the other side of the table were also untouched. Khalid Bambara had taken one look at the glasses, sniffed each of them in turn, as if someone on his staff would be so stupid as to slip poison into the water, and then ignored them. His wife and daughter had done the same.

Silas drank half of the cool water before returning it to the coaster on the table, feeling better for having something in his stomach other than butterflies.

"This isn't the eighteen hundreds. It's not as easy to take land from the felidae the way the Fatherland Party once did. They also never went up against the lions. Everyone, including you, seems to forget that they left the Shona kingdom alone, and it's not because the southern part of the continent has two seasons—hot and hell."

"We made promises."

"I don't need the reminding."

Frank blinked those big owl eyes at him. "I think you do. You see immovable barriers where I see cats in need of neutering."

Silas's scoff didn't begin to cover the depth of his concern with the contingency plan his political aspirations had him agreeing to without the ethical hesitation a less driven man would've had. Still, were they prepared to enter the republic into a war with the lions over a political promise made during an election campaign when everyone said what people wanted to hear?

"The Fatherland Party left the lions alone for a reason. They are the only felidae who've always worked together as a cohesive unit. They've only ever lived exactly where they do now. Their roots are in that land. The first felidae can be traced to the grassy plains of Earth-Borough at the very southern tip of the continent."

"Then they shouldn't have a problem with us taking some of their northern areas. They can keep their grassy plains, dry-thorn forests, woodlands, scrubs," Frank said and waved a dismissive hand, "or wherever they enjoy lying down with flies. For them to be no better than animals on two legs, they've developed quite the financial center, and it's all in northern Shona."

"They aren't stupid."

"I agree, but their strength is also their weakness." Frank retrieved a manila folder from the briefcase he'd placed on the chair beside him before the meeting began. "Take a look."

Silas opened the folder Frank slid in front of him. Inside were at least three dozen glossy pictures of the Shona royal family. None of them had been taken close-up; likely a long-range photo lens was used, but the three figures were identifiable.

As Silas flipped through the pictures of the Leothos family—laughing, smiling, and talking—Frank added commentary.

"That one was taken in Menle. Those right there in Batari. Oh, and those four in Tanset. Notice anything?"

"You have an international stalker on your payroll, and the khalid and sekhem take a hands-on approach to economic diplomacy, traveling to other felidae countries, which is how they've amassed so much wealth."

Greed and power made strange bedfellows. Silas didn't so much dislike Frank as he distrusted him. They were only six months into their term, but the pictures spanned at least two years. Even without a date on the back of the pictures, Silas could've estimated the timeframe based on the images of Asha alone. Like his daughter, a female growing from girl to young woman changed more than a father liked to notice. But changes to their face and body were present all the same.

"Everything we want is staring you right in the face and you still can't see it." Frank snatched the picture of Zarina and Asha walking on a beach, barefoot and in sundresses, Shieldmanes on either side of them.

Silas drank the rest of his water, thirsty for more than the cool liquid.

"They take her everywhere." Frank slapped the picture on top of the others and closed the folder.

"So? Asha is their only child and heir. Do you expect them to leave her at home while they globe-trot?"

"Lionesses don't leave their young."

Silas may not think the felidae equal to humans, but he never confused their ability to transmutate into cats with them actually being like the felines into which they could transform. Except a few physical differences, such as vitiligo of the cheetah felidae, little visually distinguished those with an active felidae gene from their human counterparts.

"Parents love their children. That's kind of the point of having them. Lions are social, communal, fierce. They put family and pride above everything, which is why the Fatherland Party was never brave or stupid enough to go up against them. They are . . ." Silas trailed off, not liking where his mind had taken him or the smile on Frank's face.

"You've finally caught up. Now we're on the same page, Silas. The tigers and cougars were relatively easy to kill off. The tigers were tougher than the cougars, but they lived more like loose colonies than a strong confederation. By the time they moved past their narrow-minded independence to work as a united front against our forefathers, it was too late to save them. But the lions," Frank said and opened the manila folder again, "they are a pride . . . a family. That's their weakness. They'll sign because we'll take away the one thing lions care about more than land." With a thump of his index finger to the picture of a smiling mother and daughter, Frank's hand hovered over the image of Asha, heir to the Kingdom of Shona.

Frank stretched across the table until he was able to grab the two folded sheets of paper Sekhem Zarina had left. He opened the sheets that contained the addendum, smoothing out the wrinkles. "For her, they'll sign. For her, we can get them to do anything."

Silas thought how he and his wife would feel if they awoke one morning to find their daughter's bed empty and her gone. Desperation and fear would assault him first followed by anger, but also the willingness to do anything to have her returned unharmed.

"They're staying at Sanctum Hotel, a luxury hotel neither of us can afford. It must be nice to come from a country where your currency is the third highest in the world."

Grabbing a picture from the bottom of the pile, Frank showed it to Silas. "I know where they're staying. Sanctum Hotel is expensive, true, but also secluded. Their kali may have bought them the sole use of the finest hotel in this part of Vumaris, but their wealth has also given us the perfect place to execute our plan." Frank's self-satisfied grin reached his big owl eyes. "We have friends in all the right places, Silas."

More like the lowliest of places. But Silas had both taken their money and made them promises. Failure to repay his debts was not an option.

He looked at the picture of Sanctum Hotel. The building was situated in a quiet suburb south of Minra in the center of affluent gated communities. Most dignitaries stayed at the hotel when visiting Minra, the capital of Vumaris. But none of them had the money or the clout to reserve the 180-room hotel for their stay.

A part of Silas despised the Shona for having the power to do what most humans could not, as much as he envied the slice of heaven they'd carved for themselves in southern Zafeo. Unlike Silas, Khalid Bambara and Sekhem Zarina were beholden to no one.

That would soon change, however. "Call them. But tell them not to hurt anyone beyond what it'll take to secure the girl. We can't afford an international incident, and I don't want a child's death on my conscience."

Frank's twisted grin widened. "I spoke with the shift manager at the hotel this morning. I convinced the woman she wouldn't lose her job if she supplied the deputy chief with the room numbers for the Shona. The girl's suite is across the hall from her parents'. Rogueshade is already on standby. With a phone call and a go-ahead from me, they'll be at Sanctum Hotel when the sun sets. By morning, we'll have the girl and all the leverage we'll need to get our addendum signed. Don't look so worried, Silas. In a day, maybe two, we'll have everything we need to secure our place in Vumaris history. Our party will be unbeatable once we've made northern Shona ours. A girl's innocence is a small price to pay for success."

Silas wasn't so sure, but he nodded, grinned, and eyed the picture of Sanctum Hotel again. "Okay, yeah, fine. Make the call."

Chapter 2: Pure One

The Republic of Vumaris
Batari County, Minra
Sanctum Hotel

"May I be excused?"

Ekon smiled at the sugary sweet and oh so innocent way Asha had posed the question to her mother. Everyone knew between Khalid Bambara and Sekhem Zarina, when it came to Asha, the sekhem was the disciplinarian and the khalid the Maine Coon, the sweetest natured of the domestic cat breeds.

Several hours ago, the royal family had ended their meeting earlier than expected. The Shieldmanes had surrounded them as soon they'd exited the conference room, with Ekon pulling up the rear beside Mafdet, Asha's First Shieldmane, although she wasn't a felidae lion like all the other royal bodyguards. Ekon once asked Mafdet how a felidae cheetah had become Shieldmane to the Shona family. She spoke when it suited her. Mafdet had yet to answer his question.

Only Ekon and Mafdet were in the suite with the royal family. The other four Shieldmanes patrolled the large hotel, everyone's hunger sated after a delicious meal at the hotel's restaurant.

Asha grinned up at her mother, golden-brown eyes as beautiful as the young woman. She wasn't a spitting image of Sekhem Zarina, a six-foot female with golden eyes, a curvy figure she'd caught the khalid gazing at on more than one occasion, and full lips that concealed a tongue capable of stripping flesh from bone. Her curly golden-onyx hair framed her face like a lion's mane. It was this defining feature that Sekhem Zarina had passed on to Asha. The inheritance was as much her birthright as the title of Sekhem would eventually become. The name Asha, which meant *life* in the Ebox language of felidae lions, would be relegated to her past once she ascended to the throne. When that momentous time came, two or three decades in the future, Sekhem Zarina would bestow on her daughter a different name. One befitting her new status as Alpha of the Kingdom of Shona.

"What do you plan on doing this evening?" Sekhem Zarina asked Asha. "Fill your head with human situation comedies or blast their foul music, the way you did last night? Really, Asha, I don't know how you stand to listen to and watch such inanity."

"Everything here isn't bad."

"Yes, I know. But there is much corruption in this country, and I don't want you influenced by what passes as their culture."

"Music and laughter won't corrupt me. That's what my friends are for."

Khalid Bambara laughed. Sekhem Zarina and Mafdet did not. Ekon also laughed, but on the inside.

Hands at his sides, Ekon stood near the suite door, the same way Mafdet had positioned herself in the threshold between the suite's living room, where the royal family was, and the master bedroom behind her. Like Ekon, Mafdet wore black pants, boots, and suit jacket with a white shirt—his button-up, hers a V-neck blouse. Unlike Ekon, Mafdet carried more than a high-powered handgun. In a sheath strapped to her thigh was a wicked sixteen-inch sword blade with oversized spikes on the knuckle guard handle. A month on the job, he'd mustered the courage to inquire as to her sword's name because everyone knew all blade-carrying felidae had a name for their weapon. Mafdet hadn't answered that question either. How in the hell did the sekhem expect Mafdet to train him when the Shieldmane spoke in nods, snorts, and grunts?

"Are you planning on entertaining us with what you've learned from watching Vumarian television?"

"I would, but you're making fun of me."

Sekhem Zarina leaned down and kissed Asha's forehead. "Only a little. I don't have to ask if you comprehended what transpired today with Royster and London. I know you grasped the larger point not expressed in their addendum."

"Humans are rarely satisfied with what they already possess, even when they think they are. Eventually, they will seek more and more, if they believe the acquisition will make them happier, give them something they conclude is missing from their lives."

"Quite right. Lack of satisfaction, even peace within, makes one restless, greedy . . ."

"Dangerous," Khalid Bambara finished.

"Yes, very dangerous. That's why we'll not stay in this country longer than is required. We don't trust the new Chief and Deputy Chief. We're tempted to leave tonight, foregoing a meeting with the leader of the Common Peace Coalition Party."

That surprised Ekon. To his knowledge, Shona stayed out of foreign affairs involving Vumaris. From Asha's nod, she'd known about the meeting.

Khalid Bambara settled his hand on his mate's back, an outward display of their inner love.

One day, Ekon would like to express his feelings for Asha in the same way—a taken-for-granted touch that wouldn't garner a single raised eyebrow. He possessed no desire to become khalid, but he did wish to one day stand by Asha's side as her loving and devoted mate. Again, like her ascension to sekhem, that dream was years into the future. Ekon had yet to demonstrate his worth as a Shieldmane, much less as a worthy mate to the heiress of the Kingdom of Shona.

"But," Khalid Bambara said, "Shona can no longer continue its isolationist ways when it comes to Vumaris. Today has only served to reinforce what your mother and I already know. We need allies on this side of the continent. That may mean opening our borders to them, but we are far from making such a decision. We believe, or at least we hope, Mi Sun Choi's Common Peace Coalition Party can become a trusted ally. If not . . . well, that's for a later family discussion." The hand on Sekhem Zarina's back lowered to her hip, and Khalid Bambara stepped closer to his mate. "You did well today, hafsa, and your mother is only teasing."

"I know." With a step backward, Asha moved away from her parents. "So, umm, may I be excused?" She nodded to Mafdet. "I know you'll want to speak with Mafdet about our departure plans."

Before Asha could say what she was clearly building up to, Sekhem Zarina's gaze shifted to Ekon.

He gulped. Ekon had heard people refer to the lioness's piercing golden eyes as beautiful yet frightening. He didn't disagree. Ekon also refused to look away; to do so would be tantamount to rolling over and showing the alpha his belly. If he wanted to prove himself worthy of his post and Asha's heart, it would begin with not cowering from a mother's unrelenting scrutiny.

Seconds passed between them, with no one speaking or moving. Gazing into the eyes of a Shona lioness who'd lived 120 years, a little more than middle age by felidae standards, Ekon recalled Sekhem Zarina had chosen him to serve as Asha's Second Shieldmane above older and more experienced members of the Shona pride. Her decision had brought honor to his house, and he'd vowed to live up to the faith she'd placed in his potential.

"As Asha grows into her role as sekhem, so too will you grow into your role as her First Shieldmane."

Ekon hadn't told anyone, not even Asha, of her mother's plans for his future. He wondered if Mafdet knew of Sekhem Zarina's intentions to elevate him to a post that by right should be hers. If Mafdet did, that could explain her standoffishness toward him.

Sekhem Zarina's gaze slid from him to Asha. "You may take Ekon with you but do remember there is a proper order of things."

"I know."

"There are several kinds of knowing, Asha. Take heed to all of them. Now go before I change my mind." Her eyes lifted to his again. "Protect her with your life, young Shieldmane. That was your pledge."

"Always. Until the end," Ekon voiced, repeating the same vow he'd made when he'd accepted the post as Asha's Second Shieldmane.

Asha wasted no time hurrying from the room, putting as much space as possible between them and her knowing mother. That distance was a mere walk across the hall to her suite. But once the door closed behind them, the massive suite in front of them, the distance seemed much greater.

Ekon slumped against the door, his heart racing from how an ante-lope must feel after having escaped the clutches of hunting lionesses—a rare, lucky feat that wouldn't reoccur.

A soft hand found his own and squeezed. "Mom's growl is worse than her bite."

Ekon laughed, a breathless hiccup unbecoming of Asha's sworn shield. "No one in all of Shona would believe that, not even you. Your mother is scary."

"She's overprotective."

Asha lifted the hand she held, curving it around her waist in very much the same way Khalid Bambara had held his mate. But Asha wasn't his mate and, if they didn't heed Sekhem Zarina's warning, she never would be.

Ekon pulled his hand away.

This time, the female's eyes that held his but with far less gold were Asha's. With her, his strength abandoned him. Ekon's eyes skidded down and away. "We can't. You heard your mother."

"Yes, I heard her."

Asha grasped his hand again, tugging him away from the closed door and to a circular pit in the center of the room. He removed his sidearm, placing it under a cushion but within reach. They sat on a plush, leather couch in the shape of a semicircle. The burgundy color complemented Asha's white and gold dress.

Picking up the remote from the table in front of them, the television in an open cabinet opposite the pit, Asha clicked the unit on. Sound blared but was quickly lowered.

"I thought we could watch a show. I like funny ones. But you can choose whichever one you want." Kicking off her sandals and scooting close, Asha handed him the remote control and rested her head against his shoulder.

Ekon had never met a more even-tempered, sweet girl. She could be mischievous, sure, and a little obstinate, but nothing more than what was typical for an eighteen-year-old with a strict mother. At twenty, Ekon was little better, and he had far fewer responsibilities than Asha.

"Mom only wants what's best for me."

"I know." Lowering his face, he sniffed her gorgeous mane of hair, tempted to run his hands through the dark, curly locks. She smelled of the countryside of his birth—lavender, moss, and with a hint of mint. "What do you want?"

"For you to hold me while we watch some awful but humorous television sitcom. Then for you to kiss me."

"I shouldn't have ever kissed you."

"You don't mean that."

No, Ekon could never regret crossing the line with Asha ten months ago. "You're right. I'm sorry, I shouldn't have said it. It's just, I don't want to mess up."

"You won't."

"You only say that because I'm the first boy you kissed."

Asha patted his chest. "You aren't the first boy I've kissed."

"Wait. What?" He shoved her until she sat up. "I'm not?"

"I never said you were."

"True but—"

"You are, however, the first boy I've wanted to do more with than kissing."

That stopped his mind from whirling and started his heart racing again. "You can't go around saying stuff like that."

Her smirk reminded him of what he already knew. "Okay, fine, we're the only ones in your suite. But you know what I mean."

"Actually, I don't. It's not as if I asked you to have sex with me right here and now." A sure hand found his thigh and rubbed. "Unless, you know. We could. No one would know but us."

"And your mate, if your parents don't approve of our union."

"They won't choose my mate. They'll weigh in on my decision, but they would never force me into an alliance not of my own choosing. Besides, I don't have to be a virgin when I take a mate. I only need to be faithful to him, which I will be." She patted his chest again. "You aren't ready for us to become lovers, so this conversation is moot."

Affronted, his eyebrows winged up. "Not ready? Who's twenty and who's eighteen?"

"Being twenty doesn't make you ready. It just makes you two years older than me." She nodded to the remote. "If you don't intend on selecting a show, I'll do the picking. Or," she said and kissed his cheek, "we could kiss and touch and pretend we're going to go all the way but know we really won't."

Ekon liked that idea, but her statement about him not being ready, despite his age, had pricked his pride a bit. The sad truth was that she wasn't wrong. Him not being ready had nothing to do with Ekon having had sexual experience with only one person—a high school girlfriend who'd broken up with him a couple of months after graduation. His feelings had been hurt, but she'd warranted no stronger emotion, certainly not anger or even disappointment.

Asha, on the other hand, had a way of turning him into knots. Worse, she managed the act with subconscious effort, like calling him on his unvoiced fears, while also making herself vulnerable to him by revealing her own desires.

Ekon kissed her, lips gentle, tongue patient. When she opened for him, her moan a scratch behind the ears of his inner lion, he slid inside.

Licking.

Tasting.

Exploring.

Wrapping her arms around his neck, Asha pulled Ekon atop her, thoughts of finding a mutually agreeable television show clearly forgotten. Her strong, lithe form felt wonderful underneath him. He doubted Asha would grow to her mother's height. She certainly hadn't inherited her father's tall, stocky frame either. Compared to most felidae lionesses, Asha was considered petite. Although, at five-six, she was taller than the average human female.

To Ekon, there was nothing average about Asha—neither her thick mane of hair nor the way her kisses made him want to purr at her feet—and lions could not purr. But, for Asha, he would make it happen.

Him atop her, they kissed, hands roamed, but clothes stayed on. Well, her dress did. Ekon didn't protest when Asha pulled off his suit jacket and tie and unbuttoned his shirt. No more than he complained when she rolled him over, straddled his hips, and kissed her way from his shoulders down to his belly button. He did, however, moan and curse at the feel of her hand running over his erection through his pants.

He tensed at her exploring touch, and she giggled, the only reaction that gave away her inexperience and nerves.

"Have you done this before too?"

"No." Her hand felt him again, and he fought not to explode in his boxers. "You're big."

"You only think that because I'm the first man you've touched like this." He stilled her hand. Kissing was one kind of temptation but having her curious hand on him was pure torture. "What did you watch on cable after I left you last night?"

"What did you watch, when you returned to your suite?"

They stared at each other, neither blinking. But knowing what he'd watched until three in the morning had him releasing her hand and closing his eyes, permitting Asha to touch him all she wanted.

"I had no idea humans could be so inventive when it came to sex."

"Yeah," he croaked out, Asha's fingers on the tip of his erection, circling the head and drawing precum. "They have the best pornos."

"If you'd stayed, we could've watched one together. Will you let me see you?"

Ekon's eyes popped open. He hadn't needed to see Asha to know her humor hadn't extended to her question. Like Sekhem Zarina, Asha spoke with a forthrightness that often brought one up short when not prepared for her bold—sometimes too bold—frankness.

"We agreed not to go all the way."

"Seeing isn't doing. But I would understand if you rather not. I'm curious, is all. You're handsome. That I already know."

Fingers traced his brows, arched and thick; his nose, long bridge with a wide base; and his lips, wide with a plump center. She stopped at his chin before gliding her hand to his neck then across his clavicle.

Ekon shivered.

"You're strong. Your name is quite apt. But you're also fit, muscular. Your chest is broad and your . . ." Her eyes lowered to the erection tenting his pants. "The rest of you is a mystery I want to solve. Not all of it tonight, unfortunately." Dark eyes rose to his. "Have I shocked you? I didn't mean to. I just . . ."

Asha made to roll off Ekon, but his quick hands to her waist stopped her. "Don't go, and don't be embarrassed. There's nothing wrong with speaking your mind."

"You say that now. But you didn't see your face a second ago."

"Your level of openness is rare. Sometimes, it takes me by surprise."

"I don't know any other way to be."

"It's not a bad way to be, Asha, but everyone isn't like you and your mother. We aren't all so brave."

"Or arrogant."

"That's another word, I guess. But I don't think that's the right descriptor either." With a gentle tug, Ekon encouraged Asha to lay atop him. "If I undress for you, letting you see all of me, I'll want to do more than see you in return. You're right, I'm not ready, and I don't think you are either. There's no rush." Ekon tipped up her head so that she was looking at him. "Is there a rush?"

Asha shook her head, and he kissed the tip of her nose.

"Good. Then let me court you properly. I'll have my parents speak with yours when we return home. It's what we should've done in the beginning. Do you agree?"

"Yes."

"Good." Ekon hugged Asha tightly, his erection in need of release. "Find something to watch on the television that's not porn while I'm in the bathroom."

Asha kissed Ekon, not making it easy on him to use his hand instead of her virginal body to sate his desire. Setting her away from him, his willpower a thread on the verge of breaking, Ekon escaped to Asha's en suite.

He groaned into the hand towel he shoved in his mouth as he came, spurting into his hand and over top of the open toilet. *Mmm*, the release felt good. Not as good as Asha's hand stroking him to completion or being inside of her would've felt. But it was what he needed to get him through the next couple of hours, while they watched television, pretending they wouldn't rather be having sex.

Hands washed and dried, clothes tucked in and neat, lust under control, Ekon walked out of the en suite, through the spacious bedroom, ignoring the queen-size bed, and back into the living room and . . .

Asha no longer sat on the couch in the pit. She stood near the front door. A door he hadn't heard open or close. But it obviously had because she wasn't alone in the room. A human male stood beside Asha, a gun pressed to her side.

Ekon snarled and stepped forward, claws and fangs extended.

The human lifted his gun to Asha's head.

Ekon stopped.

"Calm down, kitty, or I'll splatter her brains all over this white carpet."

Chapter 3: Most Strong

Mafdet watched young Ekon follow behind an even younger Asha, smitten by the lioness who would one day become his sekhem. Asha would grow to rule them all, not that Mafdet would be around to see the young woman mature into the big paws her mother would leave for her to fill. Her time with the Shona royal family would soon come to an end. She'd done her duty, and she was tired. So very tired. But she'd made a promise to Zarina to watch over Asha, teaching Ekon all he would require to replace her as First Shieldmane. Until that time, she would continue to use her blades and guns in the service of the Shona Kingdom and the royals who'd given her a home and a purpose when, for too long, she'd had neither.

"Come sit with us."

At the behest of her sekhem, Mafdet joined Bambara and Zarina at the rectangular marble table in the living room, sitting opposite the couple who, as always, claimed a position next to the other. Once upon a time, she'd had a mate as devoted as Bambara. But that was ages ago.

"Would you like for me to reconfirm your meeting with Ms. Choi or inquire as to whether she could meet earlier than the scheduled luncheon?"

Bambara appeared to consider Mafdet's question, while Zarina's reply took only seconds.

"No. Thank you for the consideration. It would be nice to return home a few hours earlier. But Mi Sun isn't local. She's flying in to meet with us tomorrow morning. Out of respect, we should give her time to rest before engaging in business. I would like for you to finalize everything for our departure, though. Ideally, I would like to leave for the airport as soon as our business with Mi Sun concludes."

"Of course, I'll have Virith—"

Her walkie-talkie crackled. Virith's voice, the very Shieldmane she'd been about to suggest for an assignment, boomed through the radio.

"Virith to Mafdet. Virith to Mafdet."

She sprang from the table and rushed across the room to where she'd left the walkie-talkie.

Bambara and Zarina also got to their feet. They must've heard the same in Virith's husky voice.

Anger.

Worry.

She picked the walkie-talkie up off the floor. "Mafdet, go ahead Virith."

"There are unauthorized humans in the hotel."

"Who?"

"I don't know. Some are dressed as hotel workers but not all."

"Where are you? Where are the others?"

Bambara and Zarina crowded around the walkie-talkie she held, staring at it as if it would show them the intruders Virith had described.

"Watane is pinned down on the ground floor. Adul should be somewhere on the eighth floor, and I haven't been able to reach Nochari. He should be on the same floor as you. Have you seen him?"

Mafdet knew what Virith meant by *seen him*. While the hotel contained its own security cameras in all public places in and around the building, Shieldmane security protocol twelve dictated Shieldmane use their own cameras. So, Mafdet had tasked Nochari with installing Shona security cameras in strategic locations throughout the hotel, including the floor where they stayed and its stairwells, and every major hotel entrance and exit.

"I haven't seen Nochari. I'm with the khalid and sekhem in their suite."

With the Shieldmanes scattered throughout the hotel, no one was in the suite they used as their security control office. She had eyes on nothing beyond this suite and her alphas.

"Is Ekon with the hafsa sekhem?"

At the mention of Asha, everyone's eyes darted to the closed suite door.

Bambara bolted toward it, followed by Zarina and Mafdet.

Gunfire erupted on the other end of the walkie-talkie, shaking her up but not slowing her down. Her cheetah speed had her beating Bambara to the door. Mafdet reached for the handle. Stopped. Sniffed.

Only Bambara's arm around Zarina's waist prevented her from opening the suite door. "Don't. Can't you smell that?"

"Gas?" Zarina questioned. Her outstretched hand stilled on the door handle.

It was. Mafdet didn't know what kind, but she could hazard a guess. "Probably thanol."

"Basilisk Smoke?" Zarina followed Mafdet's and Bambara's retreat. "Is that the same poison that was used against your—"

"The same one." With it seeping under the door, the scent closer, stronger, she knew for certain. "We need to stop it from getting in here."

"We need to get my daughter."

Mafdet didn't disagree with Zarina, but they would be useless to Asha if they succumbed to the toxic vapors. Thankfully, Bambara's concern for his daughter's safety hadn't clouded his judgment.

He tossed Mafdet and Zarina thick towels he'd retrieved from the en suite. "These should slow it down some, but I'm not waiting in here while whoever in the hell is out there runs free."

"I'm calling Asha's room." Zarina pointed to Mafdet. "See who you can contact who has eyes on the intruders. Bambara, your lion."

The khalid didn't require his mate's order. He'd already ripped his shirt off by the time she'd uttered his name.

It went unsaid that Mafdet would be in her human form. Her skills were better suited as a human, just as the khalid's lion was his more formidable shape. Zarina, on the other hand, was descended from the original line of Panthera Leos. Her strength, stamina, and speed remained the same, no matter her form.

"Dammit, no dial tone." The phone cracked and broke in Zarina's hand.

Bambara swore then dropped to all fours. His back, shoulder, and arm muscles were the first to break. No matter how many times she'd transmutated, or seen it done, Mafdet never got used to the brutal sound of bones breaking and popping out of sockets. Nor did she enjoy the sight of skin stretched to the point of ripping, giving way to jutting bones and torn ligaments that reformed and fused together in grinding spasms of power and pain.

Paws and retractable claws hit the carpet. Golden fur ran the length of Bambara's six-foot, five-hundred-pound body, from his wide head with a dark, long mane, down to his long, swishing tail with a tuft of fur on the end.

Bambara opened his wide mouth to roar but stopped at Zarina's hand to his side. "Let's give them no warning."

The walkie-talkie crackled again. "Virith?"

"No, Adul." His voice sounded like he'd swallowed sandpaper, normal after a transmutation back to human form. "Armed men."

"We know. Slip out and call local law enforcement."

"Can't. Tried. All exits are blocked by humans in tactical gear and with automatic weapons. Trapped."

What in the hell was going on? They weren't at war with Vumaris. Who'd sent these men to Sanctum Hotel? Sliding her gun from her holster, she turned to Zarina and Bambara.

The sekhem had ripped material from the bottom of her blue dress and had used it to cover her mouth and nose. She would still inhale the Basilisk Smoke, the same as Mafdet and Bambara, but the makeshift bandana would help.

"I don't think the gas is meant to kill us." Zarina handed Mafdet a strip of her dress. "They're trying to rout us from the suite. If the two of you are ready, let's oblige the bastards then get my daughter and then the hell out of here."

Mafdet tied the strip of material at the back of her buzz-cut head, covering her face from below her eyes to over her mouth. Whoever was in the hallway, several of them from the steps they couldn't conceal from a person with enhanced hearing, may have been waiting for them to exit. That didn't mean, however, that Mafdet would lead her alphas into a trap.

"Follow me."

Mafdet swung open the balcony doors and walked onto the enclosure. She could try screaming. But, from the height, no one would hear her. Not that she saw anyone on the street below. They'd chosen Sanctum Hotel because it was a short drive to the First Evolution Union's headquarters but also because it was far enough away from the country's capital that their presence would go unnoticed by locals and the media. Sanctum Hotel served both purposes. As Mafdet calculated her odds of getting the royal family out of the hotel and home safely, she wished they hadn't chosen such an isolated area to stay. For the first time in her long life, Mafdet would drop to her knees in supplication to see a group of humans milling about—nosy, loud, but also likely to help a felidae in need.

"We can make it onto the balcony below us or jump to the one next door."

Zarina had followed her onto the balcony. She'd removed her heels, but the sekhem was still three inches taller than Mafdet. "We should drop to the balcony below, while Bambara should claim the balcony across from us. They won't expect an attack from two separate fronts. Do you agree?"

She did. Mafdet holstered her weapon. "Hard and fast. Anyone who stands between us and Asha dies."

"That's a given. Let's go."

With graceful leaps that weren't choreographed, Bambara and Zarina jumped at the same time, landing soundlessly on their respective balconies. Shaking her head at the couple, Mafdet followed Zarina onto the balcony under her. It didn't take more than a palm heel strike to break the door's lock. She didn't hear more than a soft clinking of glass hitting the balcony floor above her, which meant Bambara had changed forms to make getting into the suite smoother and quieter than he would've as a lion.

She and Zarina entered the suite, heading straight for the front door. They stopped and listened. Mafdet heard nothing but waited for Zarina to finish her telepathic conversation with her mate before proceeding into the hallway. Not all mates could communicate in such a manner. Of those who could, the ability only existed when one or more of them were in their feline form. Yet on infrequent occasions, Zarina could reach Asha's mind, regardless of either of their forms.

"Bambara is ready. He says he heard someone knocking then going into Asha's room."

"Can you reach her?"

"It's difficult, on my best day, to get through the weeds that are a teen's mind. Lately, Asha's head is so full of Ekon that reaching her telepathically is near impossible."

Mafdet assumed as much. But she had to be sure.

Instead of reaching for her gun again, Mafdet freed her sword from the thigh sheath. Ekon had asked her what she'd named the blade. She'd never been one to become attached to inanimate objects to the point of wasting her time in naming them. So, she hadn't answered his question.

But as she reacquainted herself with the familiar weight of the sword, her right hand on the doorknob, a name came to mind.

The blade had been a gift from Sekhem Zarina, a token of the lioness's affection, trust, and loyalty. "I'm returning to you your claws. Use it well, my friend."

On silent feet, they exited the suite. On this floor, she neither smelled gas nor heard intruders. With the tip of her blade, she pointed to the ceiling.

Zarina nodded. Together, they stalked to the stairwell. As before, she paused and listened before opening the door.

Nothing.

They ascended the stairs, the smell of humans and gas increasing with each step.

Mafdet didn't have to ask Zarina if she were ready. The second her bare feet hit the landing, her lethal fangs had descended, and her fingernails had turned into vicious claws. They would soon be stained red, as would Mafdet's blade.

Slowly, she opened the stairwell door. Smoke filled the hallway, but the toxins, as Zarina had surmised, weren't powerful. The intruders had indeed been trying to flush them from their suite.

They exited at the same time Bambara crashed through the suite door. Between them were at least fifteen humans dressed, as Adul had said, in tactical gear. They wore gas masks and held automatic weapons.

Bambara attacked.

Shouting ensued. Screams.

Weapons raised. Feet thudded.

An alpha lion roared.

With Bambara's roar, the element of surprise no longer existed. So, she yanked out her gun, firing at the heads of the nearest humans.

Zarina took off down the hall. Her burst of speed was almost as fast as Mafdet. The sekhem sliced throats as she went, aiming her claws at the vulnerable sweet spot between bulletproof vest and the sealed gas mask covering at the humans' chins.

Mafdet didn't follow her alpha. Instead, she planted herself near the stairwell and the corner of the hallway that led to the other side of the floor. Bambara had claimed the opposite end, with Zarina in the middle.

More armed humans rushed around the corner. Some in tactical gear but others dressed like front desk workers—white shirt, burgundy suit, and burgundy and white striped tie.

Mafdet met them head-on, driving her sword into throats, chests, and eyes. She sliced tendons, ears, and wrists. Shot kneecaps then finished the enemy with a bullet to the brain.

She reloaded.

Gunfire and growls raged behind her. She wanted to run toward Bambara and Zarina. But more enemies poured from the stairwell and from around the corner.

Neither Virith nor Adul had known how many enemies had descended on Sanctum Hotel. Were her fellow Shieldmanes still alive? Had they been overrun by the humans? Would Mafdet and the royal couple?

She shoved her blade into the ear of the nearest enemy, a human woman with a nose ring and a gun that discharged on her way down. The bullet scored her side, blazing a path of searing pain as it went in and out. The second bullet slammed into her shoulder. No exit but a cracked bone.

Gritting through the pain, Mafdet threw everything she had at the onslaught of armed men and women. They rushed her with fists and guns. Her felidae cheetah speed and years of combat kept her upright and in the battle.

Snatching weapons from the dead, her empty handgun useless, she met their fire with her own. One by one, they rounded the corner, getting a face full of bullets. They dropped to their knees, a pile of dead and dying bodies—Mafdet's unplanned but much-needed barrier.

She chanced a glance behind her. The couple had their backs to each other, bleeding, but fighting as they lived—a unified front.

Asha flipped from one television station to the next, her mind more on the way Ekon had made her body feel than on finding a show for them to watch before Mafdet took over the post and sent Ekon to his suite. While Zarina had raised Asha to speak her mind, she had also taught her to do so with forethought and care. Zarina had a tendency to shock people, but not because she hadn't calculated the impact of her words before uttering them. But her mother had yet to teach her how to curb her thoughts when her body wanted to do the talking for her.

Foregoing the television, she clicked it off and dropped the remote control onto the couch cushion beside her. She ached in places she wanted Ekon to touch. If she were alone in the suite and in her bed, she'd close her eyes, slip her hand inside her panties and—

Knock. Knock. Knock.

Opening eyes that had closed of their own volition and dropping the hem of her dress she hadn't consciously lifted, Asha sat up—embarrassed and breathless.

The knock came again.

Asha stood. Waited. A Shieldmane would announce themself, even Mafdet who had a key to the suite. Her parents would call if they required something of her, expecting Asha to come to them, not the other way around.

By the time the third round of knocking sounded, Asha had moved closer to the door, scenting more than the human on the other side.

"Miss. Miss. Are you inside? We have an emergency. We need to evacuate this floor."

The man knocked again—hard and urgent.

Peering through the peephole, she saw a tall man dressed in the same uniform she'd seen the front desk workers wear. He appeared both anxious and impatient. If there was a fire or gas leak, the man's emotions were justified. Asha and Ekon needed to get out of there.

She unlocked and opened the door. Mistake. Asha stepped backward and the human stepped forward, shutting the door behind him.

A gun she hadn't seen through the peephole pointed at her.

"Don't scream. Don't fight. If you follow my directions, you won't get hurt."

If he didn't have a gun leveled at her stomach, Asha could've misinterpreted his smile as a sign of kindness.

"You're making a mistake."

"No, I'm making the world better for humans." Gun hand steady, the man who clearly wasn't a hotel employee scanned the outer room of the suite. "Is someone in here with you? A guard?" Green eyes tracked up and down her body. "Yeah, as pretty as you are, there has to be a guard nearby. Where? Bedroom? Bathroom?"

Asha wouldn't tell a lie only to be caught in one, but she also wouldn't reward the human's threat of violence with the truth.

"Fine. I'll take your silence as a yes." He drew closer, blond hair pulled back in a shoulder-length ponytail Asha would rip from his scalp if given an opportunity to strike. "We'll just wait right here for whoever is in that other room to come out."

They waited. It didn't take long since Ekon had already been in the en suite for five minutes. Asha knew why he'd made a quick escape. She hadn't been toying with him when she'd asked to see him naked. She'd very much wanted to feast upon his body . . . and with more than her eyes.

The door to the en suite creaked open.

The human shoved the barrel of the gun against her ribs, his breath smelling of cigarettes when he whispered in her ear, "I knew someone was in here with you. You're too important to be left alone. But didn't your parents ever warn you about opening doors to strangers?" His other hand found one of Asha's curls and twisted it around his finger. "I told them I could get you to open the door for me. It was the uniform, wasn't it? No need to answer, little girl. Now, let's see who came to play."

Ekon appeared in the living room, having reached them on soundless feet. If not for the creaking door, the human would've never known he approached. As it was, though, it was Ekon who was taken by surprise.

Asha saw the moment her gentle boyfriend morphed into her deadly Shieldmane. His eyes darkened, eyeteeth lengthened, sharpened, and his fingernails transformed into long, curved claws.

Ekon stalked toward Asha, his focus on the gunman.

In a swift upward movement, the human pointed his handgun at Asha's head. "Calm down, kitty, or I'll splatter her brains all over this white carpet."

Ekon halted.

"That's good. Real good. Put those fangs and claws away, friend."

"I'm not your friend. If you want to make it out of this room alive, you need to get that gun away from her and leave."

"Yeah, no, that's not going to happen. She's why we're here. Where we go, she goes. You're the one I don't need."

A lion roared, and Asha had never heard a more beautiful sound.

"That would be my father."

The roar was followed by gunfire, then what sounded like all-out war in the hall.

"Fuck! Fuck! What in the hell are those guys doing?"

"They're fighting my parents, which means they're dying. If you give Ekon your gun, you won't have to die with them."

"Shut up. Come here." He yanked her dress, twirling her around, her back to his front, and his gun to the side of her head. "You're my ticket out of here. We're going to wait right here. We came prepared to take this hotel. We ran into two of you felidae on the way up and neutralized both. The same with the hotel employees, so don't think I won't shoot your cute little mouthy ass too. You and your boyfriend."

"I'm her Shieldmane."

"You're a kid with a cum stain on your pants, that's what you are. You should've been out here guarding her when I knocked, instead of in the bathroom squirting in your shorts. You shut up too. I need to think."

Ekon seemed torn between lunging at the gunman while trusting Asha to get out of the way for his attack, and morbid fear of making the wrong decision and causing the human to shoot and kill her. Not for the first time, Asha wished she and Ekon shared the kind of bond as her parents. She could hear them fighting. Asha didn't need to see them to know they fought as one deadly alpha—Sekhem and Khalid.

The three of them stood there in silence, listening as the battle waged on the other side of the door. The longer it did, and the more shots she heard, the more ill she became. Her parents retreated from no foe, and neither did Mafdet, who would be out there fighting alongside her parents. If they died, were killed, what would happen to Shona? To Ekon? To her?

Asha wouldn't wait to find out. "The lion said: I am the best one to take care of my business."

"I said, shut up."

"Panthera Leo proverb."

"What?"

"It means you're lion food."

Moving quicker than ever before, Asha reached behind her, slashed the arm of the hand holding the gun with claws pushed through her fingers.

The gun fired. Went wide.

First and only chance to kill her.

Spinning, Asha darted behind the human, grabbed him by his ponytail and tossed him over her shoulder and into the circular pit.

Ekon bolted after the human and then he was on him, claws ripping through clothing and flesh.

The human screamed, fought, begged.

Asha recovered his dropped weapon, pointed it at him then lowered her arm.

Ekon's bloody mouth lifted from the gaping hole in the human's neck. He spat something onto the blood-ruined couch. Asha didn't want to know what.

She glanced down at her right hand. In her tight fist was a blond ponytail. Asha let it fall.

Wiping his mouth on his white shirtsleeve, Ekon approached, the gun she'd forgotten he'd placed under the couch pillow in his right hand. "Are you okay?"

She nodded.

"Good. Keep that gun but stay behind me."

Smoke assaulted her senses when they opened the door, as did the smell of blood. Asha raised the gun. She'd never shot one before but assumed her enhanced eyesight would help with her aim.

A hand touched her shoulder, and she nearly jumped out of her skin.

"It's me." Zarina removed a bandana from her face. "Thank goodness you're all right."

Asha all but collapsed into her mother's arms. A sob broke from her.

"We have you. No tears. There will be time enough for them, once we get out of this hotel of horrors."

A big, furry body rubbed against her, and Asha released one of her hands from her mother's neck to stroke her father's mane. They were reunited. Everything would be fine. Her parents were there.

"We need to go." Mafdet yanked off her bandana.

Asha smiled. Mafdet had also survived. But two of the Shieldmane hadn't, according to the gunman. He hadn't smelled of lies, so she'd believed him. But what of the other two?

Zarina laced her fingers through Asha's. "Adul said all the exits are blocked." She picked up two weapons from the dead, handing one to Mafdet and keeping the other for herself. "We'll have to fight our way out of here. If we hide, they'll eventually find and kill us. I have no intention of cowering in a corner awaiting my death. Ekon, the blood on you means you've protected my daughter once this evening; continue to do so. Asha, if we fall, do what you must to survive."

"Mom, I . . ." Blinding tears filled her eyes.

"There's no shame in crying or dying, my hafsa, only in not living and trying. Do you want me to give you your sekhem name now?"

She didn't. If Asha accepted her sekhem name, it would be an admission that her parents, her mother, wouldn't survive the battle out of Sanctum Hotel. She refused to think about that cruel fate.

"Don't make me. I don't want . . . I can't . . ."

Bambara's cold nose bumped into Asha's hand—his love a silent boon to her heart.

Zarina hugged and kissed Asha. Their embrace lingered, even as Asha knew they needed to get away from the pools of blood, scattered dead bodies, and waning smoke.

A hand to her lower back—Ekon's—got her going. She walked in front of him and behind Zarina. Mafdet and Bambara walked in tandem, with Mafdet opening the stairwell door for the lion, who then took the lead down the ten flights of steps to the hotel lobby.

No one spoke and, with each step, the heavier the gun felt in her hand, the sweatier she became, and the faster her heart pounded.

Mafdet opened the stairwell door that led to the lobby, peeked her head out and swore. "It's a small army out there. There's no way we can sneak past them."

"They want Asha. That's what the human in her suite told us." Ekon held her hand. "I wouldn't let him have her, and I won't let whoever is out there have her either."

"No one can have my daughter. Those spineless, greedy bastards. All of this violence because Bambara and I refused to sign their addendum. When will humans learn? Everything can't be negotiated or taken by force."

Zarina wrapped Asha in another hug. Two more massive arms engulfed them both—Bambara.

He'd transmutated so quickly she hadn't noticed.

"This isn't goodbye," her father said, his chin on the top of her head. "We'll see you again, hafsa. If not in this lifetime, then the next."

"No, Dad."

"Your mother and I need you to go with Ekon and Mafdet. They are sworn to protect you, just as your mother and I are sworn to protect Shona from people like Royster and London. It's our duty as khalid and sekhem. We will not hide or run. But, today, this one time, we need you to do both. We need you to survive. That's the only way we can leave you to do what we must."

"Don't leave. Please, Daddy. Mommy, don't leave."

Zarina kissed her forehead again. "I'll give you your sekhem name now."

"No. No. I don't want it. I don't . . ."

Ignoring Asha's teary protests, her mother whispered the name into her ear.

Asha cried. *No. No. Too soon. In twenty, maybe thirty years but not now. Not here. Not like this.*

"We love you," her parents said.

"No, please." Ekon and Mafdet dragged her up the stairs.

She kept her watery gaze on her parents until they disappeared through the stairwell door. Her father didn't roar. He gave no warning that an alpha lion approached. For two long minutes, she heard nothing.

Zarina, the alpha lioness, was hunting. She'd hunted beside her mother many times. No prey ever escaped her. But her parents were but two lions against—

The noise of gunfire ended the silence with booming percussion. More and more gunfire sounded from the lobby, and Asha made to run back down the stairs. But Mafdet shoved her toward Ekon.

"Take her. I'm going back."

"But the sekhem said—"

"I know what Zarina said. But she forfeited the right to command me when she handed her title over to Asha. And right now, Asha is in no position to command anyone. Don't let her get caught. If she does, who knows what they'll do to her."

"You mean . . . No, I won't let that happen."

"Be sure you don't. Asha? Asha? Are you listening? Do not go into shock." Mafdet appeared in front of her, her face graver than she'd ever seen it. "Do you remember what to do if you are in the clutches of men?" Fingers snapped in front of her face. "Come on. Cry later. Remember your mother's words now. What did she tell you to do?"

"T-t-transmutate."

"That's right. Stay in lion form. Stay in that form for as long as you can. I promise, if you're caught, I'll come for you. Do you hear me, Asha? I'll come for you."

"I won't let them take her from me."

"You better not."

Like Zarina, Mafdet kissed Asha's forehead.

She nodded to Ekon behind Asha, unsheathed her blade, and held it up to him. "Her name is Mafdet's Claws."

Then she too was gone. Speeding down the stairs, away from Asha, and toward a bloody death.

Stunned, Asha stared after Mafdet. Her only solace was that she still heard the ringing of gunfire. Her parents fought on, but how much longer would they last?

Ekon tugged her arm. "Come on."

Asha went.

Chapter 4:
Unwavering Loyal
One

Where *should we go? What should I do?* Ekon had no idea. But he had to do something. The alphas and Mafdet had left Asha in his care. His, a Shieldmane with a year to claim as experience. But not for this, not as the sole protector of the heir to the Kingdom of Shona.

Heir. Asha might very well be sekhem, depending on how her parents fared. Ekon didn't want to think about them not surviving or what would befall Shona if they didn't. Was Asha ready to serve as leader of their people? They would follow her, but in what direction would she lead them? He felt disloyal having such thoughts, especially in light of the role he'd been thrust into—trained but not prepared—like Asha.

She yanked her hand from his, slamming the other into the stairwell door marked with the number thirteen.

Wasn't thirteen an unlucky number in some human societies? "Let's keep going up," he suggested, unsure where to take her but knowing they needed to get as far away from the lobby as they could.

"No."

"Come on, Asha. Now isn't the time to let out your stubborn lioness."

"I'm not being stubborn. We don't transmutate into winged beasts. There's no exit on the upper floors. We need either to return to the lower level or find a place on this floor to make our stand."

"Stand? With what? Two guns? Did you not hear all of that firepower down there?"

Asha marched through the stairwell door onto unlucky floor number thirteen.

Shit. Glancing down the steps, but neither seeing nor hearing anyone, Ekon followed. What choice had Asha left him?

"They aren't dead."

"I didn't say they were."

"No, but you think they are."

Ekon did, but Asha wasn't looking for him to confirm her fears. She wanted a distraction from her painful thoughts and, if starting a pointless argument with him gave her temporary respite, he didn't mind being her punching bag.

But Asha said nothing more. She only huffed and increased her speed down the hallway, trying every suite door but finding them all locked.

"If you find one you like, I can get us inside."

"They'll check every floor for me. If they find a door unlocked, they'll search. Maybe we should break into all of them. Do you think that'll slow them down if they have to search many rooms?"

Ekon had no idea, but they rounded the other side of the floor with no better plan than they'd had when they'd run up the stairs. "I'm supposed to keep you safe."

"You can't."

"I can."

Asha whirled on Ekon, shoving him against the wall with a strong palm to his chest. "I said you can't, and I won't have you dying trying to do what my parents and Mafdet couldn't. We're lying to ourselves.

My parents wanted to give me time to escape, but I have no clue how to get out of this wretched hotel with my freedom intact."

The hand on his chest gentled but stayed where it was. Ekon covered her hand, rubbing circles on the back with his thumb.

"We have each other. Don't give up on us now . . . on me."

"I'm not giving up. I'm trying to think like my mother. Like a sekhem."

The word broke from Asha, and her body fell into his, her gun clanking to the floor. She wept. The sight curled his insides. Ekon wanted to turn into his lion, so he could hunt down and kill everyone who'd brought Asha to this place of pain and grief. Right now, Ekon could do none of those things, so he held his gun in one hand and Asha with the other.

They couldn't stay still long, but he was loath to rush her. She'd likely lost both her parents, as well as Mafdet who wasn't simply Asha's First Shieldmane but her godmother. He wished he had more to offer her than words of condolence and a chest to cry on.

Ekon kissed her temple. "Come on. Let's see if we can make it to the restaurant. It leads to a loading area. Maybe we can exit that way or find an outside line and call for help."

If they were lucky, they'd run into another Shieldmane. Unfortunately, luck hadn't favored the Shona this night.

"It's too late." Stumbling, she pushed away from him. "It's too late."

"What do you mean?"

Hands clutched her head, grabbing at hair and pulling. As if she'd been shot in the back, Asha lurched forward then collapsed to her knees. Heart-wrenching wails poured from her—the sound of a shattered heart dipped in lost innocence.

"No, Mommy. Don't go," Asha begged, her desperation reducing her to a child's state. "*Please. Please.* Don't leave me alone."

Asha's forehead dropped to the burgundy floral print runner. She tugged at her curly locks, pulling them with a force that had to hurt.

Ekon bent to help her to her feet, but she pushed him away with a strength rivaled only by the agony he witnessed in her shivering body and endless sobs.

He slid down the wall, helpless to comfort the young woman he could only now admit to loving. Why had it taken blood and death for Ekon to realize the depth of his feelings for Asha? Was it pity? Guilt?

Her vulnerability and his desire to be her hero, the Shieldmane who would save her when the others had died trying?

No. Those couldn't be the reasons. Yet, watching Asha disintegrate before Ekon's eyes, her grief sour fruit on his tongue, he was honest enough to admit that if by some miracle they survived, they would never be what they once were.

Innocent.

Trusting.

Whole.

Asha cried, screamed, swore, and threatened all manner of vile death on humans.

If the enemy came, they would find them—her hunched on the floor, a lioness on the verge of madness—and him on his ass, staring at his gun like he would his limp dick. Both useless without the right motivation.

Ekon crawled to Asha, scooped her in his arms, and held her through the worst of her tears. She didn't fight or push him away. Asha submitted to him which, in a way, was worse than her angry shove had been.

When she quieted, his shirt wet from her tears, he helped her to her feet. Asha didn't protest Ekon guiding her down a different stairwell from the one they'd ascended. She also said nothing when he pulled her into storage closets, shoved her against walls, and had her crawl behind furniture to avoid the search teams.

Reaching the hotel's restaurant had taken longer than expected, but they'd made it without being caught. Ekon pointed to the restaurant's glass walls. When they'd eaten there earlier, everyone had thought the glass added ambiance, giving the restaurant an open feel, which felidae appreciated. Now, Ekon would trade the see-through walls for drywall or plaster.

Without needing to be told, Asha half crouched, half crawled. In minutes, they'd reached the back of the restaurant and the kitchen.

"There's a phone," Asha whispered. She snatched the black phone receiver off the wall near the swinging doors that led into the dining area. The small light of hope he'd seen in her eyes, when she'd spotted the phone, died almost as soon as it had appeared. "No dial tone."

"Okay, then let's see about the loading area."

"You go, I'll look around in here. See what I can find."

"Like what? Knives?" He raised a hand, showing her the beginning of a claw. "We got cutting and stabbing covered. What we need is an exit . . . or a plan. An exit plan."

"Go."

"But . . ."

"I'm not going anywhere. But I would like a minute to myself, if you don't mind."

"Oh, umm, of course. Sorry."

"Don't be. My safety is your job."

"That's . . ." He didn't like the emotionless way she'd spoken about him being her Shieldmane as if he stayed by her side for duty alone. Once he got them far away from Sanctum Hotel, they would talk. Until then, Ekon needed to keep focused on his goal.

Saving Asha.

It didn't take him long to find the chained door to the loading area. Ekon had considered breaking the chains with his bare hands but retreated at the sound of talking on the other side of the door.

Hustling back to inform Asha of their continued run of bad luck, Ekon's lion almost broke free when he didn't see Asha by the dangling phone. But he'd calmed and followed her scent to a walk-in freezer. Asha sat on the floor at the back of the freezer, shelves of plastic water and soda bottles, and bags and boxes of food on each side of her.

"Close the door. As long as that handle works, we won't get locked in. I doubt anyone will think to look for me in here. No luck with the door to the loading area?"

"It's chained. I can break it, but that's not my concern."

Taking a second to run back to the phone Asha had left hanging, Ekon returned it to the cradle. They might not think to look for them in the freezer, but they could if they saw evidence that someone had been in the kitchen.

Sparing another look at the, thankfully, empty kitchen, Ekon closed the freezer door. He preferred the heat but didn't mind the relative safety of the cool freezer. First securing his gun on the same shelf as Asha's, Ekon lowered to the floor to sit beside her, his back against the freezer wall like hers.

"I heard men outside, that's why I didn't try to break the chain and lock. I'll check again, in a little while. For now, I think we're safe."

"For now, yes."

"Do you want to talk about what happened upstairs?"

"No." Soft. Final. Asha reached over and held his hand. "I don't want anyone else to die because of me."

"None of this is your fault."

"I know it's not my fault, Ekon. Trust me, I'm quite clear who's to blame."

"Silas Royster and Frank London?"

"Them. Their party. And whoever the group is they hired to hunt and kill us the way the Fatherland Party once did. We thought those barbaric times were two centuries behind us. We were wrong."

"You sound like you have a plan."

"Slaughtering, murdering, maiming. Do you consider that a sane woman's plan or a serial killer's weekend itinerary?"

Ekon had no clue how to answer Asha's coldly stated question, but he didn't have to because she lifted the palm of his hand to her mouth and pressed a kiss. "Until a lion learns how to write, every story will glorify the hunter."

Asha did love her Panthera Leo proverbs. She consumed books like she did water and food. Asha had been known to disappear for hours, her mother sending Ekon in search of her when she would fail to return for dinner. Invariably, he would find her either reading or swimming. Most days, she had done both by the time Ekon had located her. She would smile at him and he would, for just a second or two, forget how to breathe.

He wished she would have something for which to smile now.

"We know how to write, but the hunter's story is still the only one that's told. That must end. One way or another, it must all come to an end."

Ekon didn't like the sound of that. Nothing good bloomed from a heart buried in grief.

Asha kissed his hand again. "Will you become my lover?"

Ekon coughed up his shock. "W-what? Now? Here?"

"Yes to both. We might not get another chance. You know I want you. I have for months."

She didn't sound as if she wanted him. In fact, Asha's voice couldn't have been more devoid of the playful, passionate girl he'd kissed and cuddled with on her couch just a couple of hours earlier. Had it only been two hours since humans had disrupted their world with their guns and plan to kidnap a member of the royal Shona family?

"The freezer of a restaurant isn't the place where you should lose your virginity."

"I also shouldn't die at eighteen—virgin or not." She placed his hand back on his lap. "It's fine. It was unfair of me to ask." Rising onto her knees, she faced him—eyes watery red. "Mom bestowed on me my sekhem name. But she did more than that. She gave me a charge."

"A charge? How can a name also be a charge?"

"It simply is. No matter how well tamed a lion, he will always go back to the bush."

"Asha, talk to me."

"I am talking. Do not try to fight a lion, if you aren't one yourself."

"You're spouting proverbs. That's not talking."

Asha pushed to her feet. "I'm speaking clearly, but you aren't listening carefully." She backed away from him, their eyes locked. "I know what I must do. My charge is clear."

"What charge?" Ekon vaulted to his feet. "What in the hell are you talking about?"

Asha retreated more, stopping when her back hit the freezer door. "You're a fine Second Shieldmane, Ekon Ptah. You have honored yourself and your family well this night."

"Don't speak to me like a sekhem. We're more than that to each other."

"We are." Asha nodded. "We definitely are." Her hand grasped the door handle and twisted.

"What are you doing? Wait. If you're planning on checking the loading area door, let me get my gun and come with you."

Four seconds. Four measly seconds was how long he'd turned away from Asha to grab his gun from the shelf. Four seconds. Not long by any standard. But long enough for her to slip out of the freezer, break the door handle, and lock him inside. She'd done all of that in four fucking seconds.

Ekon rushed to the door, slamming against it with his shoulder. Again. Again. It dented but didn't give. *Shit.* "Asha, open the door." He rammed into the door over and again. He could still smell her. She hadn't gone far. "I know you're there. Let me out."

"You're strong, but it'll take you a little while to force the door off its hinges. Once you do, I'll be gone, and you'll be safe."

"Asha, don't you dare do this." He pounded against the door. If he had to, he would break every bone in his hands to get out of there. His hands would heal but not his heart, if something happened to Asha. "Let me out," he growled. "I need to be with you . . . to protect you."

"Asha is no longer here. She went away. So far away."

"No, you're on the other side of this damn door." He punched the door again, the reverberation of the blow not as painful as the dawning realization of what Asha planned on doing. "Do not turn yourself in to those barbarians. Do you hear me? Do not go to them."

"I won't let them hurt you the way they hurt Mom, Dad, and Mafdet. They'll pay. I'll make sure they do. Ms. Choi will arrive in the morning. I know you don't know her, but she's a friend. Trust her."

Ekon heard her shuffle away from the door. He pounded harder, using every part of his body to get out of the freezer and to his Asha. But the door remained intact. She believed he could escape. He despised her faith in him because she was right. He would be free. But it would take time—time he didn't have to prevent Asha from making the biggest mistake of her life.

But there was nothing he could do to stop her. She would protect him when he should've been the one shielding her from harm. "Don't sacrifice yourself for me. Please, Asha. I . . . I love you."

The retreating footsteps halted. Ekon knew Asha. She'd been raised too well to give him false hope. Once she settled on a plan, a hunt, she wouldn't be steered from her course. Not because she didn't love him but because a sekhem placed nothing above her duty, not even her own safety.

"I love you too."

Her voice faded, as did her footsteps. But Ekon could've sworn, mixed in with a man's voice yelling at Asha to "Stop right there," she'd said, "Roaring lions kill no prey."

Chapter 5: Mother of the Dead

There were so many of them. Too many. Zarina sliced the throat of her opponent, sinking her claws in deep and ripping.

Behind you.

At Bambara's warning, she ducked and spun toward the enemy behind her, evading the bullet aimed at her head. Up into his groin she drilled her claws, saving some woman the disappointment of having a child fathered by a mercenary bastard. Not that Zarina would leave the male alive. Her next strike cut through his vest and chest.

Blood and gore coated her hands—wet and sticky.

She ran toward Bambara. Her mate was an impressive lion to behold. He attacked with skill and without mercy. His big, heavy body rampaged, knocking over gunmen and tearing into them. But he also bore battle wounds, as did she.

Zarina leapt onto the woman aiming her gun at Bambara, tackling her and breaking her neck before they hit the floor.

Transmutate.

"I don't have time."

She couldn't spare the seconds it would take for her to make the change into her lion form. Zarina wouldn't risk leaving herself vulnerable and her mate without backup during her transition.

Bambara crashed into another gunman, taking him out at the knees. A shot sounded, and Zarina knew her mate had been hit again. But he made the human pay. With a *crunch* and a *pop*, Bambara ripped the shooter's arm off.

Zarina yanked the gun from the screaming man's severed arm, sending him to his death with two shots to the head. "You're bleeding."

So are you. A lot.

"For her. For Shona. I'll bleed."

Yes, for her. For Shona. Always, my love. Shall we finish this?

Another group of armed men and women converged on the lobby. They wouldn't survive to see Asha or Shona again. Pity. Zarina wasn't ready to die, and she'd nursed hopes that Asha and Ekon would one day make her a grandmother. She'd even envisioned herself spoiling her grandbabies in a way she hadn't Asha. Zarina would've made a fine grandparent, as would have Bambara.

Even if Asha had children, with Ekon or another felidae of her choosing, Zarina and Bambara wouldn't be there to witness the blessings of birth or experience the pride of watching their daughter raise her children.

Don't cry. We'll see our Asha again.

They would. But they needed to give Asha, Ekon, and Mafdet more time. Mafdet would take care of Asha, after she and Bambara were gone. Mafdet would . . .

Pop. Pop. Pop. In quick succession, three gunmen lurched forward, falling onto the floor, their brains macabre splatters of crimson. Mafdet's sword sank into the scalp of another gunman, her warrior cry all Zarina needed to shift her thoughts away from the future she wouldn't have and back to the one life she needed to save.

Zarina and Bambara charged the gunmen. Ducking and dodging, they avoided as many bullets as they could. But not all. Not hardly all.

Her speed, strength, and love of family and kingdom kept Zarina a fluid motion of claws and fangs. With each bullet she took, she killed three humans in return. Yet they still came, drawn to the sound of battle.

She wanted every last one of those barbaric humans in the lobby with them. Every. Single. One. If they were down there, they wouldn't be upstairs hunting Asha and Ekon.

"Get out of here, Mafdet. I gave you an order to stay with Asha."

The Shieldmane had the temerity to shake her head. Mafdet pivoted, avoiding an attack from behind, and then plunged her sword into the back of an enemy combatant, ripping a shrill cry from the woman. Forcing the blade down the human's back, Mafdet jammed it in deep. Bloody saliva spurted from the female's mouth, silencing her death screams.

Mafdet shoved the dead woman away from her, her sword and hand as red as the blood flowing from her gunshot wounds.

"Go!" Zarina ordered Mafdet.

Pop. Pop. Two bullets ripped into her back. Zarina stumbled forward, cringing from the burning pain but refusing to fall to her knees.

With blinding speed her mate was there, his body as damaged as her own. Yet Bambara had planted himself between Zarina and enemies with a seemingly endless supply of firepower and fighters to rain down hell on them.

One more push, my love. Do you have one more drive in you?

Zarina didn't. But for Asha, she would muster the strength. "Go to her. *Please.*" She'd never begged a soul in her life. "Save our Asha. Go, Mafdet, before it's too late."

Zarina placed her bloody hand to Mafdet's cheek, careful to keep her body between the gunmen and the friend she needed to survive.

"Zarina, I . . ."

"I know you love us, but I need you to love Asha more. Don't let our deaths be in vain." With all her might, she struck out with both hands, hitting Mafdet in the shoulders and sending her flying across the blood-slicked floor.

"Zarina, noooo," Mafdet screamed, but she'd already turned away from her.

"One last push." Zarina sank a hand into her mate's warm, bloody fur. "I love you, Bambara."

I love you, Zarina.

They charged, powering over and through the first row of combatants, wounding and killing as many as they could.

The humans fired, unloading endless rounds into their bodies.

Zarina fell first, followed by Bambara. He covered her unmoving form with his own. She wept each time his body jerked. She'd never doubted her mate's love, just as he'd never questioned hers.

Tell her. While we still breathe, let her know.

His body spasmed above her with each bullet pumped into him. Bambara wouldn't be able to hold his lion form much longer. Pain and blood loss would force the change. Once that happened, he would succumb to his injuries. Zarina would soon follow. She felt death seeping into her bones.

Tell her.

Zarina reached for Asha's mind. She focused on memories of her child. Zarina's belly round with her daughter. The sound of Asha crying her way into the world. Asha crawling onto Bambara's lap and falling asleep. Asha chasing her tail. Asha laughing and playing and . . . Asha, Asha, Asha. Zarina's mind abounded with thoughts of her and Bambara's hafsa. Their greatest achievement.

Zarina touched Asha's mind, relieved to be this close to her daughter one final time. She could sense her pain, grief, and fear. Like mother, like daughter.

Asha, my hafsa, your father and I must go now. We're sorry to leave you so soon. We're sorry we won't see you continue to grow into a sekhem who will rival those who came before. Please know, you are our pride and joy. We leave knowing Shona is in your capable hands. Love her. Protect her. And she will love and protect you. The sun, Asha. You are Shona's shining sun.

Bambara slid from Zarina's back, his human body bloody, limp, dying. He smiled his handsome smile at her, closed his lids, and slipped into death.

Zarina filled her eyes with the sight of her beloved, holding his image close for the soul's journey home. At least they would be together. If she had to die, if one of them couldn't stay behind with Asha, Zarina was comforted by the fact that they'd ended their time on this plane of existence together.

As one.

You are Sekhem Sekhmet—She Who is Powerful. Wear the title well, Asha. Take care, be fierce, and stay strong. We love you.

Chapter 6: Only One

Ekon climbed over the dented walk-in freezer door, hands bruised and bloody, eyes scanning the kitchen, and ears searching for voices, footsteps, breathing. Hell, any sound would do if it meant the enemy still lurked. If they did, that would mean Asha was still somewhere on the premises. If not . . .

It had taken Ekon twenty interminable minutes to break the freezer door down and free himself from Asha's trap. No wonder she'd gone willingly to the restaurant with him instead of demanding they make a pointless stand on the thirteenth floor or even hide in one of a half dozen unlocked storage closets they'd stumbled upon.

Running, Ekon bolted from the kitchen, through the restaurant and into the hallway. Shiny floors, tall windows, crystal chandeliers, and not a soul in sight to appreciate the elegant, expensive decor of Sanctum Hotel.

Racing against a time he already missed, Ekon rushed down the hall, around two corners and toward the main lobby. He needed to get the hell out of there and call the police. The sooner he got them involved, the sooner they could help him find Asha.

Ekon skidded around a corner, his boots slipping on something wet . . . on blood. Lots and lots of blood. He fell, breaking his fall with palms to the sticky floor. Not just blood on the floor but dead bodies.

Limbs had been savaged, throats slashed, torsos mauled, and faces sliced.

A cemetery inside a hotel lobby.

The scent of blood—metallic—mixed with the smell of gunpowder—acrid. It slithered its way up his nostrils and into a brain that needed no olfactory assistance to deduce what had occurred there.

Ekon struggled to his feet, careful not to fall again. He made his way through the carnage, glad the beasts were dead but disappointed they hadn't all been killed before Asha decided to play martyr.

A sound—groaning maybe—had his head snapping up. Body tensed. Claws broke free. Ekon stared in the direction the sound had come—near the front desk. Bullet holes riddled the cherry finish, the same as the walls, and even the floor. Broken and carved-up bodies marked a trail of grisly destruction from one end of the check-in desk to the other. At the end of the desk was . . .

Ekon rushed toward the kneeling figure, his eyes all for her until he saw what held her rapt attention. At the sight, he stumbled to a halt then dropped to his hands and knees. Tears fell, grief constricted his heart, and anger tightened his throat.

No, no, no. Not the khalid and sekhem. Not Asha's parents. He'd known, when Asha had broken down, that her parents were dead. Ekon had known. But he hadn't. Not really. Not until he'd knelt beside a weeping Mafdet, a fist balled around her spiked sword handle, the other holding Sekhem Zarina's lifeless hand.

Ekon hated to look upon his alphas' dead bodies. Hated to see the damage the arsenal of bullets had done to them. Yet there was a bittersweet beauty to the couple's death pose. Their faces were turned to the other. Their legs were intertwined. Even their blood had merged in the small space between their bodies, joining them, even in death.

He thought he would be sick. His stomach revolted at the sight of his selfless alphas. They had done nothing to warrant their fate. Yet greed and violence had come for them, a vicious storm of human destruction that had forced them to fight, to kill, and, eventually, to die.

Ekon placed his hand on Mafdet's shoulder.

Her blade flew to his throat. "Where's Asha?"

"I . . . uhh, I . . ."

"I asked you a question." The tip of Mafdet's sword bit into his throat, drawing blood. "You were supposed to keep her safe. I don't see or smell her." Mafdet drew nearer, her face right next to his, her blade hand steady . . . deadly. "You better have hidden her somewhere safe. If you didn't, if you let those monsters take her from you, I'm going to slit your worthless throat."

Ekon didn't doubt Mafdet would follow through with her threat. He gulped. If she wanted to add his life to those already claimed by her blade, then so be it. But both had failed to protect their charges. The odds hadn't been in their favor. Ekon wouldn't escape his guilt, but his rational brain whispered the truth. *There was nothing anyone could've done differently.*

"Asha locked me in a kitchen freezer and turned herself in."

A snarl hovered on the edge of Mafdet's lips, her eyes molten.

Ekon thought she would slice his throat open.

Mafdet shoved his shoulder. Hard.

He fell onto his bottom, knees bent.

"She did it to save your sorry ass, didn't she?"

Ekon nodded, feeling every bit the worthless Shieldmane Mafdet had accused him of being.

"I knew Zarina was making a mistake when she assigned you as Asha's Second Shieldmane. I knew you would turn that girl's head around." With her chin, she gestured to the bodies of Asha's parents. "This is what humans do to our kind. They've never had a problem brutalizing us. Stealing our land, breaking their own treaties, none of it was ever enough for them. They pillage, murder, rape. What do you think they'll do to Asha, now that she's in their clutches and her parents can no longer protect her?"

Torture. Murder. Rape. Ekon knew nothing of Mafdet's history before she'd moved to Shona. He may be a useless boy in her eyes, but Ekon knew the broken sound of lived experience when he heard it.

He shook his head, denying those fates would befall Asha. "No, she has a plan. I think it involves Ms. Choi from the Common Peace Coalition Party."

"Asha's plan began and ended with saving your hide. She has no plan beyond that and certainly none involving a human who ran for Chief of the Republic of Vumaris and lost to Silas Royster."

"You have no faith in the sekhem you're sworn to protect." Ekon turned to his fallen alphas, closed his eyes, and recited a prayer. ". . . Brave lions of Shona, may Goddess Sekhmet welcome you home. Be at peace, for the lion goddess will see to your souls, while we will see to your earthly forms . . ."

"They can have no peace as long as Asha is at the mercy of those who took her. And neither can I." Mafdet stood, and Ekon did the same—body and soul exhausted, heart heavy. "We need to contact the police and call home. But first, we must secure the bodies of our family. I will not allow humans to touch them. They are our responsibility."

They would have to search the entire building for the missing four Shieldmanes. Like Mafdet, Ekon didn't question whether they still lived. No Shieldmane would stand by and do nothing while their khalid and sekhem fought for their lives.

"You said you would find her."

"I did, and I will." Mafdet's bloody blade slid into its sheath. "For now, though, Asha is on her own. I hope like hell she truly does have a plan."

So did Ekon. If not, if he and Mafdet had to return home with the bodies of the entire royal family, Shona would explode and Vumaris would burn.

They'd taken her back to Minra. Not to the First Evolution Union Party's headquarters, her captives weren't that stupid, but to a warehouse in the same city where, only a few hours ago, she and her parents had sat across a conference table from Chief Royster and Deputy Chief London. They were incautious, though, or perhaps simply arrogant because they didn't blindfold Asha during the drive from Sanctum Hotel to their current location.

She'd sat in the back seat of a nondescript black SUV between two burly human males she could've killed with little effort. Asha had kept her focus on the front window, cataloging every street sign and building. The darkness hid nothing from her felidae sight. From the sense of smell alone, Asha would be able to find the warehouse again, as she would every human in and around the building.

Minra was an old city, and it showed. Not every part of the municipality had undergone a makeover like its historic district where the First Evolution Union's headquarters were housed. The part of the city she had been driven to, an industrial waterfront with rotting ware-houses and piers, smelled of sewer water and abandoned dreams.

The SUV idled in front of Warehouse 7. No one spoke. No one had since a man with a skull and crossbones tattoo on his forearm had shoved her into the vehicle with a muttered, "A lot of good Rogueshades died because of you. You better have been worth it."

Rogueshades. Asha hadn't heard of the group. But that data, like everything she'd gathered since allowing herself to be taken captive, was stored for later examination and use. Most information proved valuable at some point, but the value of the information may not be seen or even understood at first glimpse.

As she followed one of the Rogueshade men out of the truck, Asha mined for the gold nuggets she'd learned from her parents. There were many and, like so much they'd taught her, not all were useful for every situation. It was up to Asha to decide how and when best to use her parents' kernels of wisdom.

Other SUVs joined the one Asha had climbed out of, and she real-ized the driver had been waiting for the others. Ten trucks in total, with five Rogueshades in each, not counting the four who had been in the truck with her.

They piled out, wearing a combination of tactical gear and stolen hotel uniforms. Asha grieved for not only her parents and Shield-manes, but also for the human hotel employees who had the misfor-tune of working the shift that put them in the path of the Rogueshade.

No one touched her. They didn't have to. The guns pointing at her delivered their message. She'd deduced they'd been given a two-part mission. Her capture had been part one. Her signature on the adden-dum of the 1902 boundary treaty between her kingdom and Vumaris would be part two. She had no intention of signing. They had no way of knowing that, of course, but they soon would. Where would that then leave her?

Would they try torturing her into submission? Probably.

Would she escape the warehouse before they did irreparable dam-age to her body or mind? Maybe.

Would she slaughter every Rogueshade, whether in the warehouse or elsewhere, if she survived? Definitely.

Asha had her own two-part mission. One, to learn as much as she could about Rogueshade and their connection to Royster and London.

Two, to stay alive. Come morning, Ms. Choi would arrive at Sanctum Hotel. Ekon would've already freed himself from the freezer. He would've also contacted General Tamani Volt, leader of the Shieldmane Panthera Leos. She would remind him of emergency protocols, and he would relay, hopefully, Asha's message about Ms. Choi. Tamani had never met Ms. Choi but she'd been briefed. With Bambara and Zarina dead, only Asha and Ms. Choi, however, knew the finer details of their alliance. With Tamani's assistance, Ekon would arrange to have their fallen returned home. He wouldn't return with them, though. She wished he would, but Ekon wouldn't leave Vumaris until he found and rescued her or, if the worst happened, recovered her body.

Playing the role of compliant hostage, Asha walked into the warehouse. Dirt-covered windows spanned the width of the upper level of the building, cement floors the lower level. She couldn't detect any odor in the room she recognized as to what had once been stored there, but she could smell rats, roaches, and what both left behind. She also smelled lions but dismissed the thought as absurd. Asha wore no shoes, but her feet weren't cold, and it would take more than walking around a filthy warehouse to cut them.

She eyed the single chair in the center of the room and wondered if Rogueshade could get more movie cliché. Perhaps, in one of the upstairs rooms they had a cattle prod for her lion form, rope to string her up with, not that she'd seen a beam in the warehouse. Or maybe they would see how long she could hold her breath underwater or how many cuts to her tough felidae skin it would take before she cried and begged and then gave them what they wanted.

Of all her years of sekhem training, none of them included torture. Felidae had a high pain threshold. When it came to torture, that truth could prove a blessing or a curse.

The Rogueshade behind Asha shoved her toward the wooden chair. "Sit your ass down, and don't speak."

Considering she hadn't uttered a word since she let the brutes capture her, staying quiet wouldn't be an issue. Asha sat, hands on her knees. She waited for what would come next.

Except for the Rogueshade who'd shoved her, the driver from the SUV she'd been driven there in, the others took up posts on both levels. Perhaps even a few stationed themselves outside. She did hear the door behind her creak open then close.

"You're a pretty little thing. Young too. A princess."

"Hafsa Sekhem, not a princess."

"What?"

"Hafsa Sekhem of the Kingdom of Shona. That's my title." The sound of her mother's dying voice in her head threatened to flood her eyes with tears. Asha forced them down. She would not show weakness in front of this male or any other human. "That was my title before my parents were murdered. I'm now Sekhem of the Kingdom of Shona."

A sentence she'd thought she wouldn't say for at least two decades. The words felt wrong. The feeling they invoked nauseating.

The Rogueshade grinned at her. He had perfect white teeth. His dentist should be proud. Asha would make the grinning Rogueshade swallow every one of those teeth. She would also break his wide nose, pluck his dark brown eyes from their sockets, and cut his spine from his back.

Asha returned his smile, showing him her own straight white teeth.

"That's a fancy title for a little girl. I'm glad you know it because you'll need it for the paperwork."

A female Rogueshade jogged up to them. They all had a rigid, almost uniform way of walking, talking, and handling weapons that screamed human military. Whether active duty or freelance, Asha neither knew nor cared. Their fate would be the same.

The woman handed the man a manila folder and a ballpoint pen. "He wants her signature on all three pages. Make sure she signs legibly." The woman rounded on Asha. "For the trouble your parents caused, for the good soldiers they killed, we should feed your ass to real lions."

So, she had smelled lions. Asha should've trusted her senses, even though there was nothing logical about having lions in a warehouse, even ones accustomed to being around humans.

The female Rogueshade leaned close enough to Asha for her to smell alcohol on her breath and whoever's penis she'd had in her mouth before leaving on the Rogueshade's murderous mission. She also detected two distinct male scents on the female—one of which was the male in front of her, the other of a male she'd scented back at the hotel.

"Nighthide. Don't."

"We should make her sign then let the lions have her." The female . . . Nighthide, punched Asha in the face. For code names, the woman could've chosen better. As for her punch, it barely registered. If they were going to torture Asha, they would have to do better than attacks on the level of a human's strength.

"It took some doing, but London got two lions from the local zoo. They aren't as big as your daddy, whose head I would've loved to have stuffed and mounted to my wall, but the motherfucker turned back into his human form when his ass finally kicked the bucket."

"Nighthide."

She ignored the man's gravelly voiced warning.

"Not as big as dead daddy but still big." With a thumb over her shoulder, Nighthide pointed to the upper level. "We had to tranq them, but they'll be awake soon. Awake and hungry."

"That's enough."

"What, Stormbane? We lost friends tonight, and it's all her damn fault."

Nighthide struck Asha again. The same kind of punch, to the same left cheek, and with the same effect. She raised her hand to level another weak blow.

Stormbane caught Nighthide's wrist. "Leave the girl alone. We follow orders. Right now, the only order we have is to have her sign the papers you just brought me. If she doesn't . . ." He shrugged wide shoulders. "We'll wait for orders to tell us how he wants it handled."

"We know how to handle her kind." With a hard tug, Nighthide yanked her arm free of Stormbane's hold. With how much bigger the male was to the female, he'd either not been holding her wrist tightly or he'd loosened his grip so she could have the win.

"Matching bands." Asha nodded to the couple. "Until he grabbed your arm, I hadn't noticed the twin gold bands."

Nighthide's eyes narrowed and her lips twisted. "Shut up and mind your damn business."

"You're right. Your marriage is none of my business. I only mentioned it because you reek of a human male I encountered at the hotel."

"Don't push it. My wife told you to shut up."

"Of course, but do you not wonder who it is that I smell on your wife? She wasn't with you before you attacked my family and friends, was she? Maybe your group left first. Or perhaps she and he snuck away in one of those rooms I can see from here while you were preoccupied."

Stormbane's jaw tightened, and Nighthide's eyes flashed.

"Blond ponytail. He tricked me into opening my suite door for him." Asha granted Nighthide the same perfect white teeth smile she'd given to her husband—a prelude to the claws that would rip them apart. "He's dead now. But you know that because he didn't return with the rest of your murderous group. You know he's dead, the same way I know my parents and friends are. I would say that makes us even, but that wouldn't be true."

"She's lying."

"About Brightstrike being dead?" Stormbane closed the short distance between his wife's body and his own. "He's not here with us, so I count him among the fatalities. Or did you mean she's lying about you fucking that son of a bitch behind my back?"

"Can't you see what she's doing? She's trying to turn us against one another."

"Yeah, I know what the girl is doing. But I also know your lying, cheating ass. I had a feeling something was going on . . . that you were up to your old shit."

"It was her breath that gave her away," Asha interjected smoothly. "I've never engaged in fellatio, mind you, so I'm not positive about post-oral sex procedures. I assume there's brushing of teeth and tongue involved. Perhaps the use of mouthwash. I doubt either are in stock here. From what I can smell coming from your wife's mouth, she used alcohol to hide the scent. Or to minimize the taste of his cum, if she's into swallowing. I saw a woman do that on a porno I watched last night." She shook her head, as if she'd gotten lost in an erotic memory. "Anyway, I don't know what kind of alcohol she used. But I'm sure you know what she likes to drink, other than from the penis of your friend Brightstrike."

Thwack. Thwack. Thwack. Thwack.

The flurry of punches didn't surprise Asha. What had surprised her was how long it had taken for Nighthide to retaliate.

Asha's chair tipped back, but the strength of her legs prevented her and the chair from toppling over.

"How much do you love your wife?" Asha asked Stormbane, unbothered by the punches to her face and chest that left Nighthide winded but her unfazed.

"Not enough to keep putting up with her lying and bullshit."

Good answer. Asha stood, swung upward and connected with the underside of Nighthide's chin.

The woman's mouth fell open, and Asha could see three inches of her lion's claws sticking through the female's tongue.

She yanked forward, the movement bringing with it half of the human's tongue, lower lip, and part of her chin.

For the second time that day, the barrel of a gun pressed to her head.

"You said you were tired of putting up with her lying and bullshit." Asha lifted her clawed hand to Stormbane, offering him his wife's bloody tongue. "Now you won't have to."

Nighthide crumpled to the ground—sobbing and bleeding.

"That's not what I meant, and you know it. I should kill you."

"You probably should, but you won't. Not yet, anyway." Asha tossed the partial tongue to a retreating Nighthide, aided by another Rogueshade soldier who half carried, half dragged her away from Asha. "I won't sign those papers, by the way."

The barrel pressed harder against the side of her head.

Using a fistful of her dress, Asha wiped her hand clean. Well, as clean as she could without soap and water. There was still a little blood and skin under her fingernails.

Asha sat in the chair, crossed her legs, and showed Stormbane her white teeth again. "Get a video recorder. I have a message for Chief Royster and Deputy Chief London."

Chapter 7: Lady of the Many Faces

"You have completely lost your mind." Silas slammed the conference room door behind him, stalked to Frank and grabbed the shorter man by his suit lapels and onto his tiptoes. "Do you have any idea what you've done? Any idea what Shona will do when they learn their alphas are dead?"

"Get your hands off me."

"I wish I could shake some sense into you." With a hard shove, Silas pushed Frank away from him. His second-in-command stumbled and fell over the chairs behind him. "Even if I could shake sense into you, it's already too late."

Frank stared up at Silas with those big owl eyes of his, face defiant and attitude all wrong. "That will be the last time you touch me." Using the arm of a chair, Frank got to his feet. "We had a plan. You agreed to it. Don't pretend you didn't."

"I didn't agree to your hit squad assassinating leaders of a sovereign nation."

Silas kicked a chair, sending it rolling to the other side of the room. Needing to put distance between himself and a man who, with each passing day, he regretted forming an alliance with, Silas marched away from Frank. Too agitated to sit, he paced.

"One of your Rogueshade reported in. I had to drag myself out of bed to meet with him. Do you know what he showed me?" Silas didn't wait for Frank to answer. "I bet you do know. You and your damn pictures. Blood was everywhere, and the khalid and sekhem were dead." Palms slammed on the table. "Dead, Frank. Both of them."

"About four dozen of my Rogueshades died during the mission. You sound like you care more about the dead felidae than our human patriots."

"You said your group would use a felidae gas to weaken them so they could snatch the girl. That's what you said. That's what I agreed to." Silas waved his hands over his head, unsure what in the hell it meant but needing to physically express his frustration over an international incident he had no idea how to manage. "I didn't sanction the slaughter of respected world leaders." Palms slammed back down.

Frank's eyes narrowed as he took a seat and he tsk-tsked. "This is why you came to me, and why your party couldn't win without mine. You and your party lack a spine to make tough decisions." Elbows going to the table, Frank leaned forward, sneering up at him. "Your naïveté is a pain in my ass, Silas. You want power, money, and influence, but you turn a blind eye as to what it takes to get and maintain them. Yes, you agreed to have the Rogueshade sent to Sanctum Hotel to kidnap the hafsa sekhem."

Frank stood, planted his palms on the table like Silas, and asked with so much condescension Silas wanted to shake Frank like a rag doll, "How in the hell did you think that would play out, even with the use of the Basilisk Smoke? Did you really think the mission would go that smoothly? That felidae older than a century would be so easily controlled? That they wouldn't put up one hell of a fight to protect their daughter? Even your spineless ass would fight if someone came into your home wanting to take Audrey away from you and your wife." A finger rose and pointed at Silas. "We both know I'm right. The difference between the two of us is that I'm honest enough to admit it. I sent eleven Rogueshade squads and, from what I've been told, about half of them returned to the warehouse. Half," Frank repeated, his gaze hard. "So, excuse the fuck out of me if I don't shed a tear over the recently departed Khalid Bambara and Sekhem Zarina."

From opposite sides of the table, but not as far apart in ideology as Silas tried to convince himself they were, they glared at each other. This bell couldn't be unrung. "No war, Frank. We can't send Vumarian soldiers into war against the Shona."

"Why not? They have claws and fangs, but we have real weapons of war."

"If you think a nation older and richer than ours doesn't have modern weapons, then you're the naïve one. We would be fighting a blind war because we have little to no intel on the military capability of the kingdom. When have you seen footage of any kind from inside Shona? Pictures? Documentaries? Interviews? Primary or even secondary accounts? Shona leaders travel to other countries for a reason. Their borders are closed to non-Shona, but the international community accepts that foreign policy stance because they say no to everyone, including felidae from other countries. But where their borders are closed to immigrants and tourists, their financial institutions are not."

"Those facts change nothing. The felidae are animals, Silas. Animals don't deserve the same considerations and rights as humans."

Silas pulled a chair to him and sat. Listening to Frank's racism gave him a migraine. He could mention that humans also had the felidae gene, though inactive. Did their inability to transmutate into a predatory cat make them less of an animal? "We killed a girl's parents. I think that makes us the real beasts of prey. Do you have no remorse for turning the hafsa sekhem into an orphan?"

Frank also claimed a chair, sitting with a calm grace unsuited to the man. "What I made her was a queen. For our purposes, it'll be much easier dealing with an eighteen-year-old girl than her obstinate, arrogant parents." Frank's smirk made Silas want to jump across the table and punch him in his face. "You're welcome, by the way. Northern Shona will be ours in . . ." He looked at the watch on his right wrist. "Five minutes."

"What do you mean 'northern Shona?' "

"I added a couple of more pages to the treaty's addendum to include all of Shona above the twenty-eighth parallel north." The smirk deepened, as did Silas's rage. "Don't look at me like that."

"That's a third of Shona."

"I know. Think what we'll be able to do with that additional land and resources. Our party will be unrivaled, our legacy set for centuries to come."

"You're delusional."

"I'm a visionary."

"The girl won't sign away a third of her ancestral land."

"You're wrong. Like you said, she's eighteen and alone for the first time. I asked you to meet me here because I spoke with one of my men. He has a recorded message from the girl."

Silas looked around the conference room, spotting a carafe of coffee on the sideboard. He thanked the nameless worker who saved him from imprisonment after he pummeled his second-in-command to death. With the cup to keep his hands busy, the coffee to keep his insides warm, and the caffeine to keep his body relaxed, he might be able to stomach the rest of the conversation.

Silas poured himself a steaming cup of coffee, adding one sugar and two cream packets. He sniffed, tasted, smiled. *Perfect.*

"Are you done?"

Returning to his seat, Silas inhaled the rich aroma of hazelnut and drank more of the life-saving caffeine.

"You and your damn coffee addiction. As I was saying, Asha is just a girl. You saw the way she sat at this table yesterday. She looked bored out of her skull."

"News flash, Frank, all teenagers look like that. It doesn't mean anything. You would know that about them if you hadn't palmed the raising of your kids off on your ex-wife. How old are your sons? Early twenties, right?"

"My family is none of your concern."

Frank all but scowled the words at Silas, the only clue the man gave a damn about someone other than himself. *Good to know.*

"My point is that she has no more interest in ruling a kingdom than any other teenager would. Because her parents are gone, I'm sure she's hurt and angry. But she's also afraid of ending up like them, almost as much as she's terrified of running a country she's ill-equipped to handle. Like I said, she looked bored yesterday, ready to get the hell out of here as soon as she could. She doesn't want the responsibilities left to her."

"You've made a lot of assumptions."

"Thirty-five. That's how old a candidate must be to run for Chief. We're ten years older than that."

"I'm forty-seven."

"Cut the passive-aggressive bullshit and listen." Frank eyed the coffee cup in Silas's hand. A minute later, he fixed himself a cup—black—like his heart. "No country has a head of state under the age of thirty. Any head of state younger than thirty, the country risks having a ruler in office with too little knowledge, skill, and experience to be an effective leader. She may be more mature than the average eighteen-year-old, I'll give her that. But at the end of the day, Asha is a girl with a big title, an even bigger country, and huge shoes she can't possibly fill. By taking a third of her kingdom off her hands, we'll be doing her a favor."

"A favor?"

Frank gulped his coffee as if it wasn't hot. "She won't want to see it like that, and I doubt she would admit it to anyone. But she'll be glad to be rid of some of her responsibility. Her parents were too proud for their own good. But I do know teens and fuck you for implying I was an absent father to my boys."

Silas lifted his cup to his mouth. Empty. From the way Frank's fists were clenched, maybe they would come to blows after all. Ignoring Frank, he poured himself more coffee. The second cup was even better than the first.

"Stop seething and finish. You may not have anyone waiting for you at home, but I do. I don't want to be here all night."

Silas thought Frank would curse him again, and maybe he would've, but the knock on the door halted whatever had been percolating in Frank's mind.

To be continued, he supposed. "Come in."

A security guard opened the door and peeked her head inside. "Sirs, there is a Sergeant Major Javier Hernandez to see you. I was told to bring him here when he arrived."

Frank got to his feet and walked to the door, ushering Sergeant Major Hernandez in and thanking the guard before closing the door firmly in her face. Frank shook the tall, muscular man's hand, and so did Silas.

"Stormbane, this is Chief Silas Royster. Silas, Stormbane here is the elite of the elite. Rogueshade is comprised of only the best the Vumarian military has to offer." Frank's big eyes brightened, and he slapped

Hernandez on the shoulder. "I was just telling Silas about your good work at the hotel. How's our little queen?"

Dressed in crisp black fatigues, white shirt, and black boots, Hernandez didn't look like a man who'd been in a life-and-death battle. He appreciated Hernandez's good sense to freshen up before appearing at the party's headquarters.

Hernandez's dark eyes fell to the hand on his shoulder then to Silas. "Nice to meet you, Chief Royster. May I sit, Deputy Chief?"

"Of course, of course," Frank said, happier and friendlier than he'd known the man to be, except for when they'd won the election. Frank pulled out a chair for Hernandez, the one right next to his own. "Here you go. You should've brought Nighthide with you, so Silas could see we don't discriminate in Rogueshade based on gender."

Maybe not gender, but there were other forms of genetic-based discrimination.

While on the campaign trail, Silas had met his share of active duty and retired soldiers. They weren't all the same. Not in their bearings or in their beliefs. But he knew a veteran soldier when he saw one—men and women too used to taking orders and going into war. The Sergeant Major had that look about him—a man who'd traveled to a cliff's edge countless times, jumping over because someone above him, someone like Frank London, told him his loyalty and service were for a great cause. Silas would like to think the causes Hernandez had killed for were indeed great. Unfortunately, what happened at the hotel couldn't be counted as one of them, not when terrorizing and kidnapping a child had been part of his mission.

There was something else in the man's eyes. Sadness, maybe. Regret? Silas couldn't pinpoint the emotion. But the way he'd all but flinched when Frank mentioned Nighthide, a female Rogueshade apparently, Silas assumed whatever emotions he detected from the soldier had to do with the woman Frank thought would demonstrate his group's gender equality.

"Savannah is in the hospital."

Frank patted Hernandez's shoulder again. "I understand. I guess she was hurt during the mission. I'm sure she'll be fine. She's tough, just like her husband."

"Yeah, Savannah is tough. But you don't understand." Hernandez placed the item he'd been holding on the table in front of Frank. "But you will."

"Great, the video you mentioned on the phone. Where's the folder I gave Nighthide?"

"Back at the warehouse."

"You were supposed to bring it here."

"Tell us what we don't know," Silas interjected, annoyed by Frank's obliviousness to detect the undercurrent running through his own soldier. "What happened after your team secured the girl?"

Long seconds passed before Hernandez responded. His big hands were splayed on the table in front of him, and Silas could envision those hands holding a gun and ending lives. The elite of the elite. With a code name like Stormbane, Silas grasped what made him and his fellow Rogueshades the best the Vumarianmilitary had to offer, at least in Frank's eyes.

"I left a squad behind to collect our dead and dispose of the bodies of the others."

"Good," Frank agreed, with the same bland tone as Hernandez's use of the word "others" to describe those killed by his team.

"Not good, sir. When they didn't return, I sent a couple of the guys after them."

Silas knew he wouldn't like the conclusion to Hernandez's story.

"The bodies were still there, including the squad I left for cleanup and removal."

The hand wrapped around the coffee cup and making its way to Frank's mouth stilled. "What are you talking about?"

"We killed the Shona leaders and all of their bodyguards. At least we thought we eliminated all of the guards."

Frank's hand slammed to the table, cracking the coffee cup. "The royal family and six guards. That's nine felidae. Only one of them should've survived—the girl. Eight bodies. Are you telling us you don't have eight felidae bodies?"

"We don't have *any* felidae corpses. That's what I'm telling you. A lot of dead Rogueshades, including the squad assigned to cleanup and disposal, but not one Shona. We swept the hotel for survivors before we left with the girl."

"You obviously missed someone."

"I don't see how we could've."

"Yet you obviously did."

"Yeah," Hernandez said and scratched his scalp under his closely cropped hair, "I suppose we did. But there was no bodyguard with the girl when we found her."

Like Frank, Silas no longer had a taste for his coffee. He pushed his cup away instead of slamming it on the table as Frank had done his own. "Does it make sense to you, Sergeant Major, that Khalid Bambara and Sekhem Zarina would leave their daughter unprotected?"

"It doesn't. I assumed her guard had been killed and, in the melee, she ran away. We caught her in the kitchen. Most likely she thought she could escape through the loading area. Smart plan, but I'd stationed three soldiers at that post."

"When she was discovered, did she fight or try to run away?"

"Make your point," Frank barked at Silas.

"Your Sergeant Major knows my point. The girl allowed herself to be captured because she was protecting one of her guards. That's the felidae who took out the squad he left behind and who also removed the bodies of his leaders and comrades. Isn't that right, Sergeant Major?"

A stiff nod answered his question, so Silas pushed on. "Tell me you sent in another squad to clean up what the first failed to do. By clean up I also mean the security footage."

"That's what took me so long to get here. I went back to the hotel to personally oversee the mission. We had until five before the change in shift. The morning hotel crew will arrive to find bullet holes and blood but no bodies. The shift manager will call corporate and the police. There was never any way to keep what happened under wraps. But, without bodies and security tapes, the police won't have much to go on."

"Unless the bodyguard you let slip through your net goes to the police."

"Come on, Silas. We can spin this however we want. No one will believe the guard."

"Why? Because he's Shona and beneath humans? All of Vumaris doesn't think of the felidae the way you do."

"If that were true, we wouldn't have won the election. Our supporters know that no matter how rich the Shona are, how well spoken and educated, or even how attractive their human form that, at their core, felidae are dangerous animals who cannot be trusted. One guard killed an entire squad. Why would we place our trust and safety in a race of people capable of that kind of carnage?"

"But—"

"Stormbane, tell me why you didn't bring the signed papers and what's on the VHS."

Hernandez's gaze shifted between Silas and Frank, probably confused as to which of them was in charge. His dark eyes finally settled on Frank. "The girl refused to sign the addendum. She also attacked my wife. She could've killed her. She moved incredibly fast. I was standing right there. Right in front of her." He licked dry, cracked lips. "I didn't see her stand. I didn't see her fingers shift. I didn't see anything before her claws were embedded in Savannah's chin."

"My god." The statement burst from Silas. The image he'd envisioned was gruesome but also incongruent with the quiet, polite girl he'd met.

"She looks like an angel—soft spoken and mannerly. She isn't. She didn't kill Savannah, although she could've. She wanted to hurt her, to punish her. She wants to punish us all."

The two-hundred-pound, six-foot hardcore soldier shivered.

"You sound as if you're scared of the girl. Are you scared of an eighteen-year-old child who weighs a buck twenty?"

"You don't get it, Deputy Chief. We killed her parents. What do you think something like that does to the mind of someone as young as the girl? I don't think she gives a damn about being sekhem, but she cares a hell of a lot about hurting those who hurt her."

"She's just a scared little girl," Frank insisted. "We can and will control her. Okay, yes, maybe she has more balls than I gave her credit for having. Maybe she's more like her mother than I realized. But she's still a solitary lioness without a pride to back her up. She'll sign over her land to us, even if it takes destroying her will and breaking her body. Use the lions, if you must. I bet she'll sign then."

"What lions?"

"Don't worry about it, Silas." Frank slid the videocassette to Hernandez. "There's a VCR on the television stand. Put the video on so I can see what's got you shaking in your boots."

Hernandez paused and then frowned as if he'd smelled rotten food, but said nothing. Doing as Frank ordered, the Rogueshade turned on the television and VCR and pushed in the VHS. He handed Frank the remote control when he returned to his chair.

The lighting in the warehouse wasn't the best, but Silas could make out armed soldiers standing against a wall behind a seated Asha. The girl looked like she'd been through the wringer. Her hair stood up in wild curls. Her dress, different from the one he'd last seen her wearing, was torn in places and bloodied in others. She wore no shoes. Dark circles rimmed eyes that looked nothing like the ones he'd seen when she'd sat with her parents.

Silas wished his shock at seeing irrefutable evidence of his and Frank's plan to kidnap a daughter of Shona, her wrists and ankles chained to a chair, served as the cause of his pounding heart and suddenly dry mouth. But it wasn't, no matter how uncomfortable the sight of a bound girl made him feel.

Her eyes—golden-brown—neither reminded Silas of a caged animal nor of a frightened teen. They didn't shine with tears, although their puffiness revealed she had cried. Her eyes also didn't wilt when Stormbane approached from the side. They stared right into the video camera.

Flat. Cold.

"Hello, Chief Royster and Deputy Chief London."

When she spoke, the expression on her face didn't change; neither did the look in her eyes. Her voice didn't remind him of her mother's—strident and subtly threatening. Silas couldn't recall if he'd heard the girl speak yesterday. For some reason, he didn't think she had, so he couldn't be sure if her voice had changed. Common sense told him, after her ordeal, it very well may have. But it was as Hernandez had said, she looked like an angel. A bedraggled angel, but an angel all the same. But her voice—a diabetic coma level of sugary sweetness—was potentially life-threatening.

Frank paused the video. "You should've shackled her from the beginning. She won't attack anyone else with those heavy-duty chains holding her in place."

"Can she break them?" Silas asked.

"She let me put them on her without a fight or complaint."

"Meaning what?"

"It means I have no idea what she's capable of until she does it, Chief Royster. It means if I get back to the warehouse and find my soldiers slaughtered and her gone, I wouldn't be surprised." Hernandez pointed to the paused image of the girl. "She won't be gone, though. She hasn't punished us yet." The same finger shifted to Silas and Frank. "She hasn't punished you two yet. We should kill her and be done with it."

"No," Silas and Frank said at the same time but undoubtedly for different reasons.

"You already murdered her parents. That's enough. Asha doesn't have to die too."

"That decision will have us all dead. You might as well play the video and see for yourself. The girl's not right in the head. She speaks in riddles, but her message is clear."

"That she wants us all dead?"

"Wouldn't you, Chief Royster? I know I would. Why should I think because she's young and female that she would be any less bloodthirsty? If her personality ever matched her sweet face, it doesn't anymore. She's a spawn of the devil." Hernandez removed the remote control from Frank's immobile hand and pushed the play button. "We unleashed a demon. See for yourself."

"When the world around us raged with injustice and all manner of violence and oppression, the Kingdom of Shona avoided becoming embroiled in the affairs of others. We neither took sides nor offered our opinion on social issues that did not involve our people. If nothing else, we Shona know how to survive."

She paused.

Silas released his held breath.

For several minutes, Asha remained silent, staring off into the distance. It was an empty warehouse. What in the world could've captured her attention?

"We Shona believe in a higher power. When a lion and lioness ascend to alpha, they are blessed with a new name. The name Bambara comes from a Panthera Leo tribal leader who risked his life to aid the Panthera Tigris fleeing human captivity. Zarina means golden lioness of peace and protection. For my grandmother, the name Zarina exemplified what it means to be a sekhem, so she chose not to bestow Mom with a new name upon her ascension to alpha."

"This is worthless," Frank complained. Snatching the remote from Hernandez, he paused the video. "Instead of allowing her to record this garbage, you should've used the time to force her to sign the addendum. I don't need a lesson on Shona naming practices."

"Neither did I, sir. But there's a message in what appears to be the ramblings of a grief-stricken girl."

"If you say so." Frank restarted the video.

As if she'd been waiting for them, she paused again. Her eyes, once more, looked off-screen.

"What is she looking at?" Silas asked.

"Nothing. Everything." Hernandez shrugged. "She's the spookiest kid I've ever met. Give me permission to put a bullet in her brain. If not, at the first opportunity, she'll do to us what she did to Savannah. But she won't stop at a tongue and chin. She'll take all of our heads."

Silas gripped his coffee cup, raised it to his mouth, and downed the rest. It was no longer hot and the flavor of hazelnut didn't taste as good going down as it had before, but Silas needed something to calm his nerves. Room temperature coffee wouldn't be enough, but it was better than nothing.

"My mother gave me my sekhem name. I didn't want it, but she had no choice but to bless me with it anyway." Asha paused again but didn't look away. She stared right at the camera lens, eyes more gold than brown. "He who beats the drum for the madman to dance to is no better than the madman himself."

"What does that mean?" Frank asked.

"He who runs after good fortune runs away from peace."

"This is ridiculous. Is she reciting proverbs?"

"I'm not sure, sir." Hernandez looked to Silas.

"I think she is."

"A child of a rat is a rat."

"Did she call our ancestors and us rats?" Frank sounded offended.

"Yeah, that one was easy to figure out. She told me she was Sekhem of the Kingdom of Shona. But she didn't tell me her sekhem name."

"What does it matter what name her mother gave her? It doesn't change the fact that she's our prisoner and will have no choice but to cede northern Shona to Vumaris. Besides, in an international court of law, forgery would be easier to prove than coercion, especially if the supposed victim is dead."

"I think her sekhem name does matter, Frank. I'm pretty sure that's part of her message. She mentioned Shona believing in a higher power. I think she means their gods. That's likely a clue to her sekhem name. Only a handful of deities within the Shona Panthera pantheon are female."

Shona may have been an isolationist nation, but they were a learned people who were strategic in what they shared about themselves to those beyond their borders. Their polytheistic beliefs weren't a secret. Silas's wife, Claire, had found a used book on ancient Shona mythology at a garage sale. She'd picked it up, dusted it off, and added it to their home library. In preparation for his meeting with the Shona leaders, he'd pulled the book down and had read most of it.

"If your only tool is a hammer, you will see every problem as a nail."

"Pause the video."

"Why?"

"Frank, pause the damn video."

"But . . . okay, fine. It's paused. Happy?"

"Not even close. The Shona alpha lioness is referred to as sekhem."

"We know that. That's her title. Sekhem Asha. Formerly Hafsa Sekhem Asha."

"The title of sekhem is derived from the name of the Panthera Leo's lion goddess. Her name is Sekhmet."

Frank blew out a breath, rolled his eyes, and picked up the remote. "She's a girl, not a goddess."

"She's a sekhem whose mother, if I'm correct, named her after a goddess of war and destruction. According to the Legend of Sekhmet, the goddess went on a rampage, slaughtering nonbelievers and those who threatened the people of Shona. The fields ran red with the blood of Shona's enemies. They believe the lion-headed goddess is the reason why humans haven't encroached on their territory since her murderous rampage. She protects them by killing their enemies. Sekhmet can't be stopped until her bloodlust has been quenched."

Frank and Hernandez stared at Silas. The men wore different expressions. Hernandez appeared ready to deliver a kill shot to Asha. While Frank had the look of a man whose patience had run its course.

"Asha, Sekhem, Sekhmet, whatever in the hell you want to call that *girl* on the screen, she's flesh and blood and no more a threat to us than an itch on our asses. I don't care who or what the Shona worship."

"You should care because she does. It doesn't matter whether we believe in their gods. They do. It also doesn't matter how young we think Asha is to rule. Her people will rally behind her because she's the rightful heir to their throne."

"The Shona can't follow a dead girl. We only need her signature. After that, she's useless. Just like her lion goddess."

"You're wrong."

"I'm not. Hernandez, once the *goddess* signs, you have my permission to put a bullet between her eyes." Frank resumed the video.

There wasn't much left. Asha's gaze wandered again, and she paused between seemingly nonsensical Shona history facts. But there was no mistaking her threat.

"Anger and madness are sisters. I am The One Before Whom Evil Trembles."

Chapter 8: Lady of Strong Love

Eight Years Earlier
The Kingdom of Shona
City of GoldMeadow
Temple of Sekhmet

"I can't do it."

"A pout, a whine, and little faith in self. What am I to do with you?"

Asha knew she should feel ashamed, but she didn't. She also knew she should be more patient, but her knees hurt from kneeling, and she was hungry. Finally, Asha knew her mother wouldn't give her leave to break for lunch until she met her lesson's objective.

"I don't know how to convince her to speak to me."

Zarina's hand grasped Asha's, her mother on a prayer rug beside her. As always, Zarina never expected Asha to undergo a task she was unwilling to complete alongside her. That thought did bring shame to her heart.

"I'll remind you again, speaking to the goddess isn't today's lesson, my hafsa. That ability is years above you, as is aligning her spirit with your own. Both skills are too advanced for your young mind."

"But I'll be ten next month."

"Ah, yes. Ten is a notable benchmark. Do you imagine, when you move into the two digits, that your patience will double?"

Asha scooted closer to her mother, warmed by her hand over the top of hers. "Sarcasm also isn't today's lesson."

Zarina's laughter filled Asha's ears and the temple, bouncing off the stone walls and settling at their bent knees. "You mastered the art of sarcasm by age eight. I was quite proud."

"Daddy says one sarcastic sekhem in the house is quite enough."

"Did he now?"

Asha nodded.

"What did you say?"

"I told him that there was only one sekhem in our home and that I am hafsa sekhem, which is not at all the same."

"Of course not. Not the same at all." Zarina laughed again.

Asha used the lighthearted moment to snuggle even closer to her mother, dropping her head to her arm and closing her eyes. "I know today's lesson is for me to clear my mind."

"Correct. A cluttered mind is like a house with bars on the windows and doors. No one can enter or exit."

"What if I don't want to leave the safety of my house?"

"Sometimes, Asha, what appears as safe proves to be nothing more than an elaborate prison. At some point, one must open the door and venture outside, trusting their home will always be there when they are ready to return."

"I don't understand."

Lips pressed to her forehead and an arm wrapped around her shoulders. "To commune with Goddess Sekhmet, to truly be one with her, you have to open all the doors and windows to your mind and heart. She requires a willing and unafraid vessel. But no sekhem is expected to serve in that physical role. We may be long-lived, Asha, but our bodies are mortal. We aren't meant to carry the weight of a goddess."

Asha opened sleepy eyes. Her mother's gaze wasn't on her but on the six-foot standing statue of Sekhmet fifteen feet in front of them.

Shona sculptors depicted the goddess as either seated or standing, using black granodiorite combined with a variety of stones. Regardless of the position or the material used for the statue, the designs varied little from the one in the temple. Except for a lion's head, tail, and clawed hands, the statue was that of a female—naked breasts, a fitted wrap from waist to ankles, and braids that flowed down her back and over her breasts.

At five, when Zarina had first brought Asha to Sekhmet's temple, she'd hidden behind her legs, afraid to enter despite having an offering of frankincense oil. She'd seen smaller statues in her home and in most buildings in Shona. Yet stepping in the ancient temple, atop a hill where every khalid and sekhem pledged their undying protection to the people of Shona, had frozen Asha's legs.

Zarina had ended up carrying her inside. Not only that day, but every time they'd visited the temple until Asha ceased feeling as if the statue would come alive and claim Asha's body as her own. At night and alone, Asha admitted she still felt that way, though she knew better than to voice such nonsense to her parents.

Hearing her mother mention carrying the weight of the goddess as an impractical feat for a mortal eased five years' worth of unspoken anxiety. There were times when Asha had curled up next to Mafdet on the couch and watched a horror movie with her godmother. None had given her nightmares, the only reason why Mafdet relented. But Asha disliked movies that involved possession.

Most characters were possessed by demons or some other equally vile creature. The possession took two forms—forced or voluntary. Sadness and anger had her balling her fists at the awful turn the protagonist's life had taken after a forced possession, while she yelled at the characters who allowed themselves to be possessed for petty or shortsighted gains. During those times, Mafdet would hit her with a pillow and say, "Quiet it down or I'm turning it off."

Asha always quieted it down because, while the thought of possession frightened her, the fear didn't diminish her curiosity. Could a mortal control a supernatural entity or would they lose themselves—mind, body, and soul?

"I know you're still young, hafsa, so I do not expect you to master the art of meditation by your tenth birthday." Zarina bumped Asha's shoulder with her own. "But ten is pretty mature. You should at least be able to recite all ten thousand of the goddess's names before your birthday."

"W-what?" Asha squeaked.

"You do have a month, after all." Zarina stood. "You better start on creating that list of names. You left your book bag outside the temple. Hopefully, mixed in with your books and dolls, you actually have paper and a pencil in there."

Asha stared after her mother's retreating form, convinced she was joking.

Zarina walked out of the Temple of Sekhmet and disappeared into the bright late afternoon day.

Asha fell forward, her stomach grumbling. Her mother was the worst. The absolute wors—

"Mother of the Gods. That's one."

Her mother was the best.

Smiling, Asha jumped to her feet. Zarina stood in the temple's arched entryway, a pretty smile on her face. She ran toward her, wrapping arms around her waist. "Lady of the House of Books."

Zarina lowered her lips to Asha's forehead and kissed her. "Of course my devourer of literature would know that name." Zarina kissed Asha's forehead again, and she beamed up at her.

"I know more than that one."

"Do you know nine thousand nine hundred ninety-eight more names for the goddess?"

"Mommeeeeee."

"More pouting and whining, my hafsa. What am I to do with you?"

Asha darted outside, shrugged on her book bag, and didn't give Sekhmet's ten thousand names another thought.

Zarina joined her on the grassy hill. "I suppose I should feed you. That's what a good mother would do." She linked her hand with Asha's, leading her away from the Temple of Sekhmet and toward town. "Have I been a good mother to you, Asha?"

"I remember one day you allowed me to have dessert before dinner. That day you were a very good mother."

"Oh, only on that day, huh? No others?"

"Hmm, ask me again after lunch."

Zarina laughed, and Asha did love that she could bring out the less serious side of her mother. "Your father is correct, one sarcastic sekhem in the family is quite enough. Race you."

Zarina took off running. Seven strides in, she'd transmutated. Strips of her ripped dress flew off her swiftly moving form.

"That's not fair, Mommy."

Dropping her book bag but hating to ruin her favorite jeans and sneakers, Asha growled. *So unfair.* She undressed then barreled down the hill after her waiting mother.

Zarina nipped at Asha's tail then sprinted away.

Asha gave chase. She couldn't catch Zarina but matching her mother's speed was never the point. Zarina had told her, for as long as she could remember, "Each sekhem shapes the role to best suit her heart and talents. Your goal isn't to imitate anyone, not even me. All you need to be, Asha, is better than you were the day before. If you do that every day, you will be a sekhem deserving of the love and loyalty of your people."

Better than she was the day before. Every lesson her mother gave her had that end in mind.

So, Asha chased after Sekhem Zarina, not following in her footsteps but making her own.

Two hours earlier, Asha felt the sun rise. Not as strongly as she did in her beloved Shona, the air fresher and cleaner than in the overly industrialized Republic of Vumaris. But she'd felt the pull of Mother Sun, Sekhmet as much a sun deity as she was a goddess of divine retribution.

Asha did wish the warehouse's windows weren't so filthy. She would've liked to have searched for her goddess in the face of the sun. It wasn't to be, though. At least not until she either freed herself or Ekon and General Volt came for her. Surely, her Shieldmane General had arrived in Vumaris. Minra was but a short flight from Gold-Meadow, the city of Asha's birth and her home. For all that she craved to return to the peace of her native land, she dreaded going there without her parents. She didn't want to think about living in her house alone. Even Mafdet wouldn't be there for quiet comfort.

Duty and common decency dictated that Asha speak with the family of each slain Shieldmane, offering prayers, condolences, and whatever else they might require of their sekhem during their time of need and mourning. Other than Asha and Talib, Mafdet's lover, Mafdet had no family. Years ago that hadn't been the case, but Mafdet rarely spoke of the past and Asha respected her too much to pry. Zarina and Bambara had known, though, and whatever Mafdet's past held had formed a bond between her and Asha's parents.

Asha strained her eyes to catch a glimpse of sunshine, but it was no use. She settled for appreciating the few shafts of light cutting across the warehouse through random clear spots in the windows. Asha also listened to the conversations around her, as she'd done since entering the warehouse and being chained to a chair.

The chains chafed, but they weren't as uncomfortable or as limiting as the soldiers likely thought. Triple the thickness of her wrists, the chains gave them a false sense of security. They had spoken freely among themselves. Asha knew Thundersnarl and his wife were buying a new home. Ragebreaker had missed her sister's birthday party because of "this fuckin' felidae mission." Darkpelt, an abysmal code name for a person with albinism, had boasted: "This is going to be one damn fine payday. From what I hear, we're moving south. We'll finally get to see what the lions have been hiding in Feline Nation."

"Nothing special, I bet," Gore's Scream had replied. "I don't care about that. Politics is above my paygrade. As long as the Deputy Chief is happy with us, I'm good to go. But yeah, the extra cash in my bank account will come in handy."

Rogueshades weren't two-headed monsters. Nor were they like the demons she'd seen in too many horror movies—evil from birth and unable to act outside of their nature. They were intelligent men and women nurtured in a society that placed a higher value on the life of humans than those of the felidae. They were soldiers who served their country for gold and glory as their ancestors once had. Back then, their god had also factored into humans' justification for displacing and killing felidae. Perhaps, for some, their religious beliefs drove them more than notoriety and money. Asha's beliefs certainly drove her, though not to subjugation.

Asha closed her eyes. From the sounds upstairs and of the Rogueshades exiting the warehouse, the time had come. Stormbane had left for hours. When he'd returned, he'd checked her restraints.

"You're still here."

"Yes, Mr. Stormbane, I am."

"Don't do that. Don't give me that sweet tone or look at me as if I'm the crazy one for being surprised you didn't break these chains and murder my soldiers while I was gone."

"I assure you, Mr. Stormbane, this is my normal voice. I could try to sound more menacing, more animalistic, if that will better suit your notions about felidae. I will tell you, though, I've tried books on tape. I have found the voices for the characters I create in my head are more to my liking than the voice actors'. Altering one's voice to suit the mood is a talent, though not one of mine. So, you see, I don't think I can oblige you by changing how I speak."

Asha hadn't feared the human male would strike her. His hand, however, had twitched above the gun holstered at his waist. No, she hadn't thought he would hit her, as his wife had. He had barely touched her when he'd clamped the chains around her wrists and ankles. Stormbane would shoot her, though, of that she was certain. When his hand had paused at his gun, a finger grazing the handle, Asha almost welcomed the relief a killing bullet would bring.

She didn't fear that fate either. If she died, if they killed her, she would see her parents and Mafdet again in the Garden of the Sacred Flame. Her parents had promised they would be together again. By Sekhmet's grace, Asha prayed their souls would be reunited. Until that time, she had to deal with concerns on the physical plane.

The warehouse door closed behind the last Rogueshade. Asha opened her eyes. A small group of soldiers still remained on the second level, weapons trained, not on Asha, but on the creatures released from their cages. Stormbane was among the soldiers who'd stayed. His gun, unsurprisingly, was aimed at her head.

"I need you to sign the papers," he'd told her when he had returned, holding the same manila folder Nighthide had given him. "They want your signature, and I assured them I would make it happen."

"Father told me it is unwise to offer a promise when there isn't a high probability that you will be able to honor your oath."

Again, Stormbane's hand had reached for his sidearm. The human really did have excellent self-restraint, which probably explained why his wife felt so free to betray him.

"You won't sign?"

"No."

"Have it your way." He had backed away from her. "Pride will be your downfall."

"Pride, love, and hate are all you and your friends have left me."

"You're a spawn of the devil."

Asha hadn't dignified the insult with a response. She wasn't a spawn of the devil, but she would gladly become Sekhmet's mortal tool.

"Remember," Stormbane yelled at her, as far away from the lions as he could get, "you brought this on yourself. Last chance to sign. Silence, huh? Fine. Your funeral."

Two male lions broke free of their handlers. From the look of them, they weren't older than two or three years. Likely birthed in captivity, the lions had no more clue what it meant to exist as a lion in the wild than Asha knew how to communicate with a natural lion in her human form.

Not Asha's funeral. Stormbane hadn't accomplished his mission. He needed her alive to sign the addendum. However, there was an undeniable gulf between being alive and being whole.

The young lions charged down the steps, their bodies gangly in a way mature lions were not. They ran right past Asha as if they hadn't seen her seated in the chair. They explored the lower level of the warehouse, and Asha remained very still.

No matter that felidae could transmutate into cats, their minds were always that of a human. She couldn't read the mind of a natural animal—lion or otherwise. Natural-born big cats couldn't tell the difference between themselves and a transmutated felidae. She had run, played, and hunted with wild lions.

But in human form, Asha was prey. This Stormbane understood.

Asha heard the soft *tap, tap, tap* of approaching paws. She had two options, but neither bode well for the young male lions, not if the Rogueshades' guns held something other than animal tranquilizers.

Asha closed her eyes and reached for her inner lion. Her lion spirit whined at her approach, anxious to run and hunt. She knelt in front of her lion spirit—nose to snout. *I cannot bring all of you out. I'm sorry.* Matching golden-brown eyes watched each other—different sides of the same proverbial coin. *These lions need a lioness to tame them. Both are too young to do more than fight each other. But here, with us, we can give them purpose.*

She spoke to herself, she knew. The year before her first transmutation spasm, her mother had taught her a "game."

"Think of your change into lion form as having a special spirit friend inside of you. To show your friend your world, you must speak with her, get to know her, and permit her to get to know and trust you. When you do, when you and your special spirit friend are in harmony, she will visit your home whenever you ask."

Transmutation was the ultimate display of a felidae's harmony of self. Not self-control. Not skill or knowledge but harmony.

Beside her, a lion growled. On her other side, the second lion did the same. A paw slashed her chest, sending her and the chair crashing to the hard floor. Pain seared and blood oozed. The chair creaked, whined, and then broke under her.

Sharp teeth clamped onto a thigh, biting down but, thankfully, not ripping or pulling. A second set of teeth sank into a shoulder, dug deep, and broke bones.

"Come out," she whispered. "Let these males know you rule this pride."

Claws escaped hands. Muscles stretched and broke chains. The upper half of Asha's face contorted, her lioness peeking through her eyes. Pushing her lion's pheromones through her still-human skin, Asha cried out. The lion at her shoulder yanked her from the other lion, setting off white-hot pain from fangs sliding from thigh to ankle.

A growl rolled from Asha like a snowball at the top of a mountain, picking up momentum and mass as it careened down the hill. When the growl burst free, her human throat and mouth ill-equipped to handle the tremors it created, the lions stopped.

Asha opened eyes gone moist from tears. She'd torn something in her throat. A partial change had been ill-advised, and not at all an act practiced by felidae. But Asha had needed to maintain some of her human features. If not, she risked a pissing contest between the young males. As it was, they circled her as they circled each other.

Asha pushed off the broken chains, groaning in pain with each un-avoidable movement. Tossing the chains aside, she used her un-harmed arm to push herself off the mangled chair. Her right leg hadn't fared any better than the chair. Blood stained her dress and the floor.

The lions snarled, and Asha had had enough. She filled the air with more of her feminine pheromones—not sex but a clear display of the pecking order of their pride of three. Even if Asha had been inclined to have sex in lion form, which felidae certainly did, she wouldn't do so with natural-born lions. An image of Ekon in lion form came to mind, but she swatted that image away. Thoughts of Ekon would produce the wrong scent.

Dragging herself away from the shards of wood, Asha looked to the upper level. The soldiers were as they had been, their weapons pointed at the lions. Their fear reached her nostrils. They should be afraid. With her blood in the air, the lions' predatory instinct to claim prey was strong. Any available prey, although she made for the more vulnerable of their food options.

Asha's trembling arm gave out, and she collapsed to the floor. The attack to her chest must've cut deeper than she'd thought because it hurt like nothing she'd ever felt before.

"There's no pride when an ass-kicking is the price."

Asha lifted her hand to Stormbane and flipped him off.

He laughed, and she hated him all the more because there was truth to his mocking words.

A lion positioned himself overtop her—she flat on her back and he above her on all fours. The sound that rumbled from him wasn't a snarl or a growl but an odd mewing. His face, like that of her imaginary lion spirit, was very close to hers. Close enough to kill. Close enough to . . .

Asha lifted her nose to the lion's snout and her hand to the side of his face. "I am the sekhem of this pride. I do not rule you. I am your faithful servant."

Asha felt the hot breath of the second lion above and behind her. She craned her head backward to see if he was friend or foe.

He licked her face. Disgusting. Beautiful.

The lions dropped to the floor beside her—one on each side, their heads competing for space on her lap. Their weight and jostling did her injuries no favors.

Asha scratched their ears. "You belong to me, and I belong to you." She hadn't said that sentence loud enough for anyone to hear. The lions hadn't killed her, but their acceptance of her as the superior lion wasn't a happy ending. It couldn't be because torture was more than physical.

She didn't hear the bullets leave the guns' chambers, but she felt the unmistakable jolts when they entered the bodies of the lions.

More bullets followed. Overkill. The first round had done the terrible deed. But still they unleashed round after round, their skilled marksmanship and Stormbane's order all that kept them from shooting Asha too.

Blood splashed in her eyes and mouth, the metallic taste of another lost life, another innocent soul to avenge.

"Pride is a bitch, isn't it Sekhem Asha? I bet you're ready to sign those papers now."

She spat blood, wiped her eyes, and then used what strength she had left to slide from under the lions' big heads and to her feet. Blood ran, unencumbered, from her deep puncture wounds. She would heal, but it would take time because felidae strength, healing, and stamina increased with age. Compared to her parents and Mafdet, Asha was no older than the male lions who'd been used then cruelly discarded— an adult but years from her prime.

Asha hurt all over but wasn't too prideful to let the pain show on her face. Honestly, she didn't think she had much choice. The wound to her leg alone, if it didn't close soon, would lead to a terrible case of blood loss.

"I have one good arm left for signing, Mr. Stormbane. Would you like to bring me your manila folder now? Be warned, though, because you may find this human idiom to be quite true. There is nothing more dangerous than a wounded animal."

Stormbane's bullet whizzed past her head. "Fuck you. Fuck. You."

Yes, well, by the time this was over, they would all be fucked.

Chapter 9: Powerful of Heart

"I can't believe you're wearing a dress." Mafdet shook her head at Tamani's attempt to appear more human and less the imposing Shona general everyone back home knew her to be. "I didn't think you owned one."

"I don't. Ms. Choi had the garment delivered to my hotel room this morning, along with makeup, heels, and other accessories."

The green knee-length dress matched Tamani's eye color and flattered her fit form and golden tanned skin.

Arms crossed over chest and back leaned against the closed hotel room door, Mafdet waited while Tamani rechecked the results of an hour's worth of primping and prepping.

Tamani spun away from the full-length mirror and toward Mafdet. "Help me with my hair?"

"Because I know so much about hair?"

"Just because you've chosen to keep your hair cut ruthlessly short doesn't mean you can't help me with mine. But fine. A good brushing but nothing fancy it will be then."

"We don't have time for games."

"Not games, my friend." Tamani strode to the other side of the room, pushed back the steel-gray blackout curtains and let in the bright rays from the morning sun. "Our sekhem is somewhere out there. I doubt they took her beyond the city limits, but the barbarians very well may have."

"It's been thirty-six hours. They could've done anything to her in that time."

"How does that make you feel?"

Mafdet glared at Tamani's rigid back as she looked out at East Minra's metropolitan skyline—brick buildings as far as the eye could see. "I feel like shit."

"Good. You should. Our khalid and sekhem were murdered on your watch and our hafsa sekhem kidnapped. If it were me, I would feel the same. But it wasn't me. It was you, and you're going to have to learn how to deal with your guilt. She won't blame you, by the way."

"Knowing that doesn't help. Asha should blame me. I survived. Her parents are dead. She would rather have them than me."

"Of course she would." Tamani turned to face Mafdet, gaze firm and lips thin. "But Asha loves you. She would never wish for your death, not even in exchange for the lives of her parents. You know the girl's heart. As do I." A hand ran down the front of her dress. "This is strategy. We don't have time to run all over this worthless city hunting for our young sekhem. I believe they haven't killed her. So must you."

"Not killed but hurt."

Tamani waved her closer.

Mafdet didn't budge.

"Suit yourself. But this self-deprecating funk you've been in since I arrived isn't helping. In fact, it's just pissing me the hell off. From Ekon, I get it. Between his age, inexperience, and the fact that he is completely in love with Asha, I wouldn't expect more from him. But you . . ." Tamani stalked toward Mafdet, pointing a finger in her face. "Cut it the fuck out or go the fuck home."

"They were my responsibility." Arms dropped to her sides—the weight of her failure having pulled them down. "*My* responsibility."

"Did you do your best? Fight your hardest? Give your blood and your claws?"

Mafdet couldn't answer because all she could see were Zarina and Bambara running into a crowd of armed humans. There had been nothing she could do to prevent the soldiers from unloading their weapons into her friends. Stunned, Mafdet had scrambled to her feet and, having failed them, she had gone in search of Asha and Ekon, finding neither. But Ekon had later found her, but not before she'd stumbled upon a small group of soldiers who thought themselves alone in the hotel. She'd made them pay for the oversight, unleashing her fury and sorrow in every slice. They'd bled, but not as much as Mafdet's hemorrhaged heart.

"I know you did all of those things because I know the cheetah within the stubborn woman." Tamani poked her chest. "And you had me dig bullets from you instead of taking your ass to the hospital like a normal person."

"I'm fine."

"You're not. Not even close. Neither is Ekon, and neither will Asha be if our plan doesn't work. I've already dealt with the police commissioner and the governor. They both will stand down."

"You threatened them?"

"Not a threat. I explained what would happen to their city and state if they interfered with our plans to retrieve our sekhem. In exchange, I promised we would all return to Shona without violence once Asha is safely in our custody."

"Leaving without bloodshed is Asha's decision to make, not yours."

"I know that, and you know that. We will stay, fight, or leave this wretched country at the sekhem's discretion. My honor is to our country and leader. I will suffer no remorse if I must break my vow to the police commissioner and governor."

Tamani's plan hinged on too much beyond their control, much of which relied on local, state, and national leaders' fears of a war with Shona.

"The plan has to work. If it doesn't, I don't . . . I don't . . ."

Tamani yanked her into a bruising hug. "We won't lose Asha too. The gods wouldn't be so cruel as to take them all from us. We must have faith."

Tamani was wrong. Sometimes, the gods took too much. Whether that made them cruel, Mafdet didn't know.

She hadn't cried in years. But she had cried over the deaths of Zarina and Bambara and she cried at the sickening possibility of having to lay Asha to rest along with her parents.

"Shit, you got me tearing up too." Tamani pushed Mafdet from her. "Did I ruin my mascara? It's a pain to get just right. Tell me, is it fine?"

"It's good enough. You're a soldier of Shona, not a runway model."

"You're absolutely no help. None. When will the reporter and his crew arrive?"

"Twenty minutes. Enough time for you to do something about the raccoon your face has become."

Tamani's middle finger shot up.

"I knew you were the one who taught that to Asha. You're a bad influence on her."

"Like you're one to talk. You started filling her impressionable brain with gory movies when she was seven."

"Asha never cried, looked away, or threw up. She's the toughest kid I know."

"Me too. Remember that. She is her parents' hafsa. But she is also Asha. We know what they want from her, and we also know she won't give it to them."

"Which means they'll hurt her."

"Which means they've *already* hurt her. But, oh, trust me, Mafdet, she's going to hurt them so much worse in return."

Mafdet nodded, but she didn't want blood and violence for Asha. They were acceptable for movies, but Asha's life shouldn't mirror a horror film from her childhood. "Did you remember to bring the pictures?"

"Don't worry, I'm prepared. So are the others." Tamani hugged her again. "Zarina and Bambara chose you for a reason. Don't you dare insult them in death for the choice they made in life. Will you and Ekon be joining the others?"

"Yes."

"Perfect."

Every staffer and headquarter employee Silas encountered since arriving to work responded to his presence in one of two ways—with smiles and nods of approval or with frowns and headshakes of disagreement. He ignored both reactions as he made his way from the underground garage onto the floor where his office was located.

Everyone knew the royal family of Shona had met with him and London a few hours before they were murdered. Everything else they may have seen or heard would've been speculation and gossip. He didn't appreciate being the focus of either.

Silas rounded the corner. Spotting him, his secretary scrambled from behind her desk, nearly tripping over a potted plant in her haste to open his door before he reached it. "I have messages for you, sir."

"Not now, Margaret."

"But . . ." She looked from what appeared to be a dozen pink message notes in her hand and back up to him. "Commissioner Aguilar called three times. Governor Billings four. The lawyers for Mr. Lyle Rhodes—"

Silas snatched the message notes from Margaret. "Who in the hell is Lyle Rhodes?"

"He's the owner of Sanctum Hotel. Where . . . where . . ." Margaret's face turned a shade of red unbecoming on a woman with color-treated auburn hair, giving her the unflattering effect of a sour strawberry. "Where those poor people were killed. The lawyers from Mr. Rhodes's law firm would like to speak with you about damages and liabilities. Mr. Rhodes's employees were among the dead, sir."

It hadn't occurred to him when he'd agreed to Frank's plan that people other than the felidae would be at the hotel. Of course there had been human employees there to see to the needs of the Shona delegation, and he had sanctioned the raid that had resulted in their deaths. The stain on his soul kept growing.

"There are other messages, too, but those are the priority ones. Whom shall I call first?"

"No one."

"No one?"

Margaret's frown reminded him of his wife's when they'd watched the morning news coverage. "Oh my god, Silas, that's heartbreaking," Claire had said. "But I don't like the implication that the deaths and kidnapping are connected to you and our party. I'm sure you'll be able to set the record straight once you've had a chance to speak with the Shona representative." Claire had scooted to the edge of the barstool, her face inches away from the kitchen television on the counter. "Look at the photos. What a beautiful family they were. My heart goes out to the Shona princess."

Silas hadn't bothered correcting Claire. Asha wasn't a princess. She was the one and only sekhem, and her people wanted her back. He didn't need to speak with Aguilar and Billings to know the Shona had gotten to them. Silas wouldn't find help from those quarters.

"I'm not to be disturbed."

"Sir?"

"You heard me, Margaret. I have a splitting headache and a pile of paperwork to get through. Make sure I'm not interrupted." He slapped the message notes back into her hand. "Get rid of those. If Governor Billings or Commissioner Aguilar call, tell them I'm out of the office."

Her face turned that awful shade of red again. "You want me to lie to the governor and the police commissioner?"

"What I want is for you to follow your chief's orders. That's your job, unless you want to find another one."

"Ah, y-yes, sir. I'll . . . umm . . . I'll make sure you aren't disturbed."

Faster than he'd ever seen the fifty-five-year-old woman move, she all but ran from Silas and to her desk, picking up a phone that hadn't made a sound.

Silas slammed his door. Snatching the remote control from his desk, he did something he told himself not to do the entire ride in from home. He switched on the television. The interview was breaking news on every news station, and it had been replaying for the last two hours.

Standing in the middle of his office, the red, white, and green flag of the Republic of Vumaris on the wall behind the television armoire, Silas watched Erik DeGracey interview General Tamani Volt of the Kingdom of Shona—a brunette he wouldn't want to meet without a squad of Rogueshade at his back. No matter how poised and pretty or how articulate and bright she came across as, her hands reminded him too much of Sergeant Major Hernandez's—strong and steady from years of gun use.

If this interview had taken place on any other network news show, Silas could've dismissed it and moved on. But DeGracey's show, *Real Talk, Real Matters*, was respected by a cross section of Vumaris because he held no partisan leanings. If he did, no one knew what they were because he didn't use his show as an ideological platform.

DeGracey, dressed in a black pinstripe suit that fit his fifty-year-old body to tailor-made perfection, the businessman turned television personality sat on a couch beside his guest. Considering the hotel room belonged to General Volt and she had been the one to contact DeGracey, he was more her guest than she was his.

Relaxed as they were, with legs crossed and backs against the couch cushions, they looked like old friends meeting to catch up after a mutual friend's funeral.

"Walk us through this again, General. Are you saying the First Evolution Union Party's Chief Royster is behind the deaths of Sekhem Zarina and Khalid Bambara of the Kingdom of Shona, as well as the kidnapping of their eighteen-year-old daughter, Hafsa Sekhem Asha?"

"Not at all, Erik. I would never make such an unfounded accusation."

DeGracey's fingers steepled, and his nod had the same effect as if he'd said, "Go on," aloud.

"I will share details gathered from two Shieldmane survivors of the massacre at Sanctum Hotel."

Massacre at Sanctum Hotel. He'd heard those four words on the radio on his drive in, and on the lips of staff who hadn't known he was within hearing range. Massacre at Sanctum Hotel scrolled across the bottom of the television screen, a visual to solidify the verbal.

The general had also mentioned two survivors. Sergeant Major Hernandez had gotten that detail wrong. One person's testimony could be easier explained away than two.

"Fact one, my sekhem and khalid came to this country as an act of trust and diplomacy to renew an eighty-year-old peace treaty between our countries. Fact two, Chief Royster and Deputy Chief London presented them with an addendum that would've had them, if signed, ceding portions of northern Shona to Vumaris."

DeGracey turned to the camera, his salt-and-pepper goatee and short-styled hair adding an air of professional authority to his words of, "If you recall, viewers, the First Evolution Union Party ran on a platform of expansionism, nationalism, and financial solvency. In light of the events at Sanctum Hotel, we must ask ourselves: Is this what our leaders meant? Were the votes of millions of Vumarian citizens a vote for territorial expansion? If so, at what cost?" With another pointed look to the invisible viewers who kept *Real Talk, Real Matters* the number one early morning news program, DeGracey turned back to General Volt. "Please, go on."

"Fact three, Sekhem Zarina and Khalid Bambara rejected the addendum and ended the meeting early. The Shieldmanes escorted the family back to Sanctum Hotel where they all enjoyed dinner together. Sadly, that meal would prove to be their last. Fact four, later that evening, toxic gas filled the hallway where my leaders and their daughter were housed. Fact five, a bodyguard radioed to another guard, informing her there were unauthorized and armed humans in the building."

"Soldiers?"

"Most likely, yes. The surviving Shona guards contacted Minra Police Department as soon as it was safe for them to do so. By that time, however, our leaders were dead, their daughter taken, and four of my Shieldmanes killed. I forgot to continue my count."

A heavy sigh had her closing her eyes for a second and uncrossing toned, tanned legs. The general was one hell of an actress. Silas didn't doubt her sincerity. The woman was upset about the deaths of her leaders. That registered loud and clear in every enunciated word but not quite gory descriptions. That's the part that rang false for Silas. The portrait she painted was done with deliberate strokes. Royster, London, and their party as the bad guys. Zarina, Bambara, and Asha the good guys. The general was smart, though, because she avoided being that explicit, but she needn't have been. People would make their own leap, drawing the conclusion she wanted them to form.

"Show the pictures to the audience again, General."

She did.

Silas had seen them earlier. Honestly, they weren't much different from the ones Frank's stalker friend had taken of the royal family. The one difference, an important one, being that the pictures on his television screen had been taken in and around the royal family's home in GoldMeadow. They chronicled Asha's life with her parents. The final picture was of the royal family in front of their personal plane, Asha in the middle with the three smiling and waving at the photographer.

"This was taken the day they left for Minra. We had planned for their return. Now, we must plan six funerals. We hope there will not be a need for a seventh."

"We understand how difficult this must be for you and for the people of Shona."

General Volt wiped her eyes. Her once steady hand trembled, as did her lower lip. "Yes, a challenging time."

"If you are up to it, I'll show the footage."

"Yes, please do."

More eye wiping but no trembling hands or lips. *One fine actress, indeed.*

DeGracey faced the camera again, which zoomed in close enough to reveal the crow's feet makeup couldn't conceal, but also the grave expression that matched his voice.

"General Volt contacted me with the most incredible story. I didn't want to believe what she told me. But, my faithful viewers, she turned me into a believer." The camera zoomed in a little more. "On this show, I deal only in facts . . . in evidence. Well, the evidence General Volt shared with me left my mouth open and my eyes drenched. For many reasons, mainly out of respect for the dead and the good people of Shona, I do not have permission to share with you all of the camera footage that was shared with me."

Even after having seen the footage, Silas couldn't help but choke on the realization that much of the mission had been caught on tape. Hernandez had assured him and Frank that he'd taken care of the security footage. Silas had believed the soldier. But he must've lied. He couldn't figure out any other way the Shona could have security tapes in their possession.

"What I can tell you is that I saw what looked to be trained soldiers use an unidentified gas to draw the leaders of Shona from their suite. Once they were in the hallway, it was a bloody, vicious battle to save their lives. They fought. They killed. They did what most of us would do in their situation. Parents, my faithful viewers, Sekhem Zarina and Khalid Bambara were parents. Like me." He pointed at the camera. "Like many of you. They fought to save themselves and their only child."

A picture of a smiling Asha appeared on a split screen beside the image of DeGracey.

"Take a good look at this sweet young lady. She is the only surviving member of the Leothos family."

The images of DeGracey and Asha disappeared, replaced by a black-and-white video of the rear of Sanctum Hotel.

A black SUV waited by the loading area—a driver already inside. Although, from the camera's angle, Silas could see only the man's arm and his left hand on the steering wheel. Three men, tall, big, and armed with guns, escorted a young female from the hotel and toward the waiting truck. One of the men, a dark-haired guy with a beard, opened a back seat door and, not so much helped Asha inside as pushed her in.

The video was rewound a few seconds then paused on the scene with the man's arm on Asha's shoulder and she unresisting.

The screen split again, and DeGracey reappeared. "What you saw in that footage was the new Sekhem of the Kingdom of Shona being kidnapped by, dare I say, members of our own military? Can I make such a bold statement, friends? I think I can. Take a look at that tattoo—the skull and crossbones. Our army has a unit known as the Bone Cleavers. This is their symbol. I know anyone can get that symbol put on their body. But look at these men. Their outfits. Their weapons. The SUV with no recognizable tag. I will stop short of saying our national government is behind the attack at Sanctum Hotel and the assassination of two world leaders. But the question must be raised. Who else would've had motive, means, and opportunity?"

Silas clicked the television off and tossed the remote onto his desk. He couldn't stomach the rest, especially General Volt's demand for Silas to, "Release Sekhem Asha to the Shieldmane of Shona posthaste."

Posthaste his ass. He couldn't release the girl. Not only had she not signed the addendum, which was pointless after DeGracey's show because any cession of Shona land would be viewed through a tainted lens of blood and death, Asha was also the only survivor who could directly link Silas and Frank to the Rogueshade. They had also passed the point of being able to kill the girl without severe ramifications to their political career and lives.

Silas staggered to his office sofa and collapsed. His heart and head pounded—one from pain, the other from fear. *What in the hell am I going to do, and where is Frank? We need to talk. We need to—*

Knock. Knock.

"I said I didn't want to be interrupted."

"Umm . . . yes, sir, I know. But there is a General Volt on the line for you. She's the woman from—"

"I know where she's from. Tell her—"

"She said you either speak with her on the phone now or in person later at your home."

Silas swore he saw stars and his heart ceased beating. Lungs constricted and skin tightened. He couldn't breathe. Silas could barely think.

"Sir, what should I tell her?"

He licked dry lips, held the armrest and used it to push to his feet, afraid he'd fall from the weight of the house of cards he'd built falling down around him.

"Transfer the call to my line, Margaret."

"Yes, sir."

The phone rang, and Silas rushed to answer. Better to rip the bandage off the wound than to peel it back by slow, painful degrees.

"Chief Royster here."

"Ah, the man himself. This is General Volt of Sekhem Asha's Royal Shieldmane Guard."

"I know who you are."

"As I know who you are. Pleasantries aren't required. You know what I want."

"I'm sorry for your loss. I truly am, but I'm not responsible for the terrible events that took place at Sanctum Hotel. I don't know who is, but I'm willing to work with the Shona government to find the culprits."

"I didn't call to argue the truth or to be lied to. We want our sekhem returned to us. Alive and healthy, Chief Royster. That is our demand."

"Your demand? This is my country."

"And Sekhem Asha is the leader of our country. We will have her returned to us or there will be war between Vumaris and Shona."

"War, but I don't have—"

"Look out your window."

"My what?" Dragging the phone with him, Silas pulled up the blinds behind his desk, looked down, and . . . "What the hell . . .?"

"I take it you see us."

Hell yes, he saw them. Beginning at the gate to his party's headquarters and ending a block away at the oldest post office in Minra were lions. Two hundred. Maybe three.

"If you look out other windows in your building, you'll see more of us."

"More?"

"I do love the quiver in your voice. I suspect, if I were there with you, I would smell your fear. Are you sweating with fear, Chief Royster? I think you are, as well as you should. Because if our sekhem is not brought to us within the hour, no god or gun will stand between the Shieldmane and absolute destruction of Minra. That includes the Shieldmanes I've dispatched to your home. Your daughter is as lovely and as young as our sekhem. Her life means nothing to me, as the lives of Sekhem Zarina and Khalid Bambara meant nothing to you and Deputy Chief London. One hour."

Click.

Phone gripped in his sweaty hand, Silas stared out his office window. Not all the Shona were in lion form. Two rows of felidae with military-style weapons served as an armed perimeter around the lions, reminding Silas of what he'd told Frank. Shona had modern weapons of war.

Silas hung up the phone, only to have it ring again. "Chief Royster, what?"

"Finally."

Shit, Governor Billings.

"I trust you've seen who's surrounding your headquarters."

"A threat to national security. As governor, I expect you to send in the state national guard. The Minra PD should've already been dispatched to this location, but I don't see a single patrol car."

"And you won't. No MPD or national guard is coming your way. As chief, you have the power to use the federal army to engage the Shona, but I would strongly suggest against that decision."

"I won't be bullied. This is our goddamn country, not theirs. But they have surrounded my headquarters like some kind of invading force."

"If I had known this stupid, weak side of you existed, I would've never voted for you and London. Despite our rocky history with the felidae, the Kingdom of Shona have been good neighbors. Would I have liked for us to have secured some of their land like you and London promised? Sure. Did I want Shona land badly enough to kill for it? No. That's what separates us."

"London and I aren't responsible for what happened at Sanctum Hotel."

"Sell that shit to someone else. I saw the security footage, and I know Frank London. Those were our boys and girls at the hotel. I don't know what off-the-books special ops group London put together. What I do know is that we have states that border Shona, including this one. General Volt is prepared to retaliate with 'brutal and unrelenting force.' Her words, in case you couldn't figure it out, if we don't produce an alive Sekhem Asha in—"

"An hour, I know."

"In fifty-five minutes. I don't know about you, but I like my life and I don't want it to end today."

Silas sank onto his desk chair, phone pressed to his ear. "Did she send Shieldmanes to your home too?"

"My home. My office. Even to my ex's condo. We could fight them, but it would be simpler just to give them what they want."

"What makes you think the general will keep her word?"

"She may not. That's a risk I've decided to take. This is what I know. They're here. They crossed our borders in large numbers and we didn't notice. If you think the felidae we see are the only ones in our country, then you're a bigger fool than you've already proven yourself to be. I don't care what shape Sekhem Asha is in, although I pray, for all our sakes, that she hasn't been raped or tortured. I fear, if either is the case, Minra's streets will run red with human blood."

Run red with human blood. Not so different from what he'd read about Goddess Sekhmet's rampage.

"You can't make this right, but you can minimize the consequences. Tell whoever has the sekhem to deliver her to her general so she can take her people the hell out of our country."

Like General Volt, Governor Billings hung up on Silas.

Who do Billings and Volt think they are? The Chief of the Republic of Vumaris does not take orders from a governor, let alone a general from another country.

Silas looked out the window again. Golden fur and thick manes. He'd never seen so many lions. They weren't even seated. Each stood at attention, face forward and legs unmoving. The headquarters had armed guards but not enough to prevent the building from being overrun.

Sweat stained his shirt, dotted his forehead, and fell into eyes unable to look away from the deadly sight of a Shona army at his front door.

Backing away, Silas rushed to his office door and swung it open. "Margaret, I need London in my office ASAP."

Chapter 10: She Who Perseveres During Times of Struggles

Ten Hours Earlier

Asha dreamed of clear skies, warm water, and new books. Of Zarina's too-sweet tea, Bambara's prickly beard, and Mafdet's secret stash of romantic comedies. Of Ekon's boyish smile, their first kiss, and his kind heart.

Asha dreamed of home. Of normalcy. Of her soft bed and clean clothes. Of food and showers and people who loved her.

Asha dreamed of dying.

She could no longer feel her arms. After the second low-caliber bullet to her back, she'd lost feeling below the waist. She had thrown up on the same warehouse floor where they'd killed and left the lions. Her senses acute, her healing slow, eyes shut and she on the disgusting warehouse floor, Asha listened to the shuffle and chatter of the Rogueshade soldiers.

After they'd killed the lions, no one had dared to approach. As long as they had long-distance weapons, they didn't need chains. They'd calculated that the use of low-caliber guns would take her to the edge of her pain threshold but not kill her. Except, of course, for the fact that she could die from blood loss.

Against her will, she'd cried out. In fury. In grief. In pain.

Asha thought Ekon and Tamani would've found her by now. She had faith they still would, no matter how long it took them. She didn't want them to find her dead body. Not like this. Not the image of a tortured, bloody corpse that would scar their souls and birth their nightmares. Asha loved them too much to have her death haunt their lives.

Opening exhausted, swollen eyes, she peered up into an all too familiar face. Dehydration and a damaged larynx had stolen much of her voice. But Asha spoke anyway, hoarse though it came out as. "Mr. Stormbane. My torturer. Is my voice more to your liking now?"

"Why won't you just sign the fucking papers? This . . ." He flung his hand over her prone form. "This could all be over, if you sign the addendum." He withdrew his handgun. "I promise, I'll make it quick. One shot to the head, and it will all be over. We want to go home to our families."

"Oh," Asha croaked, "I'm sorry to be such an inconvenience. How thoughtless of me. Instead of honoring my dead parents' final political wish, I should've made haste with my signature so you could run home to your unfaithful but very much alive wife."

Rolling onto her side, because she knew what would come next, Asha prepared her body for Stormbane's preferred form of torture. It always came after a bullet wound—a pitiless invader that ripped through skin and burned her insides.

Her body could no longer form the fetal position, nor was she capable of lifting her arms to cover her head and face. The sad truth was that there was little she could do to protect herself. She'd lost the small window of opportunity she'd had, after breaking the chains, to transmutate into her lion form. Her body was too damaged and her mind too fractured to find the harmony required to merge the two parts of her soul. If she tried in her current state, the effort to save herself could have the opposite effect. In her more vulnerable form, she was forced to remain—a prisoner of her brutalized body.

"Will you sign?"

"You know I won't."

"Yeah, I know."

Stormbane sounded almost remorseful. But Asha wasn't fooled. He would've killed her hours ago, if he had his way. He and the others wanted this standoff over, not because they had been struck with a conscience but because Asha's "stubborn pride" had kept them from their normal lives.

The harsh spray of foul river water shocked senses she thought dulled from pain.

Asha dreamed of grassy knolls, of breezy summers, of the Garden of the Sacred Flame.

Water beat against Asha. Her back. Her face. Her perseverance.

Asha dreamed.

Of blood, of death, of revenge.

"Gore's Scream. Swifttalon. Ragebreaker."

Stormbane glanced over his shoulder at Asha in the back seat of the truck he drove. It was the same black SUV he'd used to drive her from Sanctum Hotel to the warehouse. Though almost two days ago, the time they'd spent locked in stubborn combat felt much longer. When they'd first captured her, Stormbane assumed the girl would sign London's addendum, perhaps with a few tears and curses, but nothing more. While he'd had no intention of driving her back to the hotel or . . . anywhere for that matter, he had planned on releasing her after he'd gotten what he'd wanted from her. But Asha hadn't been so easily cowed. Hell, she hadn't been cowed by Stormbane and the Rogueshade at all, which made for a long and frustrating two days.

Asha sat between Ragebreaker and Widow Maker, who cringed every time she said a Rogueshade's code name.

"Nighthide. Doommight. Darkpelt."

He'd given up on trying to get her to shut the hell up. She hadn't talked so much in the nearly forty-eight hours they'd had her. Her voice no longer held the sweet, soft timbre it once had or even the mocking sarcasm he'd become accustomed to hearing from her. Instead, she sounded like a drained singer pushing through laryngitis to give her fans a show when she should be in bed resting. But there was no entertainment found in the SUV speeding toward the First Evolution Union Party's headquarters.

Stormbane swung his gaze to the rearview mirror. The two Rogueshades had themselves pressed so close to the doors, if they weren't locked, they would've flown from them. They watched the girl with a fear he'd never seen from a soldier not on a battlefield. All the while, the girl reclined between them, head on the cushion and eyes closed—her voice the only sound in the truck.

"Rockmane. Thundersnarl. Darkstare. Spiritgrim."

Stormbane made a right onto Imperial Street and stopped. When Deputy Chief London had told him to bring the sekhem to his headquarters so he could turn her over to a Shona general, he hadn't mentioned the gauntlet of lions he'd have to go through to complete his mission.

"What the fuck?" Widow Maker leaned across the front passenger side seat. "What in the actual fuck is that?"

"Stoneshield. Battlehead. Maneater. Hellgaze."

"What the hell, Stormbane? I didn't sign up for this shit."

"We all signed up for it. We took the money. We took the girl. Now the Shona want her back. What in the hell do you want me to do?"

"Turn the fuckin' truck around."

"Too late." Unlike Asha, who wouldn't shut the hell up, Ragebreaker hadn't said a word the entire drive from the warehouse.

"What do you mean?"

Ragebreaker twisted around. "Look behind you."

Stormbane did. *Holy fuck. Where did those lions come from?* Not only big-ass lions, much larger than the two he'd sent after the girl, but armed felidae dressed in black combat shirts, tactical duty pants, and combat boots. Even if Stormbane dared to back up over two dozen lions, each weighing more than four hundred pounds, he wouldn't make it off the street before a felidae soldier shot him.

"Moltencut. Grandhammer. Singleshot."

"Shut the hell up." Ragebreaker raised her fist to Asha's face.

"Skullbow. Voidfury."

"I said shut the hell up. This is your fault."

As if in slow motion, Ragebreaker cocked back her arm. Stormbane yelled for her to stop, but it was too late. He saw it this time, Asha not as fast, not as coordinated, not even as aware as she'd been when she'd attacked Nighthide.

But she was still felidae, which made her very dangerous. Ragebreaker had forgotten. Stormbane had not.

Asha's eyes popped open at the same time her hand shot up, catching Ragebreaker's wrist and twisting.

Bones snapped.

Ragebreaker screamed. "S-shit. S-shit. Damn you. L-let go of me, you crazy b-bitch."

"I'll let go of your wrist. Is that your only request?"

"Yes, yes. P-please let it go. It hurts. It hurts."

"Do not drive us into that crowd of lions," Widow Maker yelled in his ear, more concerned about self-preservation than helping Ragebreaker.

Had they learned nothing from watching Asha take a beating? Had they forgotten how hard and fierce the felidae had fought them at Sanctum Hotel? Did Widow Maker not see there was only one way they could get out of this situation alive? That one way, that single route, ran through Sekhem Asha, not the horde of lions at their back and front.

"Don't do it, Sekhem." Stormbane pointed his gun at her, but they both knew he could no more shoot her than she would leave the truck without killing Ragebreaker.

Asha's hand shot from Ragebreaker's wrist to her neck.

"Don't."

"Are you asking me to show her mercy, Mr. Stormbane?"

"I am. This is almost over. Your people are here to take you home." Ignoring Widow Maker's curses, Stormbane resumed driving. The sea of lions parted for him. "See, I'm taking you to them. You don't have to do this."

"You're correct, Mr. Stormbane. I do not. I do wonder, though. Where was her mercy? Or yours? I was shown none. Nor were my parents and friends."

"We're sorry." Kneeling, Widow Maker twisted back around. "Okay? Is that what you want to hear? We're sorry. We're so fuckin' sorry."

"You aren't sorry. You reek of fear, but not of regret. It isn't yet your time, Mr. Widow Maker. It is, however, hers."

Snap.

"Y-you broke her . . ."

"Neck, yes, Mr. Widow Maker. It took more effort than it should've. I think I'll require assistance from this truck."

"You're crazy."

"I am what your violence has made me."

Ragebreaker's body slumped against the door, as if she had fallen asleep during a long car ride.

Leaning her head against the cushion again and closing her eyes, Asha resumed her list of Rogueshade. "Goldgrimace. Steelthorn. Fire Strike . . ."

Jostling Stormbane, Widow Maker climbed into the front passenger seat, brown eyes wild, skin ashen.

Taking his time, Stormbane drove up the street, working hard to keep his eyes straight and not on the crowd of felidae tracking his progress. There had to be hundreds of them. No wonder humans hadn't dared to venture south into Shona. Whereas other felidae lived in small, disjointed communities, easily overrun by bigger and more organized military units, Panthera Leos' strength came from their cohesiveness. Their familial, political, and military units coexisted under a single, guiding purpose—the preservation of their culture and people.

Their sekhem and khalid were symbols of both. The Rogueshades had shown them no mercy, as Asha had said. In turn, she would show them none. Stormbane hadn't been wrong. The girl was a spawn of the devil. But she was also his only chance of survival.

He stopped at the headquarters' front gate. Unlike the last time he'd been there, no guards were in the security booth.

Widow Maker shoved a walkie-talkie into his hand. "Call them. Let them know we have the girl. She's safe. She's here. She can get the fuck out of the truck, and we can get the fuck out of here. Call them."

"I don't take orders from you."

"About now, I don't give a damn. She knows all of our fuckin' names, man. All of them. She keeps saying them over and over. We shouldn't have fucked with them. We should've—"

"Your bitching isn't helping. Neither is your fear. They can smell that shit like morning coffee." He switched the walkie-talkie to channel two then held the push-to-talk button. "Stormbane to London."

Static, then, "This is London. Tell me the girl is in the truck with you. We can see the SUV from here."

Widow Maker made two circles with his hands and held them to his eyes, noting the deputy chief had eyes on them through binoculars.

Stormbane nodded. "She's here, but we're surrounded by lions. What in the hell are we supposed to do? If they're going to kill us anyway, then I'm not letting her out. I'll put a bullet through her skull then make them fight their way in here to get to us. I'm not going to turn over my only leverage without a guarantee they'll let us live."

"They'll let you leave. That's the deal. The girl. Unharmed. Then they'll leave our country. They only want the girl."

"I get that, but you wanted me to convince Asha to sign your damn addendum. You had lions sent to the warehouse. You told me to . . ."

Stormbane spied Asha in the rearview mirror. She no longer ticked off names through a raw, dry throat. Her eyes were still closed, but her head hung to the side. She hadn't slept the entire time they had her in custody, and Stormbane doubted she slept now. Her color was too dark and her breathing too shallow. Her body bore evidence of what they'd done to her, and what she'd endured.

"You told me to torture her."

Stormbane could hear swearing, but the voice wasn't the deputy chief's. Likely Chief Royster's.

"How bad is she?"

"Bad."

"Bad enough they'll want to kill us when they see her?"

Stormbane didn't have to look at Asha again. "Yes, sir."

"Shit. Okay, listen. Our hour is up. We have no more time. She wants to go home, I'm sure, and they want to take her. We upheld our part of the deal. All we can do is pray like hell General Volt upholds hers."

"A general? You really think a general will decide what'll happen to us?"

"Yes, she's—"

"Not the sekhem. Asha is. I've spent two days with this girl, and I sure as shit know why the Shona revere their leaders. She will decide our fate. Not the general whoever in the hell you said."

"Which means we're fucked. We should just do the girl now."

Stormbane thought about it. He agreed with Widow Maker. The question wasn't whether Asha would come for her pound of human flesh but when. For some reason, Stormbane didn't think it would be today. If for no other reason than the spawn of the devil wasn't well enough to kill them herself. She would want the honors. Just as he would.

"I'm getting out."

"You're what?"

"You stay here. I'm getting her out the truck. Lock the door behind me."

"You're suicidal. They're going to rip your ass in two."

Stormbane neither had a death wish nor thought the lions would harm him. Asha hadn't stated his name among the list of Rogueshade soldiers who'd held her captive. Not an oversight. The devil spawn had a mind like a fuckin' death trap. Eventually, Asha would come for them all. When she got around to coming for him, however, he would be ready for her.

Today won't be the day I die.

Stormbane opened his door and jumped out. Shit. The lions were even bigger close-up. Scarier looking too. They roared, a collective sound that had his ears ringing.

"She's here," he gritted out. "Dammit, your sekhem is here."

The crowd parted, and the roaring ceased but not the snarls.

Two women and one man approached.

"Are one of you women General Volt?"

Stormbane thought maybe the brunette because she walked ahead of the other woman, but it could've also been the female with the nearly bald head and sword at her hip. Both wore white shirts and black battle dress uniform pants with black boots. They had the bearing of soldiers . . . and killers.

The brunette nodded to the young felidae male to her right. He couldn't have been much older than Asha, and he wore the same uniform as the women—his service pistol at his waist.

The young man brushed past Stormbane and headed straight to the back door of the truck.

"It's locked. I want to get one thing straight before I turn her over to—"

The sword came out of nowhere. He hadn't seen her move, much less unsheathe her weapon.

The dark-skinned felidae pressed the blade to his throat. "You will give us our sekhem. Right. Now."

"Okay, yeah, lady. That's why we're here." He knocked on the window.

Widow Maker stared at him, face scrunched. For too many seconds, Stormbane thought he would leave him high and dry but then he heard a *click*.

As soon as the lock disengaged, the young felidae male had the door open. He looked inside, growled, and the woman's blade rose to Stormbane's eye.

"She's hurt. Badly. I don't even know where to begin with everything I see."

With no effort, the young man had Asha's limp form in his arms and out of the truck. He cradled her to his chest, his lips to her forehead but his dark eyes on him.

Murder brewed there.

Both women took in their sekhem. Expressions that began with love turned to worry then morphed into outrage.

The sword lowered to between his legs. "You deserve to die. You *will* die."

All around them lions growled.

The brunette snatched the walkie-talkie from his hand. "Chief Royster?"

"No, Deputy Chief London."

"You and Royster are cowards and bullies."

"I didn't know. I didn't tell them to do that to her."

"He's a liar. He—"

The sword cut through his pants, boxers, and nicked his dick. Stormbane shut up.

"I told Royster I wanted her alive and healthy. I was clear on both of those points. Our sekhem has been tortured."

"She's alive. She's strong and young. She'll heal. You said you would evacuate our city and country after we returned your leader. She's right there. I can see the boy holding her. She's not dead."

"And you think that absolves you of what was done to her? You think, because she still breathes, that your insignificant city and family deserve to live? They don't. But that decision doesn't fall to me."

"W-who then?"

The brunette's gaze lowered to Asha and her hand rose to the girl's cheek, caressing with a gentleness not found in her voice or eyes. "Sekhem, can you hear me?"

Slowly, Asha opened swollen, red eyes. "Yes."

"Good. We have come for you."

"I knew you would. Thank you."

If Stormbane hadn't been standing so near, he wouldn't have heard a word Asha said. But he was close. Close enough to be reminded of how they'd brutalized her, and how she'd suffered in near silence.

"I have a doctor on standby. I need to get you to her as soon as possible. Before I do, though, I need you to tell me what to do. On your order, we can leave in peace or exact our just revenge on this city, this state, and these barbaric humans." Her hand snapped out and wrapped around his throat, claws embedded in his neck. "Live or die, my sekhem. What is your will?"

"General Volt has your soldier by the throat and the other felidae female has a big knife to his . . ." Silas lowered his hand to his crotch. "What are they waiting for?"

Frank stood beside Silas. He'd come running into his office fifteen minutes ago and had handed him a pair of binoculars. "I'm not going down there. Are you?"

"I like my balls and my throat where they are, so no."

They were cowards, hiding in a building and spying on a scene from the safety of his office. Nothing that had happened over the last forty-eight hours had to have occurred. The needless violence and bloodshed. The deaths. The danger his decision had placed his family and nation in. None of it should've happened, but it all had because Silas wanted what didn't belong to him.

From his perch, Silas found he didn't mind the role of coward, not when playing hero could've had his life in the literal hands of two hardcore felidae females.

"You gave them permission to torture the girl."

"How the hell else did you think we were going to get her to sign? You're worthless, Silas. Spineless and worthless."

"Spineless? I don't see you down there with your Sergeant Major. If your spine is made of sterner stuff than mine, then go down there and tell General Volt it was you who gave the order to have her sekhem tortured. You go, and I'll stay here and watch you through my nice binoculars while she rips out that spine you think so highly of."

"Shut up. . . . Did you hear that?" Frank lifted the walkie-talkie between them. "The general said something to the girl."

"Her hand is still on the PTT button?"

"She must want us to hear what's going on."

"What did she—"

"Shush."

"Live or die, my sekhem. What is your will?"

"Did she just?" His fingers on the binoculars tightened.

"The girl decides our fate."

Silas had feared as much, but Frank sounded stunned. "She's their leader. It's her right."

"She's a girl. Eighteen. A child. Our fate shouldn't be decided by a child." Frank pressed the lens of his binoculars against the pane of glass. "It's for show. All of those felidae won't listen to a girl barely out of high school. The general, sure, but not a child. She rules nothing. Not a goddamn thing, Silas."

It began as one, maybe two roars, then grew to twenty. Fifty. A hundred. More. More. Within seconds, the hundreds of Shona who'd converged on his headquarters were roaring. Lights in his office flickered, the building shook, and Silas thought a tornado had touched down right outside his window.

They raged. The sounds of their fury an ear-splitting, heart-pounding prelude to death. Silas was sure they would rush the gate, break down the doors, and swarm inside. Any moment he would hear the scratch of claws outside his door then feel the prick of sharp teeth at his throat.

"Too loud. Hurts." Frank dropped to his knees, binoculars and walkie-talkie skidded across the floor, and hands covered ears.

Silas wanted to take cover like Frank. Instead, he watched his office windows crack. Warm air seeped through the fragments, and still the Shona roared.

Lions.

Tigers.

Jaguars.

Leopards.

Cougars.

They'd all come to return their sekhem to Shona.

The sound intensified, and Silas thought he would pass out. They would come—claws and fangs. He'd killed his wife and daughter. He'd killed himself. The Shona would . . .

The roaring stopped. Not decreased but . . . no sound. Silence.

Silas picked up the binoculars he hadn't known he'd let slip from his moist hands. Wiping the sweat from his face, he pressed his eyes to the eyepieces.

Sergeant Major Hernandez was hightailing it away from his truck and toward the security gate. General Volt and the other felidae female looked down at Asha. Silas recognized the woman with the short haircut and the male who held Asha as two of the Shieldmanes who'd waited in the hall outside of the conference room while the royal family had been inside with Silas and Frank.

The two survivors. Not one.

Silas no longer cared. What mattered most was what Asha would do next. He sensed Frank moving beside him but didn't look away from the girl.

Asha raised her hand. With a single finger pointed away from his headquarters, the Shona turned and, in military formation, marched down the street. The lions took the lead, followed by the Shona in human form.

A white SUV limousine with gold rims and a gold and white Kingdom of Shona car flag on the hood pulled beside General Volt. The driver hopped out, opened the rear driver's side door, and helped the young Shieldmane with their sekhem. Once Asha was inside, the driver climbed back into the truck and General Volt and the two Shieldmanes joined their hurt sekhem inside the luxury vehicle. Then they were off. The remaining Shona cats ran behind the vehicle.

In less than five minutes not a single felidae remained on Imperial Street. A finger. That was all it had taken to command hundreds of felidae.

Silas collapsed to the floor, his heart in his throat. For ten minutes, he and Frank sat in silence. They'd survived but . . .

"That's way too much power for a girl to have."

"Not a girl, Frank."

"A devil's spawn, like Stormbane said then."

After Asha's command, Silas wouldn't argue against Sergeant Major Hernandez's contention. "I don't care what in the hell she is, as long as she's gone." *Is the girl really gone, though? God, I hope so.*

Silas should've felt relieved. His life had been returned to him. In time, Vumarian citizens would forget about the Shona royal family and Erik DeGracey's interview with General Volt. He would turn his party's lawyers loose on Mr. Lyle Rhodes's little nothing law firm. The owner of Sanctum Hotel would prove to be a nonissue. In time, he too would turn his focus to other matters. He would give it six months, maybe a year. They would be fine. The First Evolution Union Party would be stronger than ever and, fifteen years from now, Silas would win another term for his party. He would drop Frank from the FEU ticket, of course. But that would come later.

For now, Silas held shaky hands to chest, slowed his breathing, and counted his blessings.

The walkie-talkie crackled. It was on the floor somewhere with them. There, under his desk. He crawled to it but stopped when a hoarse voice came across the line.

"Stormbane. London. Royster. Death does not knock on the door."

Chapter 11: Lady of the House of Books

Kingdom of Shona
City of GoldMeadow

Snuggled under her duvet and eyes closed, Asha listened as first Tamani and then Ekon left her bedroom. Asha didn't think either believed her to be asleep, but she would rather not deal with seeing them watch her for signs of pain—emotional and physical. So, she kept her eyes closed and duvet pulled to her chin until her silent message prompted Ekon and Tamani's reluctant action.

The bed dipped and, without opening her eyes, she turned toward a mirage made real. Asha wrapped an arm around Mafdet's waist and buried her head in her lap—not wanting to cry but unable to stop the tears from falling.

"It's all right. You're safe now. You're home and you're safe. I have you, my sekhem."

Mafdet's sekhem, not her hafsa sekhem. Yes, Asha was home and safe, so were Mafdet and Ekon. But not Zarina and Bambara. They were forever lost to her. But the gods had spared Asha and they'd returned Mafdet to her. For those two blessings, Asha would always be grateful to her gods.

Still . . . her heart hurt and, while having Mafdet alive and at her side filled her with relief and joy, a bleeding hole had formed in her chest. A hole, Asha feared, that would never mend.

"They're gone," she said through sobs punctuated by a runny nose. "I felt them leave me. In my mind, I heard Mom take her final breaths, and I wanted to go with her . . . with them both. I shouldn't be here. I should've died too."

Strong, tender hands cupped Asha's damp cheeks and lifted her face. She shifted with the movement, rising onto her elbows and looking up at Mafdet.

Her godmother stared down at her, penetrating eyes bordered by worry lines above and dark circles below. "If you wanted to die . . . if you believed you should've died, you wouldn't have fought so hard to live. I promised I would find you. But I didn't. I failed you and your parents."

"No, Mafdet, you—"

"I. Failed. You." Mafdet emphasized each word, her guilt an invisible tether between them. "But you didn't fail yourself. Sometimes, Asha, when the world seems to conspire against you, the best you can do is endure . . . survive. You did both."

Mafdet leaned in and kissed Asha's forehead—the gesture heartwarming and an unpleasant reminder that she would never again feel Zarina kiss her in the same way.

"I'm so very sorry for your loss, Asha. I mourn them too."

"I know. You loved them as much as I did."

Mafdet nodded, her own tears seeping from wilted, red eyes.

How many hours has Mafdet gone without sleep? When Asha had first awakened, Mafdet had been by her side, as had Ekon. But Asha had no idea how long ago that had been or how long she'd been unconscious after she'd passed out on the drive to the airstrip. One day? Two?

Asha lowered her head to Mafdet's lap again—selfish in her need to keep her close for a little longer.

Mafdet stroked her hair the same way she'd kissed her forehead—like Zarina. Whether deliberate or not, Asha didn't know, but she craved the familiar touch even if the hand didn't belong to the woman she most wanted to soothe her broken heart. But she loved Mafdet, so she soaked in every ounce of her affection.

"I'm here. You aren't alone."

I know, but it's not the same.

"You're tired." With a squeeze to Mafdet's waist and a kiss to her cheek, Asha turned away and curled into a ball. "You need your rest. With the bullets removed, I'll heal quickly." Not that she recalled being operated on, but common sense and closed wounds were clues enough. "I don't need a babysitter but thank you."

Asha buried her head under the covers, a silent but rude dismissal. If Mafdet stayed, her guilt a suffocating fog, it would only add to her own depression.

"Sleep well, Asha."

She tried, but she slept fitfully, dreaming of callous humans.

A cold spray of water slammed her head against the warehouse floor, cracking her skull and cutting her face. Asha's eyes flew open. Room dark, the shaft of moonlight through the open blinds cast spotlights on two figures at the foot of her bed. Asha's heart leapt, as did her body, vaulting from her bed, happier than she'd been in days.

"Mom. Dad."

A dream. No, a nightmare. Everything she'd experienced had to have been a dreadful nightmare. Asha dashed to the foot of the bed, grin big and arms open wide.

"Mommy. Daddy." She reached for her parents, desperate to feel them . . . to have them hold her.

Her arms met air. Asha tried again, but she couldn't touch her parents. But they were right in front of her as Mafdet had been.

No, not like Mafdet.

Asha sank to the foot of her bed. Her parents had returned home, but not in the same way as Asha, Mafdet, and Ekon had. *Ghosts. Restless souls.* Zarina and Bambara smiled at Asha, and her heart ached anew.

Mafdet was wrong. Asha was very much alone.

Although Ekon stayed upwind of Asha, he knew the second she'd caught his scent. She didn't shift in his direction, but she did snap her book closed and wrap a beach towel around it. He had no idea what book she didn't want him to know she was reading. Likely, it came from her mother's personal library. Other than the beach, Asha spent most of her time in Sekhem Zarina's home office.

Removing his flip-flops, Ekon strolled from the sand dunes where he'd been watching Asha, and down the hill, digging toes into the hot sand as he moved closer to his MIA sekhem.

Yanking off his T-shirt but leaving on his shorts, Ekon dropped the shirt and shoes a few feet from Asha's outstretched legs. "It's a scorcher out here." Ekon smiled down at Asha, happy to see her.

Reclined on her back, nothing between her body and the grainy, hot sand, Ekon couldn't tell if Asha's eyes were open or closed, thanks to the dark shades she'd put on after sensing him. Asha didn't smile. That much he could see.

Ekon plopped down next to her, legs bent at the knees and gaze on the brilliant blue of Tideless Depths Ocean instead of on Asha. While it may have taken her two weeks to fully recover from her injuries, her body no longer bore outward evidence of her torture. She was all lean, bronze sexiness in a barely there red bikini.

"I'm home now, Ekon. I don't require a Shieldmane to follow me everywhere I go."

"What about a friend?" Ekon glanced over his shoulder. Asha still wore her black shades, but she'd pulled them atop her head, using them to keep her bangs out of her eyes. "There you are, my sekhem."

With the bright sun beaming down on them, Asha's eyes should've glistened with vibrance. They used to twinkle like gold coins unearthed on the ocean floor—the finder blessed for the discovery. Ekon indeed felt blessed to have Asha safe and at home, no matter how dim her eyes and spirit had become. When he'd seen her in the black SUV, eyes closed and body marked with abrasions, blood, and bullet wounds, he'd wanted to kill every human who had dared to lay hands on her.

Only Asha's need for medical attention had kept Ekon from turning savage and murdering the driver and passenger. Following General Volt's and Mafdet's lead, he'd controlled the beast within. The human soldiers had hurt Asha, and he hadn't been able to keep her from harm.

"I'm sorry. I should've been a better Shieldmane." Ekon hadn't gone in search of Asha for himself. Yet, every time he saw her, he found himself wracked with guilt. Unwilling to maintain the distance Asha had become too comfortable placing between them, he reclined next to her on his elbow.

"You look sad, Ekon."

"I was thinking the same of you. And tired. You aren't sleeping, are you?"

"I see too much when I sleep."

So did Ekon. So too did Mafdet, probably, not that the Shieldmane would admit to having nightmares. Of the three of them, only Asha had returned to Shona unlike the person she'd been before leaving.

Ekon scooted closer, wanting to kiss her, but they hadn't been that close since the fateful night at Sanctum Hotel. Did Asha still love him? He hoped so because his feelings for her hadn't changed.

"I think you spend more time on this beach than anywhere else."

"The water is soothing, and the open space makes me feel free."

"They can't hurt you anymore. You'll never again be their prisoner."

Asha rarely spoke of her two days with the Rogueshade soldiers. None of what she had shared included details of her torture. If not for Dr. Ochill, Ekon, Mafdet, and General Volt wouldn't have known the extent of what she had endured. Asha had undergone hours of surgery to reset bones, close gashes, and remove bullets. For three days she slept, with Mafdet and Ekon sitting vigil.

When Mafdet and General Volt had taken Dr. Ochill aside, out of Ekon's range of hearing, he'd known what they'd asked the doctor. When they'd returned to the family waiting area, the women's faces had still been tight from worry but some of the tension around their mouths had eased. No female should be a victim of sexual assault, especially a virgin. As awful as the Rogueshade had been to Asha, none of them had raped her.

Leaning closer, Ekon's face hovered over Asha's. "Promise me you'll never stand between me and protecting you again."

"No."

"No? That's it? Just no?"

"Would you prefer I lie?"

"I would prefer you stop being so . . . so . . ."

"What? Quiet? Distant? Cold?" An eyebrow arched, and that was the most emotion he'd seen from Asha in months.

"I'm here for you, if you want to talk. Even if you don't want to talk, I'm still here. Distant is an apt word. We don't hang out anymore. We don't laugh or joke. We don't hold hands or kiss. I can't remember the last time I've seen you smile."

The last sentence wasn't strictly true. Asha had smiled when she'd used the Rogueshade's walkie-talkie to deliver a parting death threat to the three most responsible for killing her parents and of torturing her. The smile, however, hadn't come from a place of joy but from Asha's deep pain.

"When I awoke, Mafdet was seated in a chair beside my bed. I smiled then."

"You cried. I was on the other side of your bed, Asha, remember?"

"Yet another reason for me to be happy."

"Come on. Let me in." Giving in to temptation, Ekon pressed his lips to Asha's. Nothing demanding. He wouldn't dare. But he lingered for a few seconds, hoping she would reciprocate.

She did not.

"Do you feel nothing for me now?"

Reaching up, Asha wrapped her arms around his neck and pulled him down to her, hugging him close. "I'm trying, but I can't."

"Trying what?"

"To feel something other than hatred and grief. I'm full to overflowing with both. I breathe them. Eat and drink them. They rule my sleeping mind and fight me for dominance during the day."

Ekon wished he had the right words. For what she'd lost, and how, there were none. A year was but a morsel of time.

"I know it hurts." Squeezing her tightly, he kissed her cheek and wiped away her tears. "No one can make you hurt less. Nothing can do that but time. I'm not going anywhere, Asha, not as long as you want and need me. I'm your Shieldmane, unless you reassign me. Whether I'm also still your boyfriend, that too is for you to decide. You owe me nothing. I won't hold you to anything you said when we were in the walk-in freezer."

Slowly, Ekon withdrew from their embrace, wanting to hold on but giving action to his words. Asha had too much going on in her life to fit him into it the way he would like. Being sekhem kept her busy, even with the help of her advisors. Young Asha may be, but unintelligent and arrogant she wasn't. One of her first decisions, after she was healthy enough to begin her duties as sekhem, was to create an advisory council.

Asha stared up at him. They'd gotten her back, but in pieces.

"I don't want to lose you too, but I no longer know what I have to offer you. My lengthy silences and absences would be unfair. I can barely stand to be in my house. I hear my parents' voices. See their noncorporeal forms. I smell them too." Asha's hand rose to her heart. "I feel them in here, but also everywhere I go. They aren't at rest. Their souls deserve to be at rest in the Garden of the Sacred Flame."

Removing her sunglasses, she tossed them onto the sand. Limp bangs cascaded down, concealing an eye but not Asha's emotional confession.

"I look in the mirror and no longer recognize myself. When I speak, for a moment, for dizzying, confused seconds, I wonder who gave the visitor leave to speak in my stead. I used to be a normal girl. Now, all I think about, all I read about is divine retribution."

Ekon glanced to the book wrapped in Asha's beach towel. Divine retribution. Only one of their gods dealt in revenge.

Asha sat up, forcing Ekon to shift from above her. "It'll be a year next week. My parents' souls have been restless for a year, and it's my fault."

"It isn't your fault."

"It is. My list is incomplete. I've searched. For a year, I've searched. I'm close, but I need all ten thousand of them."

"Ten thousand of what?" Ekon mirrored Asha's position, legs crisscrossed.

She didn't answer him, but her gaze shifted to her book before casting out to the ocean.

"Despite how it appears, I do still love you, Ekon. You, Mafdet, Tamani. But most days, it's more of an intellectual memory than a true feeling. I know I love you because I remember how it felt to have you deep in my heart." Lifting a hand, she placed it over her heart. "What I feel for you is still in here, but it's trapped in a castle with no drawbridge but a moat."

"What's in the moat?"

"Vile images and ideas. My fury and self-doubt. My fear and heartache."

Asha spoke of finding peace for her parents' souls, but it was she who had no peace of mind.

"If you like, I could help you with your research. Ten thousand of anything is a lot."

To his surprise and delight, Asha smiled. "When I was in the warehouse, I thought of your kind heart." She kissed him, a short peck to his lips. "I never doubted you and Tamani would find me. That knowledge helped me stay strong when, too many times, I wanted to die."

"Because they hurt you."

She shook her head, curls limp from the humidity. "No, because dying was preferable to living without my parents. I still don't know how to manage without them in my life."

"You've been doing it for almost a year."

"Poorly."

"But you're still doing it."

An eyebrow arched. "Have you always been an optimist? I don't recall."

Ekon thought he detected a hint of humor in her voice, although that could've been wishful thinking.

"Would you like to take a dip?"

"Umm . . ." Asha glanced at her book again. "I was in the middle of a chapter."

"A chapter you've probably read a dozen times over."

"You couldn't possibly know that."

"That's a yes." Ekon jumped to his feet. "It's hot, but the ocean is cool. Let's go for a swim."

Asha hesitated, and golden-brown eyes stared up at him—contemplating his offer. It was rare for a felidae mated couple to have only one offspring. Ekon had seven siblings. The average number of children for felidae households was five. But alphas often had children later in life, choosing to put the ruling of Shona above that of starting a family. Such was the case with Sekhem Zarina and Khalid Bambara. While one child made for a quaint family of three, the loss of her parents left Asha with few touchstones in her life that could come close to matching the bond she shared with her parents. The bond of siblings could serve such a role. But Asha didn't have even that to help staunch the bleeding of her parents' passing.

With a nod, Asha took Ekon's offered hand, permitting him to help her to her feet.

His eyes dropped to Asha's sexy, skimpy bikini.

Of course, she noticed.

"I did ask if you wanted to become my lover." Two fingers wiggled in front of his face. "Twice."

"I know, but you weren't ready. Not really."

"No, I suppose I wasn't."

"Will you ask me again, when you are?"

"Maybe. Rejection, even for the right reason, hurts."

An exploring finger ran the length of the top of his shorts, playing with the smattering of hair on his lower stomach. If she went farther south, she'd find even more hair to wrap around her teasing fingers.

"I promise, the next time you ask I won't say no."

"Even if I ask now?"

Ekon slid Asha's hand from his stomach, up his chest and over his heart. "You said it yourself, you don't feel much of anything beyond sorrow and rage. When we make love for the first time, you want to be present, in every way possible. I want that too. But it won't happen until you settle your heart and mind."

"Until I find my harmony, you mean."

"Yes. When you do, when you've reawakened that part of yourself, you'll come to me for the right reasons."

Standing on tiptoe, Asha kissed him.

Ekon returned the kiss, mindful not to touch her beyond her mouth. His parents raised a gentleman. But even a gentleman could be tempted by a female in a bikini whose kisses were as sweet as ripe berries plucked from a tree.

"A swim sounds good. The company definitely is." Asha's soft fingers laced with his. "I don't require help with my research but, once my list is complete, there is another way in which you can be of assistance."

Ekon didn't know if he liked the sound of that, but they both knew he would help her no matter what she asked of him.

Hand in hand, they ran into the water.

Asha sat on her mother's office couch across from her glass tabletop desk. As a girl, Asha used to sit in the same spot, reading a book or coloring while her mother worked at her desk. They rarely spoke during those times. Companionable silence, her father would say, his deep voice intrusive, his laughter at their identical frowns all the reaction he wanted before returning to his own office.

Pulling her feet onto the couch, Asha dropped her forehead to bent knees, and arms wrapped around her legs. She didn't want to see the image of Zarina hovering beside her desk. Not today. Not when she'd spent an enjoyable hour swimming with Ekon. Neither Ekon's company nor the swim had been a strong enough distraction to keep Asha's mind from whirling. But the old normalcy of both had reminded Asha of simpler, happier times.

For that hour, Asha's entire world hadn't revolved around fulfilling her mother's dying wish. Zarina's and Bambara's wandering spirits hadn't followed her into Tideless Depths. Body submerged in the blue tropical waters of the ocean, the weightlessness had added to her sense of freedom. Under the water, no responsibilities existed, no spirits lurked, and no one noticed if she cried.

But on land, in her home, in her mother's office, all she'd ignored while in the ocean's watery bosom came flooding back the moment she'd stepped foot onto the beach. Sound—invisible footsteps. Smell—rotting flesh. Sight—silent specters.

Asha dared to peek between her arms and at her mother's desk. Zarina's spirit hadn't moved. Dressed in one of her favorite outfits, a royal blue sleeveless turtleneck design Ankara maxi dress with yellow and black accent shapes, Zarina watched Asha—her expression bland in a way it hadn't been in life.

"I'm trying. I know it's taken a long time, but I am trying."

Just once, Asha would like her mother's spirit to speak to her, even if it were to scold her for her lack of progress. But the spirit only ever stared at Asha with lackluster golden eyes.

"Tell me what to do. Where to look. I've been through all of your books. The ones down here, as well as in your bedroom. I've read them from cover to cover. I have pages of notes and names, but not ten thousand."

As they'd done in the ocean, tears fell but there was no water to conceal her weakness. Her head dropped to her knees again. She wasn't worthy of her sekhem name or the title, not if she couldn't honor her parents by avenging their deaths. Asha could think of no other way to free their spirits so they could move on to the next plane of existence.

"I'm sorry," she mumbled.

"Who are you talking to?"

Wiping her face with the back of her hand, Asha looked up to see Mafdet frowning at her from the threshold of the office.

"What happened? Why are you crying?" With her usual long, confident strides, Mafdet entered the office, a book under her arm.

"That looks like one of Mom's books."

"You're drenched, and I can smell the salt of the ocean on you. Why didn't you shower and change before—"

Asha leapt from the couch, uncaring. Mafdet was right about her sullying Zarina's couch with a wet, dirty beach towel wrapped around an equally wet and ocean-soiled body.

"That's definitely one of Mom's books. Why do you have it?" Asha reached for the book, but Mafdet sidestepped her. "Give it to me."

"I intend to but not yet."

Asha reached for the book again, but Mafdet pushed her hand away. "Give me Mom's book. It isn't yours. It shouldn't be in your possession."

"You're correct, it did belong to Zarina. Like everything else of your parents, this book now belongs to you."

"That's right, now give me the damn book."

Mafdet's face took on that granitelike expression that came over her whenever someone said or did something to anger her. "I know you're upset and are sekhem, but you'll never be too old or too powerful to show proper respect."

Shame had Asha apologizing but not retreating from her point. "You had no right to remove anything from Mom's office without asking."

Mafdet maneuvered around Asha, careful to keep the book on the opposite side, as if she expected Asha to snatch it from her. Mafdet wasn't wrong. But she shouldn't have to take a book by force that belonged to her.

Glancing from Mafdet to Zarina's spirit, Asha turned away from them both. She walked to the sliding glass doors, taking in acres of verdant land and a rock-edge gravel path that led from the house to Sekhmet's ancient temple at the top of the hill. Asha unlocked and opened the doors, letting in the heat and a muggy breeze.

"Tell me why you have Mom's book and why you refuse to return it to me."

"I haven't refused. But I want to understand first."

Asha stepped onto the path, the gravel sun heated. She couldn't see the temple from her position but that didn't stop her from feeling the pull of the statue within. Asha hadn't been inside since her return home. But she soon would. The anniversary of her parents' murder neared.

"Why have you purchased Sanctum Hotel?"

"How I choose to spend my inheritance doesn't concern you, especially since you refused to accept a seat on my advisory council."

Mafdet's rejection had hurt her deeply. She still didn't understand her decision, and she wouldn't command her to act against her will. So, that had left Asha with two Shieldmanes from her time as hafsa sekhem, neither whom she had officially elevated to the post of Shieldmane to the Sekhem, as Adul and Virith had served Zarina.

"There are others better suited to serve in that role. You don't need me to represent the Acinonyx Jubatus."

"None I trust as much as I do you. Don't worry, I won't ask again. Keep your secrets, Mafdet. I can only assume you don't trust me with them."

That too hurt but being sekhem and Mafdet's goddaughter did not entitle her to Mafdet's deepest, darkest secrets.

Her response of, "Tell me what you intend on doing with the contents of this book," confirmed her speculation.

Mafdet didn't trust Asha the way she had Zarina. With Mafdet and Zarina's long history that was to be expected. One day soon, they'd need to speak of Mafdet's role, not as her godmother but as her Shieldmane. Asha wouldn't hold Mafdet to a promise she'd made to Zarina more than eighteen years ago.

"What I choose to do with my book isn't your concern."

"Just because your parents are gone, Asha, that doesn't mean you aren't accountable to the elders in your life."

Asha turned, only to find Mafdet had approached on silent feet. She'd mourned her for two days, along with her parents. Ekon had been correct. Asha hadn't smiled but cried when she'd realized the woman seated beside her bed wasn't an illusion.

"What do you want from me?"

Not an illusion but a solid presence with her own unreachable castle of pain. "I only want the truth."

"I've never lied to you. I won't begin now."

"Then tell me your sekhem name."

Asha's eyes dropped to the book under Mafdet's arm. Dressed in a romper-style one-piece, black workout outfit, Mafdet's two-toned legs and arms, what humans incorrectly diagnosed as vitiligo, were on full display. The blotches in skin color were normal for felidae who could transmutate into a cheetah. Unlike other felidae, their cat skin also appeared on their human skin. Asha thought it beautiful.

"Is my name the price of Mom's book?"

"You know it isn't. I also know I can't keep this book from you any longer or prevent you from doing what you feel you must."

Mafdet handed Asha the leather-bound book. Taking the book from her, she pressed it to her chest like the precious gift it was.

"Thank you."

"Don't thank me. My instincts are howling to take the book back and lock you in your room until the notion that blood and revenge will heal your heart passes."

"I know killing the humans who ruined my life won't bring Mom and Dad back."

"Then why risk what's in that book?"

Asha turned away from Mafdet. A chill ran up her spine, Zarina's spirit having passed through her. Her mother stood on the gravel path in front of Asha. Seconds later, Zarina was joined by Bambara's spirit. Together, they floated up the path, holding hands the way Asha and Ekon had earlier.

"There are only two reasons why I would risk calling on the goddess."

Asha stepped back into Zarina's office. Her parents may have gone to the temple, but it wasn't yet her time to follow them. She closed and locked the sliding glass doors.

"I know you want to protect me, not out of duty but because of love." Asha kissed Mafdet's cheeks. "You are the closest person I have to a parent. I would do almost anything you ask of me. Give you anything within my power to grant you, but not this, Mafdet. My parents' eternal rest is at stake. I know you can't see them. Some days, I'm not even sure if their spirits are real or a figment of my imagination. Whatever the case, they've been with me a year. Whether my actions will give them peace or only me mine, I must try."

Foregoing the couch, Asha sat at her mother's desk, clicked on the desk lamp, and opened the book to chapter one: *Invoking Goddess Sekhmet, One Who Was Before the Gods Were.*

Asha reminded herself to add that name to her list. She began to read, her conversation with Mafdet forgotten.

"You said there were two reasons you would risk everything for revenge. What's the second reason?"

"That's simple."

Asha flipped the page. She'd spent a year reading and researching. It hadn't been a waste of time. No one book had all the answers she sought. But the book Mafdet had withheld from her might prove to be the final piece of the puzzle. With a quick glance at Mafdet, who hovered by the door again, she thought of phrasing her answer as a proverb but settled on a straightforward response.

"They deserve to die. Every last one of them."

Chapter 12: Awakener

"Are you sure? Being my Shieldmane and friend doesn't make you obligated to take this step with me. I'm capable of proceeding alone."

Ekon and Asha stood in front of the archway to the Temple of Sekhmet. While Ekon had been to the ancient temple dozens of times, he'd never been there at the cusp of sunrise, the most dangerous time to appear before the goddess. He'd also never gone there with the intent of invoking her spirit. Technically, Asha would do the invoking.

He held a basket of offerings she'd prepared. When he'd arrived at her home to escort her to the temple, he'd carried a bottle of red wine, the preferred offering of the temple's keeper.

"For what we intend to ask of the goddess, a single offering won't be adequate," Asha had told him, looking at the bottle of red wine in his hand.

Ekon had appreciated her inclusion of him in her phrasing. For too long, Asha had kept everyone outside the proverbial castle she'd mentioned at the beach a few days earlier. He'd read old stories of Sekhmet, like every Shona child. Tales of her bloodlust and vengeance. Her protection of Shona from incursions by humans. While he believed in their gods, Ekon didn't think it possible to invoke their spirits to do the will of mortals, even the will of a grieving young woman of unshakable faith.

Asha had handed Ekon a wicker basket, took his other hand with hers, and led him through the house, to her mother's office and out the sliding glass doors. In silence, they'd walked a gravel path, the sounds of their footsteps swallowed by the fading darkness of the approaching morning.

"Being here with you is my choice. As your Shieldmane. As your friend. But also as the man who loves you." Cupping Asha's jaw, he tilted her head upward and kissed her lips—a slow, gentle kiss of desire but also of eternal devotion. "I've come this far, don't push me away now."

"That's not my intention. I've read everything Mom had on Sekhmet and invocations, but I can't be certain what will happen if I manage to invoke Sekhmet's spirit. What I do know is that, once invoked, I have from sunrise to sunrise. One day."

"What will happen after that?"

"I must return to the temple by the second sunrise or I forfeit my corporeal form to the war and destruction part of Sekhmet." Asha's brows knitted together. "I might have gotten the translation wrong, though."

"Asha," he ground out. "This is too important for you not to know the consequences."

"Either my body or my soul. I'm unsure which. The words are the same, but the definition varies depending on the context. Hubax is an ancient Panthera Leo language I read only a little better than I speak it, which is mediocre at best."

Ekon gripped the handle of the wicker basket tightly instead of hoisting Asha over his shoulder and marching her down the hill and away from the Temple of Sekhmet.

"You're saying your plan, if not executed within a certain timeframe, could leave you a body without a soul or your body could become the vessel for the worst aspects of Sekhmet?"

"I don't like the way you stated that, as if I don't know what I'm doing."

"You don't. You've read and researched. That's what you do. I don't doubt you know everything there is to know about the invocation.

None of which means you know exactly what's going to happen in the temple once you get started. Tell me, in all of your research, have you read of any felidae performing the invocation ritual?"

"Mom once told me that mortals aren't meant to carry the weight of a god's powers."

"Perhaps then you should listen to your mother."

"I am listening to her." Asha shivered as if a blast of freezing air cut through her body. She stared past him and into the temple.

Ekon followed her gaze but saw nothing but flickers of light from the Candles of Eternal Flames lining the walls of the temple. The setting and rising of the sun triggered the flames, their red glow the only light inside the structure.

He had no idea what she saw that he couldn't. Whatever it was, it resulted in Asha stiffening her shoulders and setting her jaw.

Stubborn.

Resolved.

"The First Evolution Union Party will be in power for another fourteen years. Royster and London have Vumaris's entire military to draw from, not only the Rogueshade. You know I want revenge. I won't pretend otherwise. I recite the names of my enemies—a daily, corrosive mantra." Her hand rose to the chest torn open by lion's claws. "I can't forgive. A weakness, most likely, but one I've decided to embrace. Even if I hadn't, I will not permit Shona to fall like every other felidae nation. Humans are like sharks when they scent blood. At the slightest hint of weakness, they come in for the kill. With me as sekhem, they think Shona weak. I understand Tamani's strategy to reveal what happened at Sanctum Hotel, but the consequences of her actions could prove fatal."

Ekon hadn't thought of the repercussions of General Volt's decision to secure Asha's safe return through the use of manipulation, intimidation, but also of the media. No Shona leader had ever been interviewed live on international television and revealed so much of Shona life and culture to outsiders. Not even Mafdet had interfered with the general's plan. But desperate times were known to birth questionable decisions and actions.

"Mom and Dad's assassinations and my kidnapping revealed to the human world a chink in Shona's proverbial armor. To keep our borders secure, our people safe, and to minimize the perception of me being easy prey, especially when I travel abroad, I must send a message no one will soon, if ever, forget."

"Divine retribution?"

"Yes. I will make them fear our kingdom. So much fear, Ekon, that the thought of challenging us will have them trembling. We won't ever be prey again, not if there are steps I can take to prevent that from happening."

Asha's points were valid, even if they aided her self-delusions and granted legitimacy to her rationalizations. She wasn't wrong about sharks, blood, weakness, and humans. Clearly General Volt possessed similar thoughts if the extra combat training she'd instituted was a clue to her unvoiced concerns about the potential for invasion.

"Violence, blood, death?" Ekon questioned, summarizing her contentions to three simple but impactful words.

"Yes, but not only those." Asha freed the basket from his hand. "Safety, protection, love." Slipping from her sandals, Asha entered the Temple of Sekhmet, her red wrap dress flowing behind her.

Red—Sekhmet's divine color.

Red—the color of blood.

Ekon followed Asha's lead and removed his leather sandals before entering Sekhmet's sacred temple. Once inside, he pulled his bottle of red wine from the wicker basket.

The flames from the red candles cast a shadow, giving the illusion of Sekhmet's statue as twenty feet tall instead of six. Kneeling in front of the figure, Ekon recited a prayer then offered the red wine, placing it at the statue's base. Other offerings were already there—old flowers and even older pomegranates.

Asha knelt beside him. Removing a piece of heavy red velvet from the basket, she laid it out before taking her time and situating each of her offerings atop the fabric: red beer, frankincense, mushrooms, bloodstones, red roses, a pack of raw meat, a jar of sand, and a bottle of warm milk. She said her own prayer to the goddess—silent as Ekon's had been.

Grasping her hand, Ekon brought it to his lips and kissed the palm. "Tell me what you need me to do."

Asha had brought nothing with her, not even the books she coveted.

"The sun will rise in two hours. That's how much time I have to invoke Sekhmet's spirit . . . to recite her ten thousand names."

Ekon blinked at Asha, an attempt to clear the fog her declaration had created. "Wait, that's what you meant by ten thousand. That's a myth. Sekhmet has many names, more than any of our other deities, but not ten thousand of them."

"You're wrong." With care, Asha pushed aside the bouquet of withered yellow flowers and rotten pomegranates. Long, sure fingers ran over words chiseled into the base of the statue under Sekhmet's bare feet: *Speak my name and I will live.*

"Mom knew. Not that I'd end up here seeking vengeance in her and Dad's names. But she knew. She understood the importance of a sekhem aligning her spirit with that of the warrior goddess's, of being focused of mind and of heart. Without focus, without faith, Sekhmet will not hear my voice, much less consider my plea. I know her names. I only hope I am worthy."

What could a mortal possibly grant a goddess to prove their worth? Certainly not meager offerings available to anyone with the will and time to gather them.

"You may want to grab a prayer mat from the corner over there."

Ekon did, getting one for Asha too. "Where do you want me?"

"As far away from me as possible but also away from the archway I'll exit after I am imbued with her powers of divine retribution. Sunrise is when Sekhmet is the most powerful, which also means it's when her harsher elements are the most lethal."

The temple wasn't bigger than the size of a large master suite, about three hundred fifty square feet, much of which was taken up by the statue and offering area.

Prayer mat in hand, Ekon decided on a spot south of the statue. From this vantage point, Sekhmet's statue was to his left but in front of him. The position also gave him an unobstructed view of Asha and the archway.

"That's a good enough location as any, I suppose. There won't be any need to stay here while I'm gone. Mafdet will expect a report from you after I've left. You being in the temple with me and my promise of a swift report from you are the only reasons she isn't here being an overprotective godmother." Asha sat several feet from the statue, cross-legged and on the soft, gray prayer mat he'd given her. "Mafdet has never spoken of children, but I suspect she used to have her own. Be sure to put her mind at ease, Ekon." Asha's lips quirked up at the corners. "I should've kissed you before sending you away from me."

"That can be easily remedied." In seconds, Ekon was on his hands and knees and in front of Asha.

She laughed, and he loved the sound. But he loved the way she cradled his face more, her fingers toying with the stubble there before pulling him closer and grazing his lips with her tongue. Ekon sighed, opened his mouth, and waited for Asha to make the next move.

She did, sucking his lower lip into her mouth and biting it with an arousing sexiness that had him moaning and wrapping an arm around her waist.

Then finally, finally, she kissed him properly, her tongue in his mouth and her soft lips moving against his.

Ekon wanted to press her back against the temple floor and wedge his hips between her thighs.

"Will you permit us to be together, when my heart is no longer full of rage and vengeance? When Sekhmet's bloodlust ceases to haunt my waking and sleeping hours? When my parents' spirits are at rest? Can we be together then, Ekon, or will you claim, once more, that I'm not ready for us to become lovers?"

Ekon had promised Asha they would become lovers the next time she asked. He'd meant the words, but she obviously hadn't taken them as a promise she expected him to uphold regardless of the circumstances surrounding her proposition. She'd outlined criteria under which she would be "worthy" to become his lover—an emotional prerequisite he would've never suggested but one he appreciated because it would make the moment about them.

In Sekhmet's temple, this moment was about Asha and her parents, not about Asha and Ekon.

"When you're ready, I'll come to you in any form you prefer."

"You tempt me." Asha nibbled his jaw. "I do love your lion form." Her hand slipped around his neck and pulled him in for a long, wet kiss. "But, for our first time, I want this Ekon. Your mouth." She kissed said mouth. "Your hands. Your . . ." Asha laughed when he caught the hand moving south. "You should return to your prayer mat before we forget where we are and why."

She sounded like Ekon's old Asha. For that to last, Asha needed to exorcise her demons. He didn't know if he wanted the invocation to work or not. Which result would bring Asha fully back to herself? Which one would condemn her to another year or more of psychological torment?

Giving Asha one more kiss, a too short exploration of her neck, Ekon settled himself again on his mat. He would do as she asked. Ekon assumed, once imbued with Sekhmet's divine retribution spirit, Asha would use the goddess's power to go in search of the men who'd wronged her and her family. Ekon would report to Mafdet then return to the temple. He'd packed his truck with supplies before he'd left home: sleeping bag, fruit, water, sandwiches, flashlight, and CD player with CDs, headphones and extra batteries.

Ekon watched Asha. Her hair reminded him of her father's lion's mane—curly, big, and dark brown with gold highlights. Palms of hands on her knees, she sat with her back straight, eyes closed, and face turned in the direction of Sekhmet's statue.

Ten thousand names in two hours. Will that be enough time? She has no notes. She couldn't have memorized all ten thousand names, could she?

"Goddess Sekhmet, you are ancient and wise. The Kingdom of Shona stands as a free and independent nation because of your strength. We breathe because your sun has granted us life. You are known by many names, for you have touched the minds, hearts, and souls of all felidae. We may not all speak the same language or all call Shona home, but felidae from every corner of the planet honor you in prayer and in deed. We are your children, and you are *Mother of the Gods*, *the Source*, *Powerful of Heart*, and *Ruler of Lions*."

Four names, and a hell of a lot more to go. Apparently, Asha had memorized every one of Sekhmet's names, not that Ekon could imagine there being ten thousand of them. It wouldn't have hurt, though, if she'd brought her notes.

"You can read my heart and my mind because you are *Most Strong* and *Lady of Strong Love*. You know why I am here, why I've come to you on the one-year anniversary of my parents' murders. *Pure One*. *Only One*. When I dream, I see my parents. Beside them, I also see you, *Lady of Many Faces*, *Mother of the Dead*. This past year, I've known grief. I've been weak. I've cursed and cried and wished for vengeance and death. This you, too, understand, *She Who Perseveres in Times of Struggles.*"

He thought Asha would simply state Sekhmet's many names. Doing so would've been the quickest strategy but, as he listened to her out-pouring of pain and hard truths, there was no strategy to be found with Sekhem Asha. Sure, her mind was as quick and as tactical as anyone's would be with Sekhem Zarina and Khalid Bambara as their tutors and role models. But the young woman had approached the invocation without a hint of self-protection or calculation. Asha had come to bare her soul, apparently, and perhaps that was why she questioned if the goddess would find her worthy.

With such innocent vulnerability, how could the goddess not?

"Dad taught me the importance of friendship and family, *Unwavering Loyal One.* Such lessons are easier learned when raised in a house-hold of love, where intellectualism is valued but not above kindness. You are *Lady of the House of Books.* I have traveled beyond the con-fines of my mind when I read, but it is at home with my friends and family where I am the happiest."

Ekon glanced at his watch. The flames from the eternal candles were beginning to wane as the dawn of a new day approached. Even if the invocation didn't bring forth Sekhmet, he was so proud of Asha. Not only had she lowered the drawbridge to her fortified castle, she'd obliterated the structure stone by stone, leaving nothing but a nine-teen-year-old young woman who loved and missed her parents.

"I beseech you, *Great One in the Places of Judgment and Execution,* come forth. I beseech you, *Satisfier of Desires, Drier of Tears,* come forth. I beseech you, *Overcomer of All Enemies,* come forth." For the first time in almost two hours, Asha's eyes opened, and she stood. "I beseech you, *Victorious One in Battles,* come forth." Asha stepped for-ward, her hands outstretched toward the statue. "*Sekhmet of the Knives. Burner of Evildoers.*" Palms touched the statue's lion face. "*De-vouring One, Terrible One,* I invoke your ten thousand names. *The Awakener, Sekhmet, Beloved Teacher.* I invoke you." Tears fell but Asha's hands and words didn't falter. "*Sekhmet, Lady of Radiance, Re-vealer of the Ancient Paths,* I invoke thee. Come forth, my goddess, come forth." Asha's forehead lowered to the statue's chest, just under the lion mouth. "*Finder of Ways, Keeper of the Light, Lady of All Pow-ers.* I invoke you, *Beloved Sekhmet.* Awaken. Awaken. Awaken."

The sun rose, the first rays of light heralding in the new day. Out went the Candles of Eternal Flames, casting the temple in semidarkness. No sounds or smells penetrated the temple's walls—an unnatural phenomenon Ekon couldn't explain.

He rose but stayed where he was.

Asha had recited every one of Sekhmet's ten thousand names, her voice no less sure and strong on the last name than it had been on the first.

Ekon watched and waited. The air in the temple felt unnaturally stale and muggy. The hairs on his nape and arms rose but the odd sensation he sensed didn't raise his hackles.

"Asha," he whispered. "Are you all right?"

No answer.

Ekon lifted his foot to move toward Asha but stilled at the sight.

The granodiorite statue crumbled. Not slowly or even in parts but at the same time and completely. All the while, Asha remained where she was but not under her own power.

A woman's arms with clawed hands held Asha close. Very close, so close that Asha's body melted into the other woman's. No, not melted but merged.

Ekon stumbled backward.

The woman turned to him—her golden lion's face no longer frozen in granodiorite. Fur and bone. Asha had invoked the warrior goddess. Braids fell past breasts, claws curled, golden eyes glowed, and Asha's bloodred wrap dress fit every curve of the goddess's divine form.

Asha had been worthy, her plea accepted. She'd awakened the deadliest part of the goddess. Yes, Asha had been worthy, so worthy Ekon knew her unspoken sekhem name.

"Sekhem Sekhmet . . . ?"

The lion-headed goddess turned to him and nodded. Her solid form thinned around the edges, her tail whipped, and her eyes shimmered from red to gold. Rubble crunched under bare feet. More of her form thinned like a receding tide from a shore—vanishing.

Ekon was losing her. "Asha, don't—"

She disappeared.

Chapter 13: Lady of Slaughter

The Republic of Vumaris
Lower North Ngaso
Motel Escape

"You're beautiful. Come back to bed."

Mirrors didn't lie but horny men did. Savannah couldn't help it; every mirror called to her. The one in the motel room was no different. Bathroom door open and she inside, she stood in front of the full-length mirror that hung on the sturdy door. Most women when standing naked in front of a mirror would examine the shape of their ass, the lift or sag of their breasts, the fine lines on their face, the size of their stomach, or even the *V* of their sex.

Not her.

For the past year, when Savannah neared a mirror, she would stop, stare at her mouth and jaw, and recall how she'd gone from truly beautiful to damaged goods. A year. Had it been only twelve months? It felt longer. The number of surgeries she'd had and painkillers she'd consumed made the single year seem like a dozen.

Large hands encircled her waist. Tongue and mouth sought her neck. Kissed. Licked. "You're gorgeous. Don't worry about the scars. You have a great plastic surgeon because they're barely noticeable. You survived." Dick pressed into her ass. "That alone makes you badass and sexy as hell." Cade spun her around and kissed her. Not on the mouth. He knew better. She didn't kiss or give him blow jobs. But Savannah did permit Cade to fuck her in the ass, so he didn't much care that her mouth was off-limits.

Well, off-limits to him, not to Javier. She owed her husband. As angry as he'd been because, well, he was always furious when he'd learned she'd taken another lover, Javier had felt sorry for her enough to stay. He'd scheduled every one of her doctor's appointments, held her hand after each surgery, and even cried with her when she'd seen her face after the first operation. The man was loyal to a fault. His dad had been a shit husband and father, so Savannah supposed Javier thought he could make up for what his father lacked by staying with a wife whose childhood was worse than his.

Savannah loved Javier. She truly did. Her heart would shatter if he ever left her for good. But what Javier didn't know wouldn't hurt either of them.

Cade's mouth descended to her nipples, sucking with a greedy roughness she'd long since stopped trying to convince Javier she liked. His beard scratched, leaving red marks, and she liked that too.

"You taste so fuckin' good."

She grabbed his dick, stroked fast and hard the way they both enjoyed.

"Fuck, yeah, like that." Cade bucked into her hand, biting her breasts each time she circled and squeezed the pink head of his dick. "Shit. Shit. Come here."

Holding her by her wrist, he dragged her from the bathroom, pushed her onto the bed, and pinned her under him, his dick inside of her before she could lift her legs and open wide.

Savannah moaned, Cade's deep, hard thrusts exactly what she needed to take her mind off things better left in the past. She and Javier hadn't been good for each other for years. But she always returned home to him and he invariably forgave her transgressions.

A part of Savannah hated him for that, just as a part of Javier hated himself for loving a lying, cheating bitch. He'd called her that more times than she'd allowed Cade to fuck her. As big as Cade's dick was and how well he used it, Savannah would work damn hard to even the score.

He hit the right spot inside her, and moans rumbled up and out. The man knew how to make her tingle and squirm and squirt a river for him. Shit. Why in the hell had it taken her so long to get onboard with what he'd been offering since before the clusterfuck that had been Sanctum Hotel?

Grabbing a fistful of Cade's black hair, Savannah yanked him down to her breasts. He had the most amazing mouth, second only to the dick pounding into her.

"Yes, yes." Arching her back and slamming her pelvis into his, she took from him as much as he demanded of her.

Savannah would shower before she jumped in her car and headed home. Javier would still be out, so she'd have time to take another shower, using the white jasmine bodywash Javier liked to smell on her. She would cook them dinner, watch him lock the house down and check his half dozen guns, and then go to bed alone because Javier would stay awake half the night waiting for the "spawn of the devil" to return.

If the little bitch hadn't come for them already, she wouldn't. The first few weeks after the felidae had left Minra, Savannah had been as paranoid as Javier. But she couldn't live in a state of constant fear. It wasn't healthy, and she was tired of being a prisoner in her own home.

Cade on his knees, holding her legs up and at the ankles, he kept her open wide for him, his hips in constant, hard motion. "So wet, baby. So wet."

Cade hit that sweet spot inside her again, and Savannah's eyes fluttered shut. Damn but he knew his way around a woman's body. Whenever she was with him, he left her wanting more. During those times, Javier would benefit from the work Cade had put in earlier in the day.

Cade slammed into her again, and Savannah smiled at the thought of having Javier's big, strong body under hers after having spent an indulgent afternoon with Cade. Javier's paranoia may have been a pain in the ass, but his concern over her safety translated spectacularly into the bedroom.

Cade's sweat dripped onto her belly . . . her breasts. Yes, he should be sweaty. Savannah certainly was. More sweat splashed onto her hot flesh. His hands fell away from her legs, and she pouted.

"You want to switch positions already?"

Cade didn't answer or move.

Savannah guessed he did want to switch. That was fine. He liked doggie style, and so did she. She opened her eyes, her mouth already forming the words to let him know she was cool with changing positions.

Cade dripped onto Savannah.

Not sweat. Oh, god, not sweat.

Blood. So much blood. But only from a single wound—a hole in his chest. A hole through which a clawed, bloody hand penetrated, the same way Cade's deflating dick still penetrated her.

The hand withdrew from Cade's body, while the other pushed him off the bed. *Thud.*

Savannah wanted to scream. Wanted to run. Wanted to rub her eyes and will the terrifying sight away. But she couldn't. Her body wouldn't act on the screams in her head.

Not real. This isn't real. I'm dreaming. Please, god, let this be a dream. A nightmare. Anything. Anything other than a woman with a lion's head.

It wasn't a dream, but it damn sure was a living, snarling nightmare.

Savannah's shaky hand rose to her reconstructed jaw. The doctors had called her recovery "a miracle." Her speech would never be the same, but she wasn't mute, so she'd counted that as a win.

The creature stared at her, golden eyes glowing with nothing she'd seen before outside of documentaries on predators—serial killers, rapists, and wild animals. The growling woman . . . thing combined the worst of humanity and animality.

The clawed hand with pieces of Cade's heart impaled on the ends pointed toward the floor. God help her, the creature opened its mouth and pointy teeth glistened but the voice that emerged was as gentle to the ears as cotton on satin.

"First blood is always the tastiest, but rarely the most filling. My belly is empty, and Mr. Skullbow's death was but an insignificant hors d'oeuvre unworthy of my claws." The thing sniffed. "You smell of sin and fear."

Savannah scooted away from the lion-headed creature with the dulcet voice of a demented angel. When her back hit the headboard, she cast her eyes around the motel room. How in the hell had the thing gotten in there? Sure, fucking Cade was mind blowing but not so much that a trained soldier would miss a half-woman, half-lion thing enter her motel room. The door was closed—the metal chain still in place. There was only one window in the room—to her right with drawn curtains. The thing hadn't come in that way, either. So how?

Savannah shook her head. It didn't matter. She was naked, unarmed, and the creature stood between her and the locked door.

"Two Rogueshades. One room of lust and lies. I would say your husband would miss you, mourn your well-deserved death, but he won't."

The hand free of blood and Cade's innards reached for the blue comforter and yanked, pulling the sheet and Savannah to the edge of the bed.

She scrambled backward, screaming when claws raked across her chest, slicing off breasts in one brutal swipe. Blood spurted, and Savannah couldn't stop her screams.

"He won't miss you because Mr. Stormbane won't live long enough to know of your wretched demise."

She didn't see the second slice. Or the third. The fourth. The fifth. But she felt them. Pieces of her body fell to join Cade on the floor.

"You're soaked, though not in the way you seem to enjoy most."

She cried. Bled. Begged.

"Speak my name."

Savannah shouldn't have known the creature's name. Yet the second the command roared out of its mouth the answer materialized in her pain-addled brain.

"M-m-mistress of D-dread."

"I prefer Lady of Slaughter, but your response will do. Come now, Mrs. Nighthide, my stomach needs filling and you are but one meal I intend on devouring this day."

The lion-headed thing crouched over her. Sniffed. Growled. When it lunged at Savannah, rows of deadly teeth gleaming, another name formed in the space between life and death.

Lady of Terror.

Kabo Row
Salty Night Bar and Lounge

"**Another** round of Rotten Bloods?" Kendrick slammed his glass on the rickety table and snorted. "Rotten Blood—great drink, stupid name."

Lennox pushed to his feet. "I'll get the next round." He shoved Cree's shoulder. "Your cheap ass can pay for the one after that."

"Why me? There's five of us at this table?"

Lennox shoved Cree again, harder than the first time. "Yeah, five people, and you're the only one who never pulls out his wallet."

"You're a freeloader," Riggs added, his meaty hand wrapped around his glass, mustache wet from his drink. "A cheap-ass freeloader. Thanks for the first round, Widow Maker, but I don't want another Rotten Blood. I want to try that new Burning Barrage beer."

"No problem, but watch it with the code names, man. After the year we've had with the media on a hunt for members of London's team, we gotta keep that shit low."

"Right, right. Government names only. Got you." Riggs tipped his glass to Lennox. "A Burning Barrage. We're celebrating."

"We damn sure are." Zane's chair scratched against the floor when he stood, unsurprising since the man topped two-fifty. As bald as a cue ball but without the smooth exterior, Zane stretched, burped, and farted, all at the same time. "I'll assist with the drinks."

"You need to take your funky ass to the bathroom." Kendrick waved a hand in front of his nose. "And lay off those Cognac Eye wings. You're foul, bro."

"Shut the hell up. You had just as many wings as me."

"Yeah, but you don't see me bringing them up from both ends."

"All right, all right. Shit. Is this a celebration or what? If it is, then we need more drinks." Lennox pointed to the men around the table. "A Burning Barrage for Riggs, a Rotten Blood for Kendrick and me. What do you want, Cree?"

"Honey Howler."

"Honey Howler?" Kendrick threw peanut shells across the table at Cree. "You pussy. That's not a real drink."

"And Rotten Blood is? It sounds like a venereal disease."

Kendrick laughed. "Yeah, it kind of does. Fine, whatever."

"Come on, Zane. Let's go before these assholes change their minds."

Music ricocheted off the walls—some heavy metal shit Kendrick could've done without. But Salty Night catered to its diverse customers, which meant a country boy like Kendrick had to sometimes put up with bands like Placebo Surrender who thought yelling was the same as singing. What did he expect, anyway? It was a Wednesday and the best bands performed on Friday and Saturday nights.

He supposed they could've waited until the weekend to have their celebration. At least then he could've savored his drinks as well as the music because Taste of Perfection tore up the stage, leaving him horny and in search of a woman with a fat ass, big tits, and no aversion to screwing in the back of a minivan with car seats.

But no, the celebration had to be then. He'd invited all the in-state Rogueshades from his last mission, but soldiers were more superstitious than athletes. Most had declined, giving bullshit reasons why they couldn't, although more likely wouldn't, drag their asses from their hiding holes. That was all good, though. Kendrick hadn't lost his balls. They were right where they were supposed to be. When Royster and London finally managed to quell their detractors and the public moved on to another sensational story, Rogueshade would be back in business.

He hadn't been called Widow Maker in too long, and his wife refused to call him by his code name in bed. *Her loss.*

"Okay, the heroes have returned." Zane handed Cree and Riggs their drinks.

"Thanks." Kendrick took his drink from Lennox.

The five friends smiled at each other, fresh drinks in hand and the scarred wooden table far too small to accommodate their long legs. But they made do.

"Since you got us together," Riggs said, "you do the honors."

Kendrick thought back to the night at Sanctum Hotel. These men, his brothers, had had his back. It hadn't been their first mission together, but it had been their toughest.

"This time last year, we kicked some serious felidae ass."

His friends stomped feet on the floor and pounded fists on the table.

"I mean, don't get me wrong, those Shona weren't easy to take down. But we bagged and tagged them, that's for fuckin' sure."

"That's because ain't no lion shifting motherfuckas tougher than us." Riggs tossed back half his drink, hissing. "Shit, that's strong."

Lennox punched Riggs in the arm. "You asshole, Kendrick wasn't finished, and we're supposed to drink at the same time."

"Oh, yeah, go on."

"Well, umm, I was pretty much finished. Just, we made it out alive. That's worth celebrating."

"Hell yes it is." Cree clinked glasses with Zane and Lennox, who flanked him. "I wasn't trying to go out like the others. Here's to the fallen."

Cheers and stomping followed but a little more subdued with the reminder of the dead Rogueshades. Kendrick may not have liked every soldier in London's special ops unit, but they were human like him, and humans didn't deserve to lose their lives to felidae.

They ordered more rounds, and Kendrick was pretty sure Cree didn't pay for any of them. After his sixth drink even Placebo Surrender sounded good to him. He staggered to his feet. The music and a sexy female in a tight-ass red dress called to him. Kendrick may have been a little drunk and lights in the bar set low, but he knew one fine piece of ass when he saw one.

"I'll be back, and Cree, if you touch my drink, I'll break your fingers."

"I don't want your damn drink. I can buy my own."

"Yeah, that'll happen the same day your wife finds your tiny dick under that gut you call a six-pack. Meaning never."

Cree threw up fingers at Kendrick. They could've been gang signs, for all he cared. He walked away from his friends and toward the seductress in red. Her long braids would be perfect for running his hands through, just as her ample hips would feel amazing pressed against his.

She didn't dance, although she stood on the dance floor, back to him.

Kendrick approached, his breath hitching the closer he drew. He didn't know what it was about the woman, but he couldn't stop his legs from moving toward her.

Kendrick didn't make it a habit of picking up women and screwing them. It was just that, well, ever since Jackie had gotten sick things between them hadn't been the same. Between chemo and the kids, his wife was too tired and too sick to take care of him the way she used to. Kendrick knew that made him a selfish bastard, but no one gave a shit about what he was going through. No one asked how he was doing or what they could do for him, not even the assholes he called friends. Everything was Jackie this and Jackie that. Well, fuck Jackie, and fuck cancer for slowly taking his wife from him. *I'm tired of being fucked over. I'd rather do the fucking.*

Kendrick danced up to the temptress, pleased with his only slightly drunken two-step, and the fact that everyone who had been clustered around the woman had cleared a path. *That's right. Get out of my way. Shit, it's been months since I got some. And she looks like she'd give it to me good and nasty.*

But . . . wait. Why isn't anyone moving, and why did the music stop?

Kendrick swung in the direction of the stage. Three guys and two girls, Placebo Surrender were still on the stage dressed in jeans and T-shirts, their normal gig gear. They were frozen in place.

He laughed. *I'm hallucinating. Those Rotten Bloods must've hit me harder than I thought.* Kendrick laughed again. Maybe he should've had a weak Honey Howler like Cree. If he had, he wouldn't be seeing things, like his friends jumping up and down and pointing at him.

What were those assholes doing? See, he knew he was drunk because they yelled nonsense at him. He flipped them off.

"What? I can't hear you?" He could hear them just fine, since the band had obviously decided to take a break. Cupping his ear, he pretended to fall for their stupid joke. "Say what? Oh, okay. Yeah, there's a lion behind me?" He grabbed his crotch. "I got your lion right here."

Warm breath blew on his nape, and Kendrick's dick twitched. He hadn't hallucinated the temptress in red. Good. He didn't know why his friends had decided to yank his chain, but he was tired of playing their game.

"You smell delicious."

That voice. Could a woman have a sexier sounding voice?

"You don't smell like rotten blood to me."

"What?"

"Fresh. Ripe. Delicious."

Okay, sexy voice and nice ass aside, the chick was crazy. Kendrick didn't do crazy bitches. But when her hot breath hit his nape again, doing wonderful things to his skin, he reconsidered his standards.

Kendrick's friends broke out in a run. Not toward him but . . . Damn, her breath was hot, hotter than it had been the first time.

Before he got more than ten feet from their table, Zane jolted to a stop. Then Cree and Riggs. Lennox got a little further, but he too snapped to attention. His body lurched forward then backward, whiplash without a vehicle.

Kendrick had to help them, but he was so hot. So damn hot. Was his neck on fire? His hair?

"Fresh. Ripe. Delicious."

That voice. Against his ear. *Owww*, his ear burned. More than that. Drooping. Melting.

"It is good to see you again, Mr. Widow Maker. It's been too long. Have you missed me?"

Each word was like a branding iron—burning and marking his skin.

Kendrick watched, with wide eyes, his friends yanked into the air. They screamed, and so did he.

A tongue licked his other ear, and his scream intensified. Acid? Whatever it was, his second ear burned like the first.

"Fresh. Ripe. Delicious. Your blood is moving now. Fear has that effect on mortals. Your heart is racing, pumping even more blood. Each one of you has a different taste, which makes my meals all the more scrumptious."

Riggs fell, his body smashing through a table before slamming into the floor. He groaned but was soon wrenched back into the air.

"Nighthide tasted of adultery. Skullbow of fornication. Swifttalon of cowardice. Darkpelt of envy. Thundersnarl was a rewarding blend of deceit and anger."

Kendrick swallowed. How many Rogueshades had she killed before coming after him and his friends?

Zane dropped to the floor followed by Cree and Lennox. Then they were snatched back into the air, an invisible power controlling them like a marionette. The same power held him hostage because he damn sure couldn't move. Unlike everyone else in the bar, who'd been turned into statue-like figures, Kendrick and his friends were the focus and at the mercy of the faceless female behind him.

She kind of sounded like that little Shona princess but grown up and with a hard edge he'd stupidly mistaken for sex appeal.

"I wonder what sin you and your friends will taste like." Her belly rumbled. "Hmm, I'm still hungry. Famished, in fact."

His friends' bodies smashed to the floor over and again. Kendrick could do nothing but watch.

Flaming arrows appeared from nowhere.

Kendrick screamed.

The arrows flew toward his friends.

Thunk.

Thunk.

Thunk.

Thunk.

Heads exploded, a popping eruption of brain tissue and blood. The four flaming arrows hissed, slithered to the floor and walls, lapping up gory remains.

Kendrick threw up in his mouth.

"Rockmane—abuser of self. Darkstare—covetous. Spiritgrim—greed. Hellgaze—hypocrisy. Riggs Muller. Cree Aubrey. Zane LeRoy. Lennox West. You wanted to shoot me in my head. Will this do instead?" She nuzzled his neck and, were those whiskers he felt? "What do you think of the Seven Arrows of Sekhmet?"

"S-seven?"

"Ah, of course. How can I expect you to make an informed decision when I haven't presented you with all of the facts?"

She shoved him forward, knives scoring his back and the same invisible power that had dominated his friends had him in its grasp. It whipped him around and he saw the face of his temptress in red.

Kendrick wished he hadn't. Nothing like her should exist. But she did, and she'd tracked him and his friends to Salty Night Bar and Lounge. Kendrick thought of Jackie and their children. They were at home. He'd promised his wife he wouldn't get drunk or stay out too late. She hadn't believed him, but she'd nodded, kissed his cheek, and told him to, "have a good time and drive safely."

He cried. Seven Arrows of Sekhmet. The lion-headed woman had used only four. That left—his body flew through the air, propelled by the force of three flaming arrows sinking into him. He crashed into the wall behind him, a flaming arrow in each leg and one in his stomach.

Kendrick couldn't scream, move, or even choke on the blood that had gathered in his mouth.

The creature floated up to him, her maw coated in blood. "Lusting after women. That is your sin among many, Mr. Widow Maker."

The arrows burned . . . and so too did Kendrick.

Chapter 14: Lady of Transformations

Kingdom of Shona
Temple of Sekhmet

"Where in the hell is she?" General Volt marched to the temple's archway, hands on her hips and a growl in her throat. "I don't see her."

"I don't think that's how it works." Ekon finished rolling his sleeping bag. He still had a few more items to clear out of the temple, but his progress had been slowed by the general's and Mafdet's arrival. "Asha disappeared. She didn't exit the temple like a normal person, so I doubt we'll see her jogging up the path to meet the sun."

General Volt spun around, the bottom of her black suit jacket whistling upward with the harsh, abrupt movement. At this time of hour, why General Volt and Mafdet were dressed in their full Shieldmane uniforms, he had no idea. Ekon had foregone his suit, boots, and tie in exchange for comfortable sandals, shorts, and a T-shirt.

Mafdet shook the trash bag she held in her left hand. "I'll take this granodiorite mess to the house."

"That can wait. We need to figure out what to do about the sekhem."

"Don't bark at me, Tamani. I'm not in the mood for your attitude."

"I wouldn't have an attitude, if one of you had informed me of Asha's plans before she vanished."

"She didn't exactly vanish," he interjected. "I mean, she did but we know where she's gone."

"Do you really want to speak to me right now, Ekon?"

"Asha invoking the spirit of Sekhmet isn't his fault. She's an adult and sekhem. If you were here, what would you have done differently?" Mafdet held up the trash bag to General Volt. "These pieces are all that's left of a centuries-old statue. None of us thought it possible to truly call on the gods, but Asha did. She believed. Don't be angry with him for going along with Asha's plan."

Ekon took the trash bag from Mafdet. No need for them both to make a trip back to Asha's house when he had to go down the hill to drop his supplies off in his truck.

"I'm not angry with Ekon, but, shit, Asha goes from depressed and distant to calculating and vengeful in the blink of an eye."

"It wasn't in the blink of an eye," Mafdet said, voicing his thought. "Asha has been plotting this for a year. We all saw the wheels turning. Her extensive research. Her disappearances for hours. She eats but only to prevent me from complaining. As far as I know, she hasn't been in her lion form since returning home. She speaks to her parents. I'm convinced she think she sees them. Asha roams the house at night when she should be asleep. She cries more than she'll admit to anyone. And she swims in the ocean until exhausted because that's the only place she feels she can release her anger without hurting herself or anyone else."

"I know, but—"

With a shake of her head, Mafdet patted General Volt's shoulder. "No offense, my friend, but you don't know. You've never lived with Asha. If you had, you would truly understand the toll her parents' deaths have taken on her. I don't have to ask how you felt the day we saw what those monsters had done to Asha. Each of us would've killed to avenge her, along with Zarina, Bambara, and our Shieldmane brothers."

"It's our duty to serve and to protect. But how can we do that if she won't let us?"

"Little of what she has done is about us." Mafdet and General Volt turned to face Ekon. "Asha thinks she's fulfilling her mother's dying wish."

General Volt's brows knitted together then an eyebrow arched. "Did Asha tell you her sekhem name?"

"In a way." Ekon nodded to the remnants of the crumbled statue in the trash bag he held. "We should've guessed it. Sekhem Zarina gave Asha the alpha name of Sekhmet. Considering it was bestowed before her mother was murdered, it makes sense Asha would assume her mother meant for her to avenge her parents as her first act as the new sekhem of Shona."

"Too much sense," General Volt agreed. "She invoked the worst aspects of Sekhmet, I gather?"

"That's what Asha said. War, destruction, plagues."

"Divine retribution in its most awful forms. Sekhem Sekhmet." General Volt sounded as if she was testing the title on her lips and found it not quite to her liking. "There's a reason why sekhems aren't traditionally named after the gods." General Volt snorted a laugh, slapping Mafdet on the back. "But you're named after a god, my friend, no wonder Zarina had no issue gifting her daughter with Sekhmet's name. Goddess Mafdet—judgment and justice but also execution. That's the problem with gods, they don't know whether they want to help or hurt mortals. No wonder Asha is confused."

Ekon slung his sleeping bag over his shoulder. "I don't think she's confused. What Asha is doing in Vumaris is an attempt to staunch the bleeding in her heart. Until the humans who stole her innocence and security are no more, she'll continue to be blinded to the real reason Sekhem Zarina named her after Sekhmet."

General Volt scanned him, as if taking his measure and finding whatever she sought in the gaze that didn't flinch from her scrutiny. "Ah, now I remember why I didn't complain . . . too much . . . when Zarina elevated you to Asha's Second Shieldmane. You'll make a fine khalid one day."

"I don't care about becoming second alpha of Shona. My only goal is Asha's happiness and safety."

"You made Tamani's point but, like Asha, you can be blind to the obvious." Mafdet pointed to the archway. "The sun has risen but our sekhem hasn't returned. You said Asha had from sunrise to sunrise, correct?"

"Yes. She must still be in Vumaris chasing her demons."

"Sekhmet's bloodlust." General Volt sighed, hands going to her hips. "If Sekhmet's bloodlust has taken over, we may not be able to save Asha a second time."

In an uncharacteristic public display of affection, Mafdet granted General Volt a one-arm hug. "A wise but annoying person once told me to have faith in my sekhem. I return that advice. Have faith, Tamani." Mafdet reached out her free hand to him, and he took the offer. "Have faith, Ekon. Asha will return to us. We'll make sure we're here when she does."

"What if, when she comes home, she's more Sekhmet than Asha?" Ekon asked, terrified that would prove the case.

"The sad, unforgivable truth is that we didn't save Asha a year ago. That's not who we brought home. We've spent the past year pretending otherwise. Sekhem Sekhmet has been with us all along. It was the goddess who set the sekhem free, not the other way around."

The Republic of Vumaris
Lower West Ngaso

"I knew you would come. I told Savannah you would be back. I told them all. But no one would listen."

Bam. Javier's double-barrel shotgun exploded. Two perfect shots to the chest. He reloaded. Shot again. Again. Again. All dead center. None of them kill shots. He pulled a Glock from his waistband and unloaded the weapon—seventeen direct shots to the head.

Perfect aim.

Nothing.

He kept shooting, moving from one gun to the next.

Load. Shoot.

Load. Shoot.

What would it take? Fuck, what in the world would it take to kill her?

"Why in the hell are you just standing there? Say something." Javier shot again. Like all the other bullets, they went in and out. No entry or exit wounds. No blood. No damage except to his wall behind whatever in the hell had entered his home after he'd dozed off while waiting for Savannah to return home.

While Javier may have never seen the lion-woman who'd materialized in his bedroom, he damn sure could figure out who was responsible for it being there. He didn't know if Asha was somehow behind that lion's mask or whether she'd summoned the creature to do her bidding.

"Stop hiding and come out and face me." He let his useless gun slip from his hand and onto the floor. He'd unloaded every bit of ammo he had into the creature. The second he'd run past her and out his bedroom door, without her moving a clawed hand to stop him, he had given up what little hope he'd had of fleeing his house. There was no escape to be found. Neither through a window nor out a door. He'd tried each one, and they had all led back to his bedroom and the silent but watchful creature within.

She sat in a chair in the corner near the window. His chair. Many nights, including this one, he'd reclined there, a gun in his lap, waiting for Asha to return for her pound of Rogueshade flesh. Javier should've known the girl would choose the night of her parents' deaths to come for him. Had she hunted the others too? From the dried blood on her face, hands, dress, hell, even on her toes, she'd made many stops before seeking him out.

Javier glanced to the body in his bed. Not Savannah's, although the person rested on his wife's side of the bed. Rest wasn't an accurate descriptor, though. Nothing as peaceful as that four-letter word could explain the condition of the damned soul taking up half of Javier's marital bed.

"Where's Savannah and why did you bring Deputy Chief London here?"

The devil's spawn didn't answer.

"Talk to me. Did you kill my wife because you damn sure did something foul to London?"

Not only had Javier awoken in his chair to find the creature in his room but a sweating and vomiting London in his bed. The older man had swollen lymph nodes over his entire naked body, groin included. He'd had two seizures since arriving. His jaw had stiffened but the rest of him had jerked in rapid succession. London's face had turned blue and, for a minute, Javier thought the man would lose consciousness. It would've been a kinder fate if he had. Instead, Frank London was as awake and as cognizant as Javier.

"He's dying."

The creature had to know that, of course, but nothing in her countenance registered an ounce of sympathy.

London groaned and, as much as Javier wanted to help him, he didn't want to catch whatever plague he carried. Bubonic, based on the look of the swollen nodes.

"You did this to him."

The accusation fell flat. Javier was scared shitless but a strange part of him suspected he would've felt better if he heard the spawn of the devil call him *Mr. Stormbane*. Instead, her golden eyes had closed, and her breathing had slowed.

Not asleep but also unconcerned with him as a threat. For as many times as he'd shot her, her body no worse for his efforts, his threat level ranked up there with a gnat.

Savannah wouldn't be returning home, he realized. The thought of her death should've grieved him more but all he could muster was a depressing sense of relief. The fraud they'd called a marriage was finally over. Strangely, he had the inhuman creature to thank for his marital liberation.

Javier slid down the wall on the same side of the room as a groaning London but across from his would-be killer.

"You're going to make me watch him die. That's why you brought him here, isn't it? You know the deputy chief is the one who sent us after you and your parents. All the intel we needed came from him. The zoo lions were also his idea. But you know that already. I know you do. To be so young, you have an evil streak."

Javier had spent the past twelve months looking over his shoulder for Sekhem Asha or one of her Shieldmanes. She'd all but told him she would return his cruelty with her own. Not a day had gone by without his mind revisiting the night at Sanctum Hotel and the two days at the riverside warehouse.

During his time in the military, Javier had gone on many missions and killed countless people. They had no names worth remembering or faces he could recall. They had been targets in need of eliminating. Good soldiers followed orders. Javier Hernandez had always been an excellent soldier.

Dressed in a tank top and jeans, Javier raised his knees to his chest. He didn't know where to look, so he stared at his bare feet.

Javier hadn't been able to forget Asha's name or her angelic face. Her defiant golden-brown eyes. Her sarcasm and deceptively sweet voice. He also hadn't forgotten the sound of her pained cries or the acidic smell of her urine because he'd given an order for the guards not to permit her to use the bathroom. "If the stubborn devil's spawn wants to relieve herself, she can piss where she sits." With as much dignity as she could muster, she'd squatted and done her business in front of men and women who'd already thought her no better than an animal in the bush.

No, Javier hadn't been able to forget Sekhem Asha. Obviously, she hadn't forgotten him either.

"I'm sorry." He'd spoken the apology low and more to his knees than to the creature. Javier lifted his head, cleared his throat, and repeated, "I'm sorry. I'm sorry for what we . . . for what *I* did to you, Asha. To your parents. To your friends. I'm truly sorry."

Eyes opened and, if Javier weren't mistaken, they were less lion gold and more golden-brown like the Asha from his nightmares.

Javier thought she would speak, perhaps tell him she could smell his fear but not his regret, as she'd done to Widow Maker. He had indeed come to regret his actions. But regrets changed little. They certainly couldn't resurrect the dead or erase a girl's memory of two days of unjustifiable brutality.

Her only response to his apology were cold eyes that took in Javier then London.

The deputy chief looked awful—swollen, pasty, and flushed. As he watched London, the man's toes and fingers shifted from red to brown to black. Impossible. Gangrene didn't kill body tissue in a matter of minutes. Then again, everything he'd seen since awaking should fall within the impossible category. But it didn't. It was all too real. Horrifying but real.

Javier couldn't watch London suffer any longer, so he left his bedroom. Again, the lion-headed creature permitted him to exit. When he reached his living room and sat on the sofa, a shivering London appeared beside him. Javier moved to the dining room. The kitchen. The basement. Hell, even the half bath on the first floor. No matter where he went in his house, a plague-tortured London soon appeared. Resigned to having to watch the man responsible for bringing hell to the Shona, Javier returned to his bedroom, sliding down the same wall where he'd taken refuge earlier.

Seconds later, London materialized in front of his feet.

"K-kill m-me. K-k-kill me." Tongue licked dry, cracked lips and London repeated his plea.

Javier had expended all his bullets on Asha's lion demon. There was a sharp chef's knife in the kitchen. Javier had never favored knives, but he knew how to kill an enemy with one. The deputy chief wasn't his enemy, but the man was suffering.

"You've made your point. You can let him die now."

A manila folder appeared in the small space between Javier's feet and London's prone form.

He picked up the folder, opened it, and then swore. *The fucking addendum to the treaty.*

The irony had Javier laughing and crying. She could've killed him while he slept. The same with Deputy Chief London. He didn't doubt, however, that she would eventually take both of their lives.

"Two days, huh?"

Her eyes slipped closed again, her clawed hands folded in her lap, and her silence couldn't have been more terrifying than if she would've come after him with her sharp teeth.

Two days. They'd shot her. Starved her. Withheld fluids. They'd set real lions loose on her while chained and with no way of defending herself. He'd ordered his own version of waterboarding, spraying her with cold, dirty river water. She'd suffered their mockery and taunts, their insults and curses, their absolute disrespect of her personhood. The Rogueshade had treated Sekhem Asha as less than an animal. In Vumaris, animals had more rights and legal protections than that of the felidae of Shona.

For two days, Javier stayed in his bedroom, using the closet as a makeshift bathroom. When he'd first had to take a piss, he'd opened the door to the upstairs bathroom but promptly slammed it shut before the group of lions feasting on a downed but not yet dead antelope spotted him. She had turned every room in his home into a supernatural highway, connecting his house to what he assumed were locales in Shona.

A rain forest.

A mountain peak.

A savanna grassland.

All dangerous. None routes to freedom.

Faucets ran red with blood and all the food in his house had molded. She hadn't missed anything, including turning ice cubes into small blocks of stainless-steel link chains.

Not once, during the forty-eight hours she'd kept them hostage, did she move from the chair or open her eyes, not even when she'd used her powers to further torture London.

Vomit, fever, shock, abdominal pain, cough, diarrhea, chills, weakness, Frank London was forced to endure them all. He should've died long ago, but she'd kept him alive, infecting him with one plague then another.

Asha had to have hated Javier and London to subject them to such depraved treatment. Then again, hate hadn't been the Rogueshades' and the deputy chief's motivations for what they'd done to the Shona.

On his hands and knees, Javier crawled to the chair where Asha sat, sitting back on his haunches when he reached her. She gave no indication she knew he was there, but he hadn't expected an acknowledgment. His fear hadn't diminished. She could kill him at any moment. In fact, the two days had left Javier with nothing but time to torture himself thinking about when and how Asha would end his life.

"I-I know you can smell truth from lies, just as my scent reveals my fear." Javier scooted closer, his body inches from the woman he'd wronged. "I can't see any of Sekhem Asha in the lion face you're wearing, but I know, somewhere deep inside is the respectful, sarcastic, and stubborn young woman I helped to victimize. I know I'm going to die. I know I deserve everything you've done to me because I did worse to you and with far less provocation."

Javier didn't know the exact time Asha's plane had landed in Shona, but he assumed that had been the first time since her kidnapping that she'd felt her life returned to her. Not the same life she'd had when she'd left home, though, but the new life she had to forge from the ashes of her pain and loss.

"R-R-oyster. G-guilty."

Javier didn't bother looking back at London. Even at the end, the deputy chief refused to take responsibility for his crimes. Worse, he'd spent the last two days both cursing Royster's absence from the hell Asha had turned Javier's home into and reminding Asha of Chief Royster's equal culpability.

As far as Javier knew, Chief Royster could already be dead. If not, Javier wouldn't do or say anything to hasten Royster's judgment.

Risking Asha's wrath, Javier laid his hand atop hers. Despite the ferocious claws, her hand radiated heat, her skin smooth and soft.

Lids parted and only Javier's guilt and remorse kept him from withdrawing his touch.

This close he could see she truly had the head of a lioness, while the rest of her body was that of a woman. A woman taller and stronger than the Asha he'd known but no less a version of the same girl who'd looked him in the face and refused to sign away her people's land, knowing pain and indignity would follow.

The lioness snarled, a shallow baring of teeth.

Javier's heart pounded so hard he felt it in his eyes, but he didn't back away. He wouldn't.

"You have every right to despise my guts. What I did to you and what the Rogueshades took from you are unforgivable. Crimes. Sins. For years, I told myself I wasn't a bad man despite doing bad things to awful people. But that was bullshit. I never cared who the person was on the other end of my bullet because I didn't want to care. You can't do my job if you look beyond the surface. Caring makes you soft and gets you killed. So I lived to fight other battles, go on other missions because I chose not to give a fuck about the blood I shed, the lives I denied, and the families I destroyed."

He caressed her hand, going so far as to travel the length of a finger down to the beginning of a claw.

The rumble of sound in her throat had Javier withdrawing his hand but not his body.

"I recorded a replay of the episode of DeGracey's show with your General Volt. I have no idea how many times I've watched it."

Once he'd stopped lying to himself, he'd broken down, crying each time General Volt or DeGracey had displayed a picture of the smiling and happy Leothos family. He'd sobbed even harder and longer at the video footage of them taking Asha into custody. He'd been the driver of the SUV, although no one knew his identity thanks to the angle of the camera that caught only a portion of his arm.

Javier recalled precisely what he'd been thinking when Asha had been shoved into the back of his truck—anger over her parents' audacity to fight back but also a sense of privilege and entitlement as a human. How could humans not be superior to a race of people who loped through much of their lives in animal form?

He'd come face-to-face with his racism and prejudice, the single-minded belief that led him to devalue the worth of an entire group of people to the point of having no compunction executing them for money.

Javier had one final confession. Glancing over his shoulder, he met London's watery green eyes. *He must feel it too—death nearing. Our final judgment.*

He cleared his throat, more afraid than he'd ever been but never more committed to finishing something he'd started. "I was there, when your parents died." *No, that's a cop-out.* "I mean, I was part of the group that shot and killed your parents. Your father tried to protect his wife. He shielded her body with his. We shot him." Javier lowered his eyes. Ashamed. "A lot. Until he died and shifted into his human form. By that time, your mother was close to death. She'd fought hard. They both did, but they were outnumbered and outgunned. I don't know what her final words or thoughts were. At the time, I didn't care. She wasn't our mission. You were. So we fired on her."

After the number of bullets they'd pumped into her parents, he couldn't imagine the Shona would've been able to have open-casket funerals for their murdered leaders. Had Asha seen what they'd done to her parents? Had a Shona medical examiner submitted a report to the new sekhem? Javier hoped not but a part of him suspected Asha would've wanted to know every detail of her parents' deaths, no matter how much the knowledge would've gutted her.

Taking a deep breath, Javier lifted his head, ready to die for his crimes against the royal Shona family. Asha's lion would put him out of his misery. He deserved nothing less than her eternal scorn.

Javier choked on the sight before him. Hell, tears fell, and he . . . shit. His heart hurt.

No braids.

No claws.

No golden eyes.

No lion's head.

Not a spawn of the devil but a beautiful young woman. *An angel with golden-brown eyes.*

"Sekhem Asha." Javier's voice trembled; so too did his hands.

"Mr. Stormbane."

That voice—sweet with a touch of vinegar.

Javier's deliverer.

His Glock materialized in his right hand, and he knew what she wanted him to do and it wasn't to grant London's two-day wish. The deputy chief would die soon enough, his torture well-earned.

So was mine.

How many times had he contemplated disobeying orders and shooting Asha in cold blood? Worse, how many times had he threatened the eighteen-year-old with death by a bullet to her head?

Once would've been too many, and Javier had threatened her more than a single time.

He didn't check the gun's magazine clip to know it was full.

Like Javier's, tears ran down Asha's face. He had no doubt she would mature into a wonderful woman and leader of her people. He would be years dead, but the thought of her living a long, happy life despite the wrongs done to her younger self, made the weight of the Glock that much lighter in his hand.

Javier raised the barrel of the gun to his head and pressed it against his temple.

His deliverer leaned back and closed her eyes. "Say my name, Mr. Stormbane, and I will live."

He smiled. His angel. His . . . "Sekhem Sekhmet."

"Thank you. I forgive you."

She forgives me. Me . . . Rogueshade. Stormbane. Sergeant Major Hernandez.

Javier's heart filled with relief. His lips formed a smile of content-ment. His finger pulled the trigger.

Bam.

Chapter 15: Only One

The Republic of Vumaris
Upper West Minra

"You don't have to do this." Silas stepped in front of the guest bedroom closet, throat tight, mind and heart racing. His breaths came in heavy pants. "Come on, don't do this. I can't believe you're going to throw away twenty-three years of marriage."

"We've talked about this."

Claire crossed arms over her chest, cocked her head to the side, and glared at Silas with eyes so pale blue he could see the red of the heart he'd broken.

"You talked. I never agreed to the temporary separation."

"You don't have to agree, and it won't be temporary. Once I'm settled, I'll have my lawyer contact yours."

I thought this bump in our marriage would blow over.

DeGracey's show had started the ball rolling, and other media outlets had jumped on the bandwagon. Silas and Frank had been crucified in the media, and those damn pictures of the Shona family had been everywhere. Even a year later, Silas couldn't go a week without a reminder of what had happened at Sanctum Hotel.

"I told you, I didn't have anything to do with the deaths."

Claire's clicked tongue called him a liar. Her stomped retreat to her dresser expressed so much more. Yanking open the dresser drawers, she took no care in pulling out clothing and tossing it onto the bed and into her suitcase.

"The two lion handlers from the local zoo confessed. They received a personal call from Frank." Claire's head snapped up from her packing. "I never liked Frank, but you picked him as your deputy chief, so I tried to be supportive. We watched the news program with the former zoo employees together. What kind of man is so arrogant as to call in that kind of crazy favor personally? Worse, what kind of sick, cruel asshole thinks up a plan to torture a child? I suppose the prick thought it funny to have actual lions attack a girl who could turn into a lion." She threw a balled-up shirt at Silas, hitting him in the chest. "It isn't fucking funny. It's a sign of a warped mind. And you had that psycho in our home and with our daughter."

They'd gone from sporadic arguments to shouting matches—with Claire accusing him of awful things and Silas flat out denying each one. There were many upsides to a long marriage, such as the comfort that came with knowing your partner. Part of that knowing was . . . well, realizing when a spouse was feeding their partner a big helping of bullshit.

Silas had lied.

Claire had cried, yelled, swore.

Silas had kept lying. Once he'd started, there was no way in hell he could confess, not after the awful way Claire and Audrey had spoken about the "amoral cretins" who'd "hurt the poor Shona princess and her parents."

He'd lied.

Claire had moved out of their bedroom the day after they'd returned home from settling Audrey into her dorm room.

"I told you, that was all Frank. Okay, okay, I'll admit that Frank came to me after DeGracey's interview with that Shona general." Silas took a chance and moved around the bed separating them and closer to his wife, stopping at the foot of the guest room's queen-size bed. "Frank said he was worried about us not being able to keep our campaign promises. I told you, Sekhem Zarina and Khalid Bambara wouldn't sign the treaty's addendum."

"You say that as if their stance was wrong. My god, Silas, what would you say if the president of . . . pick any country you want, all but demanded that you cede part of Vumaris? It would be offensive at best and arrogant at worst." Claire shoved more clothing into her suitcase, not taking her normal care with her packing. "You keep trying to lay everything at Frank's feet. I have no problem believing the idea of the addendum and everything that followed was that asshole's brainchild." She slammed the suitcase shut. "But you aren't a stupid man, Silas. Far from it. Frank would've known better than to take action on that grand of a scale without the go-ahead from the chief. I'm not stupid either, so stop speaking to me as if I am."

After DeGracey had interviewed the two lion handlers and showed footage of the riverside warehouse where the Rogueshade had kept Asha, the public had called for Frank London's resignation. The Rogueshade had cleared out of the warehouse long before DeGracey's film crew even knew the warehouse existed. But they'd left two dead lions behind and a ton of other evidence that supported the lion handlers' and General Volt's claims. A surprising number of concerned Vumarians had wanted to know what had happened to Asha after her kidnapping. Where answers weren't available, the public filled in the rest with wild speculations. As a result, the First Evolution Union Party's approval rating, especially Silas's, had tanked.

No evidence existed that directly linked him to Sanctum Hotel, the Rogueshade, or the warehouse, so he had managed, barely, to keep his head out of the legal and social noose. He did worry about Frank, though, but the man, despite having resigned under a gray cloud, had maintained his innocence. Like Silas, Frank neither had the courage to retreat from his lies nor the stomach to accept the full ramifications of his actions.

Silas slumped onto the bed, his mind grasping for words to change Claire's mind and to salvage his marriage. He couldn't lose his wife. Not like this. Not over a handful of dead felidae. Would Silas have made a different decision had he'd known Frank's plan involved assassinating the leaders of Shona? Of course.

What angered Silas, however, was everyone's reaction, including Claire's.

"You have a doctorate in Vumarian history and are the chair of the history department at a college so expensive that, were you not an employee and entitled to tuition remission, we wouldn't have been able to send our daughter there."

Claire tugged her suitcase off the bed and propped it next to the dresser with open drawers and scattered clothing. She managed to grab a second suitcase from under her bed and glare at him while doing it.

He didn't care. If she intended on moving out and divorcing him, he may just as well say what he'd been holding inside for months.

"As a professor of our country's history, tell me, Claire, how did humans come to have a nation of our own on this continent?"

"What?"

Claire flipped dark hair over her shoulder, but Silas wasn't fooled by the display. She knew what in the hell he meant.

"War, genocide, slavery, treaties? Tell me, how did humans come to create and rule Vumaris when felidae were here first?"

"Don't be ridiculous."

"I'm not, and you teach early Vumarian history. You've written dozens of scholarly articles on that time period."

Silas leaned against one of the bed's columns, manufactured wood in a white finish, sadly enjoying the glint of shame that crossed his wife's face.

"Everything we have we secured through lies, manipulation, trickery, and outright violence. Those rough days of land grabs and broken treaties weren't that long ago. You know the historical details better than I do. We celebrate Vumarian founders as "great men," as "visionaries," and as "brave pioneers.""

"Don't you dare."

"You wrote those words, Professor Royster. I only read them in a book that earned you the status of best-selling author. As a people, we grow, expand. Name one country whose founding didn't involve a battle or disagreements."

"I can't believe you're actually sitting there justifying torturing a child the same age as our daughter."

"Yet you're fine with viewing your husband of two decades as a villain when you've written glowing prose about men responsible for the near extinction of the cheetah and tiger nations. Men who broke every treaty they brokered with the felidae of Zafeo. Your great men of vision wanted this entire continent as their own and only the might of the lion shifters of Shona stopped them. It was never my intention to hurt anyone, Claire. I was open to negotiations. I would've honored the addendum to the treaty. I would've—"

The phone rang.

"Don't pick it up. We're talking. It's probably just . . ."

Of course Claire answered the phone. She wouldn't even grant him that small request.

"Slow down, sweetie, I can't understand what you're saying. Yes, your father is right here. He's fine. No, we aren't watching the news."

Claire snapped her fingers, pointing to . . . ah, the remote control near his leg.

"What channel?" Silas mouthed.

"Audrey, sweetie, please calm down. What are you saying about Frank and dead bodies?"

That had Silas scrambling off the bed and toward the other side of the room. He opened the television armoire, the white finish the same as the four-poster bed.

"What channel?" he snapped.

Wide eyes and a gaping mouth were his only responses from Claire. Fine, he'd just have to flip through . . . he turned on the television, then stumbled backward until his legs hit the foot of the bed. Silas wouldn't have to flip through the stations.

"I repeat, former Deputy Chief Frank Bartholomew London is dead at age forty-six. This is breaking news. We do not have all the details. What we do know is that the body of former Deputy Chief London was found on the lawn of a home belonging to a Javier and Savannah Hernandez. Mr. Hernandez was found dead in his home. We do not yet know the cause of death of either man. We also don't know the whereabouts of Mrs. Hernandez who, according to police, wasn't in the home with her husband."

Silas heard the remote control crash to the floor, but he was too stunned to register much beyond the reporter's declaration of Frank's death. Why hadn't he been notified? Who in the hell approved the reporting of Frank's death? He knew who—Governor Billings and Police Commissioner Aguilar. The men had taken advantage of Silas's contentious relationship with their party to make moves that, if successful, would have their party tossing Royster on his ass come next election cycle, and sliding them onto the political ticket.

Claire came and stood beside him. To his surprise, her arm settled across his shoulders, holding him in a loose hug.

"We've had unsubstantiated and hard to believe reports coming in from all over the state and country of a lion-headed woman in a red dress. Details are sketchy but customers at Salty Night Bar and Lounge, a popular watering hole in Ngaso, swear a lion-headed woman froze everyone in the bar then proceeded to brutally kill five men. Once the men were dead, the lion-headed woman disappeared, leaving everyone else unharmed."

Claire kissed his temple. "Ngaso is only sixty miles from here."

Ngaso was also home to Fort Lekate, the base for many of the Rogueshades involved in the Sanctum Hotel attack. Claims of a lion-headed woman, no matter how absurd it sounded, along with Frank's death, and the involvement of Sergeant Major Hernandez and his wife were too many points of convergence for Silas not to think the Shona were involved.

"One year and two days, Silas."

He'd spent the anniversary of the attack on the felidae keeping himself busy so as not to drive himself crazy remembering the girl's parting words. *Death does not knock on the door.*

"It has to be a hoax."

"I would be inclined to agree, if there weren't people who could actually transmutate into predatory cats. It does sound crazy, though. But Frank is dead only two days after the anniversary of the massacre at Sanctum Hotel." Claire pressed the phone into his hand. "Talk to our daughter. She's convinced the lion-headed woman will come after you next."

Silas didn't want to speak with Audrey. Her concern for his safety only served to remind him that his daughter, like his wife, thought him guilty. He was, dammit, but it hurt like hell to have his family know that kind of terrible truth about him.

Phone cord pulled taut, Silas held the receiver to his ear. He did his best to soothe his daughter's fears, all the while saying nothing as his wife removed clothing from her closet.

Silas had lost his party's trust and his credibility with the public. Silas was losing his wife. He might also lose his daughter. Frank was dead. No great loss there, but his death signified another turning point in his life. The lion-headed woman hadn't come for him, at least not directly. It seemed young Sekhem Asha cast a bigger shadow in life than her parents did in death.

"I'm fine. I'm safe."

Silas hadn't heard Audrey cry since a pimply faced kid she affectionately called her "boyfriend" had dumped her for another girl. Silas had been secretly pleased. The boy wanted more than his daughter was willing to give. He'd felt every bit the proud father that day, happy he'd raised a girl unafraid to stand up for herself and to stick to her beliefs. But taking a stand, even when right, could hurt, and wasn't that a sad epiphany for a forty-eight-year-old man?

Silas had no idea how long he spoke to his daughter on the phone or the last words he'd said to his wife after helping her load her car with suitcases he'd bought for family vacations. What he did recall was going to bed alone in a house once filled with love, laughter, and joy but had slipped into a depressing state of silence.

Closing his eyes, and drifting into a fitful slumber, he dreamed of a girl roaming the halls of an empty house, tears rolling down her cheeks and two ghosts trailing behind her. The scene replayed over and again.

The same sorrowful girl. The same dark house. The same protective ghosts.

A dream. A nightmare.

Lonely is one, a honeyed voice spoke in his mind. *Sleep well, Chief Royster. Sleep well, for where a woman rules, streams run uphill.*

Silas's eyes popped open.

Chapter 16: Great One of Healing

Kingdom of Shona
Temple of Sekhmet

She heard them before she saw them—Ekon, Mafdet, and Tamani. They were her family, the only reason she'd returned home instead of hunting down Chief Royster and then gorging on the blood of humans.

"Do you know how many times I've trekked up this hill to a temple without a statue or our sekhem?"

"As many times as Ekon and I have. I told you I would call when Asha returned. Go to work."

"How am I supposed to work when the sekhem is MIA? What do you suggest I tell her council?"

"Tell them their sekhem is making the world safe for Shona," Ekon said.

"Right now, Asha's safety is my greater concern. It's been three days. I think we need to have a serious conversation about next steps. We can't keep wasting our time returning to this temple with the hope that Asha will miraculously appear."

"Asha will come home."

"Mafdet, shit, you keep saying that but she's not here."

She crashed to the temple's floor, silencing the bickering. Splayed facedown, and momentarily disoriented from Sekhmet's magic and her graceless landing, she didn't move.

Footsteps ran toward her.

She pushed to her hands and knees, head down, claws extended and cutting into the floor. She growled.

The footsteps halted.

She could smell them. Their blood. Hear them. Their heartbeats. She scrambled backward in a defensive crouch.

"It's all right, Asha. You're home now."

Mafdet. But the Asha she'd known, cared for and loved hadn't been all right. She'd died, like so many Rogueshade had by her vicious hands. Hafsa Sekhem Asha had perished, along with Sekhem Zarina and Khalid Bambara.

"You really have turned into Sekhmet." Tamani's scent floated to her—love but also sadness. "Look at you, my sekhem."

She hadn't wanted them to see her this way—covered in blood and smelling of death. *So much death. So many sins.*

The Rogueshades but also hers.

She scooted farther away until her back hit the wall where Goddess Sekhmet's statue had once been. Raising her head, she saw them. Worried and tired but also relieved. They'd waited for her to return, having faith in her when she'd spent three days questioning her sanity and morality.

Mafdet and Tamani stood next to each other, dressed in their familiar Shieldmane uniforms and wearing twin expressions of concern. She'd been gone too long, and she'd worried them. She hadn't meant to do either.

But it was Ekon's smile that gave her pause, confused her even. She'd turned into something unrecognizable, a creature of war and destruction. She'd relished the power from her goddess, as well as the fear the mere sight of her invoked in her enemies. Yet, with her family and coated in the blood of those she'd slain, the form her revenge had taken wasn't the image she'd wanted them to have of her.

But she didn't know how to transmutate back into her human form. The transformation had happened only once, with Stormbane, and that hadn't been deliberate. After he'd shot himself, she'd transformed back into Sekhmet. Again, without conscious thought.

Ekon moved around Mafdet and Tamani and toward her. In an eerie similarity to how Stormbane had knelt in front of her, his hand atop hers, Ekon also knelt, his body wonderfully close. He reached out to her, but not in the same way Stormbane had.

Ekon cradled her lion's face with his large, gentle hands.

She wanted to weep, to bury her face in the crook of his neck, to seek his forgiveness for sins committed against others.

"Sekhem Sekhmet is a title worthy of Hafsa Sekhem Asha."

She'd terrorized without mercy. How could Ekon say her name with tenderness and reverence?

"Mi Sun Choi called when you were away." He scratched behind her ears. "She said the Common Peace Coalition Party is ready to move forward with your parents' plan whenever you are."

For a year, she couldn't fathom any plan that didn't involve blood and death. Could she now? Was she capable of leading Shona in a direction separate from her grief? Had her bloody rampage set her parents free or did their spirits still wander the mortal plane?

One of Ekon's hands traveled to her chest and over her heart. She hadn't felt it beat in three long days. The organ fluttered, leapt. "Sekhmet may be a warrior goddess of war, destruction, and plagues, but she is also a sun goddess of healing. You choose. War and plagues or sun and healing? Answer this question, my sekhem, which version of Sekhmet do you believe your mother named you after?"

She'd done little the past year but think. She thought about vengeance and justice, not about growth and the future. Raising her hand, she placed it over Ekon's heart. Dried blood caked her fingernails.

Fingernails not claws.

She thought she understood why she'd transformed at Stormbane's home.

Truth. Vulnerability. Pain but not anger . . . forgiveness.

Closing her eyes, she gave in to the power of Ekon's truth. Not a revelation but the opening of a door she'd kept closed because walking through it had been a more terrifying prospect than floundering in sorrow.

Self-pity looked suspiciously like defeat.

Mafdet and Tamani joined them, completing her family circle. They hugged her. Kissed her. Accepted her as she was—wounded but ready to begin the healing process.

Her choice. Warrior goddess or sun goddess? War and plagues or healing?

She sank into Ekon's arms, her face, her human face, pressed to his solid, supportive chest.

Mafdet kissed the top of her head and Tamani wiped away her tears that, for the first time in a long while, weren't born of sadness.

Tears of hope.

"Sekhem Sekhmet." She lifted her head from Ekon's chest, permitting him to help her to her feet. "Duality. Harmony. I cannot be one or the other. I must accept that I will forever be both. Warrior and healer."

She'd brought destruction and plagues. But she had yet to learn the difficult art of healing. Sekhmet would begin with herself.

Following Tamani and flanked by Mafdet and Ekon, she left the temple of her transformation, and walked down the path to a house that she'd forgotten had once been a home. It wasn't a magnificent structure by any standard. Not a mansion or palace, not even a sprawling compound like the First Evolution Union's headquarters in Minra.

The two-story white stone façade surrounded by a landscaped garden had never ceased to conjure a smile from her. No matter how many countries she'd visited with her parents, returning home felt like taking a deep breath after a spring shower—refreshing, cleansing, and freeing. She inhaled through her mouth, appreciating her home in a way she hadn't in twelve long months.

Tamani hugged her. "Take a shower, eat . . ." Grinning, Tamani leaned back from Sekhmet and laughed. "Then again, you've had Rogueshade buffet for three days. I doubt you're hungry. Maybe you'd like a glass of warm milk to wash down your breakfast, lunch, and dinner."

Mafdet tsk-tsked. "You're not funny."

"Who's the general and who's the Shieldmane?"

Mafdet ignored Tamani but asked her, "Who remains, or did you devour them all?"

"All except for Chief Royster."

Almost imperceptibly, Mafdet's right hand shifted to the knife sheathed at her waist. "Good to know. You won't ever hear me say this again, but Tamani is right. You need to wash the filth of those humans off you. Eat, if you're still hungry. Rest, if you're tired. There are matters Tamani and I must tend to, so you'll have the house to yourself. Ekon will be here. Let him be of assistance."

Ekon shifted beside her, giving movement to the sudden burst of awkwardness she felt at Mafdet's not so subtle implication. Not a suggestion, of course, but an acknowledgment of the inevitable.

Tamani slapped Mafdet on the shoulder. "You're the least tactful person I know."

"I'm friends with your mate and mother, so I know you're lying." Mafdet shrugged off Tamani's hand. "What would you like for us to call you? Are you ready to accept Zarina's gift?"

A gift as opposed to a burden. The difference in perspective had her turning away from her house and gazing out at the expanse of land. She'd traversed every inch of the acreage with her parents—on two feet as well as on four. Asha in Ebox meant life, which was what her parents had given her in every sense of the word. They'd loved her, taught her, guided her, even scolded her, when needed. They'd also trusted her to lead her best possible life, making decisions from the place of *us* and *we*, not from *I* and *me*.

She shifted back to her family, their gazes expectant. Smiling, she kissed each of their left cheeks. "I thought Asha dead. When I look at you all, as well as my home, I know that's untrue. Asha still lives inside of you, but also inside of me. But I am no longer wholly Asha, as I can never be fully Sekhmet. As Mom once told me, mortals aren't meant to carry the weight of a god. But a part of me now does."

A difficult confession but one that had to be made.

"I didn't take Mom's words literally enough." She raised her hand to her heart. "Protectress of Shona, Great One of Healing, those are the names the goddess whispered to me when I accepted her powers into my body. But they aren't mere names or even titles, but charges. My charge. The same charge Mom gave me before she died."

She kissed them again, but on their right cheek, a formal display of affection from a sekhem to her loyal Shieldmanes.

They lowered to a single knee and raised their eyes to hers.

She'd refused the formal induction ceremony of a new alpha. No one questioned her legal authority to rule. She'd been the Shona's hafsa sekhem, so the transition to alpha had been politically seamless but emotionally jarring.

She still had no interest in a formal induction ceremony. But there, among her family, she would pledge her soul to them, as they had already pledged their bodies to her.

"I am Sekhem Sekhmet of the Kingdom of Shona. Alpha of our land. Protector of our people. We are bountiful and blessed." In turn, she touched their heads. "We are deadly in war—strong of heart and sharp of claws. We are glorious in peace—sparkles of light and harbingers of faith. I am daughter of Zarina and Bambara Leothos, and you are my beautiful lights, my forests of rose petals."

Sekhmet's fingers grazed Tamani's upturned face, an unspoken request for her to rise. The general did with lithe crispness. "You are Tamani Volt, Guardian of the Gates." She kissed both of her cheeks.

"And you are Sekhem Sekhmet—Protectress of Shona."

Tamani's smile, more so than her words of loyalty, warmed Sekhmet. She nodded to Tamani, giving her leave to proceed with her day. Hopefully, less worried about Sekhmet's safety and mental well-being.

She listened to Tamani's retreat then shifted her focus to Mafdet. Her godmother had been a staple in her life, as much as her parents had been. Perhaps one day Mafdet would share her complete story with Sekhmet—maybe when Sekhmet was older or the heartache she'd caught glimpses of in Mafdet's eyes, over the years, ceased to burden her heart.

Without Sekhmet's silent request to rise, Mafdet stood—tall and lean, and so very beautiful of form and spirit.

"You are Mafdet Rastaff, Slayer of Serpents." Sekhmet slowly lowered her gaze to the blade Zarina had gifted to Mafdet decades ago. While Mafdet held many secrets, not all were hidden from Sekhmet, so she lingered on the blade's handle, guaranteeing Mafdet wouldn't miss the meaning of her next words. "Mafdet, Great Cat of the Nation of Swiftborne." She kissed Mafdet's cheeks then whispered in her ear, "Not very subtle, my felidae cheetah, but neither are the condoms you keep leaving in my bedroom."

Sekhmet kissed Mafdet's cheeks again. She really did cherish her godmother, even more after Zarina's death.

Mafdet's gaze slid from Sekhmet to Ekon then back to her, mouthing, "Use them." Aloud, Mafdet said, "And you are Sekhem Sekhmet—Great One of Healing."

Mafdet cut her eye to Ekon once more before strolling in the opposite direction than the one Tamani had gone.

Sekhmet tugged Ekon to his feet, grinning up at him from a face in need of a thorough washing. Hand in his, she led him toward the sliding glass doors. "Tamani was right, I need to shower. Wash my back?"

"Umm, what?"

"As eloquent as ever."

Halfway through Zarina's office, Ekon stopped, forcing Sekhmet to do the same.

She turned to face him. "What's wrong? Do you not wish to share a shower?"

"More than anything, but that's not it." Ekon fidgeted with the hem of his shirt for only a blessed second before he spoke his mind. "You gave Tamani a title, Mafdet two, but me none." Ekon shrugged, but there was nothing nonchalant in the gesture.

Her unintentional slight and his hurt had her wrapping her arms around his waist and resting her head on his shoulder. "Like Sekhmet's ten thousand names, I have many titles for you. Of them, one is closest to my heart."

"I—"

She hushed him with a finger to his chin but wanted to place her lips to his. *Not yet. Not until I can come to him unsoiled of mind and of body.*

"Ekon Ptah, you are the Beautiful Soul, Lord of Truth, He Who Listens to My Words but Also to My Heart. You are my Finder of Ways, my Inspirer of Felidae Kind." Sekhmet kissed his throat, his pulse strong and fast, his skin salty and delicious. "Sublime One. Adorable One."

Yes, adorable, especially when he smiled at Sekhmet with youthful jubilation. She caressed his grinning face, loving the way it lit up even more from her touch.

"Are those a sufficient quantity of titles, or must I stroke your ego by listing more?"

His boyish smile gave way to a roguish man's smirk. "My ego isn't the part of me in need of your stroking, my sekhem."

She opened her mouth to offer a teasing reply but snapped it shut. Two figures hovered beyond the sliding glass doors. Fingers laced with each other, they nodded to Sekhmet, turned, and then floated in the direction of the Temple of Sekhmet.

"I have to go."

"What do you mean you have to go? I thought—"

She kissed him—quickly, dismissively, but not without regret. "I'm sorry, Ekon. There's something I must do before we can be together. Meet me in my suite in an hour?"

He glanced over his shoulder, likely wondering what Sekhmet had seen that had prompted her abrupt change in plans. "Your parents?" Ekon turned back to her. "Do you really see your parents, the way Mafdet believes you do?"

Mafdet may not have been able to see Zarina's and Bambara's ghosts, but she saw through Sekhmet with ease.

"I can. I know you can't, but they're making their way to the temple. Please accept my apology, but I must meet them there."

Before he could delay her longer, she darted through the office and out the sliding glass doors. Racing up the hill, she followed her parents.

Her father transmuted into his lion form. Her mother did the same.

Corporeal. But how?

So slow, my hafsa. You are alpha now, show us the worth of your lioness.

Sekhmet gritted her teeth, pumped her legs and arms faster, and charged after her parents, enjoying the sound of Zarina's playfully taunting voice in her head but not how far of a lead her parents had on her.

Humid wind whipped through her unruly hair. Grass crunched underneath her feet. The sun beat down on her skin, but memories of old warmed her heart.

Her father's infectious laughter. Her mother's quick wit. Her father's good morning hugs. Her mother's goodnight kisses.

Sekhmet stumbled and fell.

Her father's praise. Her mother's wisdom.

Bones broke—hard snaps that bowed her back and split her skin.

Her father's prickly beard. Her mother's golden-brown eyes.

Limbs elongated and jaw widened, producing roiling spasms of liberation and gasping shocks to her senses.

Their devotion—to each other, to Shona, to her.

Fur sprouted. Claws formed. Fangs descended.

Through golden eyes, she spotted her parents at the top of the hill. *Waiting for me.*

Pushing to her paws, unsteady at first but more sure-footed with each step, Sekhmet continued up the hill. Devouring the distance between them with long, resilient strides, she surged forward.

Zarina and Bambara had indeed waited. Their magnificent corporeal forms stood in front of the archway to the Temple of Sekhmet. She thought they would enter upon her arrival. Instead, her mother nipped at her tail and her father nudged her neck with his snout.

She knew what both behaviors meant. But they couldn't possibly want to play. Could they?

It seemed they did because Zarina nipped Sekhmet's tail again, sprinting away before she could react.

Bambara tackled Zarina and Sekhmet paused for only a second before joining the fray. As always, she aligned with her mother.

Lionesses versus lion.

Sekhems versus khalid.

Her father swatted them away—his paws large but his attacks gentle.

Sekhmet ran, rolled, and roared. With each nuzzle and nip, each pounce and parry, Sekhmet fused with Asha.

Grief ebbed.

Bloodlust retreated.

Harmony beckoned. So too did the Garden of the Sacred Flame and her parents' overdue eternal rest.

Together, they loped into the Temple of Sekhmet. Her parents claimed the freshly cleaned offering area. Bambara sat facing the archway with Zarina reclined beside him.

Equals in life. Equals in death.

The first time they'd left her, she hadn't had an opportunity to say goodbye. Sekhmet nuzzled her mother's neck and then her father's, inhaling their scents one last time. They did the same to her. It wasn't enough but she wouldn't cry or complain. Instead, she would relish the moment for what it was—a gift from the gods.

Instinctively knowing what she had to do, Sekhmet walked behind her parents to where the goddess's statue had once stood. Focusing within, on the love she had for Zarina, Bambara, Ekon, Mafdet, and Tamani, she envisioned Asha and Sekhem Sekhmet. They sat beside each other on the sand at Tideless Depths Beach, looking out at the crystalline water, a book with an image of the lion-headed goddess between them.

They spoke in unison, the froth of the ocean inching up the beach and toward their bare feet.

"Great One in the Garden of the Sacred Flame who rouseth the people, who reduceth to silence our enemies, we are pure, aware, beautiful eyes which giveth life to two forms."

Power crackled inside Sekhmet like fire in a hearth. Her body transmutated—a new creation, an old form. Stepping back on human feet, Sekhmet slumped against the wall behind her, drained from the final merging of her two halves but also from the return of the goddess's power to its proper place of containment.

Using the temple's wall to steady herself, Sekhmet walked the interior of the temple until she reached the archway. Stopping at the opening, the sun shining behind her, Sekhmet wept but also smiled at the sight before her.

Sekhmet's granodiorite statue had returned. No longer on a dais, she stood behind a statue of a lioness in repose, her hand on the lioness's head, her other hand on the shoulder of the statue of a male lion to her left.

Goddess Sekhmet but also Sekhem Zarina and Khalid Bambara. Immortalized.

One temple. Three resplendent statues.

Her parents were finally at peace.

Protected by Sekhmet's sun. Thank you, my goddess. Thank you.

Chapter 17:
Complete One

Ekon felt awkward, if not intrusive, being in Asha's . . . Sekhmet's bedroom without her. This level of intimacy would take time to get used to, as would thinking of and calling Asha by her sekhem name. Out of all the names Sekhem Zarina could've bestowed on her daughter, why had she chosen Sekhmet?

Ekon strolled from the desk chair where he'd been seated and reading one of a half dozen open books on the desk, to a bay window that faced the Temple of Sekhmet. The house was too far down the hill for Ekon to see the temple, but he could make out the rock-edge gravel path just fine. The sun was high in the sky, and Sekhmet's requested hour was nearly at an end.

Sekhmet. Zarina's faith in her daughter was unmatched. She had to have known how Asha would've interpreted her new name.

A nude figure appeared on the path—walking with purpose but not with speed. *That's my sekhem. You've rediscovered your balance.* He looked forward to running again with her in lion form. It had been too long.

Ekon removed a purple wrap from the foot of Sekhmet's bed, hung it on the outside doorknob and then closed the door. She may have had no choice but to return home without her dress, but he wanted to ensure she did have a choice when it came to when and how to share her naked body with him.

He returned to the blue leather chair, careful not to interfere with Sekhmet's organized mess. Except for her desk, everything else in the room reflected her tidy nature, including her made bed, which, according to Mafdet, she rarely slept in since her parents' deaths.

Full bookcases took up most of the available wall space. Even more books were piled in neat, small stacks in front of them, all with worn spines and dog-eared pages.

The doorknob turned, and a rush of nerves had him jolting to his feet.

Sekhmet entered, wearing the vibrant wrap he'd left for her. He'd never seen her in such disarray, and she smelled like an awful mix of blood, sweat, and sickness. Yet, to Ekon's adoring eyes, she was the most beautiful woman he'd ever seen because every foul scent, every bloodstain, and every wild curl flecked with gore were testaments to a war waged and won. Not against the Rogueshades but her aggrieved heart.

Smiling at Ekon, Sekhmet closed the door behind her.

Sekhmet. Yes, Ekon comprehended Sekhem Zarina's choice of name. Who knew a daughter better than her mother? With or without the name of Sekhmet, Asha would've sought revenge, likely on her own because the young woman was too stubborn and independent. But with the name of the goddess as her sekhem right, Zarina had indirectly yet masterfully sent Asha on an intellectual journey that would either result in her invoking the goddess or end with her exhausted from the search but having burned through her fury. A gamble but one Sekhem Zarina must've felt she had no choice but to take to protect her daughter from herself.

"Thank you for my wrap . . . and for waiting."

Sekhmet glanced around her room, arms behind her back. Her nerves helped ease his own and made her infinitely more desirable.

"How are your parents?"

"At rest." The smile that followed her response was like pulling back a curtain and letting in the rays from a newborn sun. "Finally. I have a surprise for you, Mafdet, and Tamani."

"What kind of surprise?" Whatever it was, Ekon would love it because it brought a cheery smile to Sekhmet's face.

"You'll see tomorrow. We'll go to the Temple of Sekhmet together."

Sekhmet walked to her closet, opened the door and stepped inside. The walk-in closet comprised an entire wall, in front of which were four wide bookcases. Considering the number of garments felidae tended to ruin during their transmutation, most Shona homes were built with large closets. Within seconds, Sekhmet emerged from her closet, a white robe in one hand, a cosmetic bag in the other.

"Give me a few minutes to wash my face, brush my teeth, and then get in the shower."

Sekhmet stared at Ekon, and it dawned on him that he hadn't moved since she entered the bedroom. He laughed, expelling a breath he'd been holding.

"Nervous?"

"A little, yes."

"Only a little? My heart feels like it's going to burst from my chest."

So did Ekon's. He didn't have much more experience than her, but he knew enough to make her first time a pleasurable one for them both. He appreciated her forthrightness. That hadn't changed about her.

"Will ten minutes be enough time?"

She nodded.

Ekon watched Sekhmet walk to the same side of the room where he'd spied her descending the hill. Entering her en suite, she left the door cracked, presumably for him to follow when ready.

A drawer opened then closed. Water ran.

Ekon broke into movement. First, he dashed to the bedroom door and locked it. He couldn't imagine anyone barging in on the sekhem, but he wouldn't chance an overzealous housekeeper walking in on them. Second, he thumbed through Sekhmet's music selections. Finding a band they both liked, he started the disc. Ambient music drifted from the radio CD player, suffusing the bedroom with textual layers of slow, instrumental music—piano and flute emulated through a synthe-sizer.

Third, he stepped out of his sandals and yanked off his clothes, toss-ing them onto the floor before recalling he wanted to make a good first impression. Letting Sekhmet see how he would upend her tidy space with his dirty clothes, if they shared a room as mates, was a truth best left for another night. Ekon picked up and folded his clothing, placing them neatly on Sekhmet's dresser next to . . . a box of con-doms?

Jealousy and possessiveness reared their ugly heads, but common sense had Ekon backing away from the dresser and his insensible thoughts of Sekhmet with another male. There was no romantic rival for her heart. But Sekhmet did have two mother figures in her life who would do anything to protect her, including from an unplanned preg-nancy.

His heart slowed and his fists relaxed. He even laughed, when he noticed she'd used a strip of condoms as a bookmark in a book entitled *Sekhmet: Goddess of Love*. Only his Asha would be so oddly practical as to use whatever was in reach to save her spot in a book.

He heard water beating against the shower floor. How long had it been? Five minutes? Ten?

Ekon started for the bathroom but changed direction. Snatching the strip of condoms from Sekhmet's book, he rushed to the bathroom door, pushing it fully open. Steam tickled his nose but didn't obscure the sight of a naked Sekhmet behind a glass shower door, washing her hair under a spray of water.

He gulped at the sight. Breasts hung like tempting fruit. Hips flared with womanly sensuality. Legs, toned and strong, called to him, beg-ging to be caressed, licked, kissed.

Ekon tore one of the condoms from the strip. Someone must either have an interesting sense of humor or poor taste in condoms. He held a green glow-in-the-dark condom with a smiley face. Ekon laughed. The condom was strangely perfect for their first time together.

At the sound of his voice, Sekhmet turned her head to the side, wa-ter sloshing down her back. Her grin had him fisting the condom and his dick twitching. Sekhmet's eyes lowered to said region, and her wink gave him the last push he needed.

Ekon opened the glass door and joined Sekhmet inside the shower. Glass mosaic tiles led from the bathroom into the walk-in shower, a seamless transition. She turned to face him. The skylight let in the natural light, under which she stood.

He tossed the condom onto the built-in bench.

Her giggle was like a hug at the end of a long workday. "I see you found one of Mafdet's many safe sex reminders."

"No reminder needed." Ekon wrapped an arm around Sekhmet's waist and pulled her flush against him, repressing a moan at the softness of her body. "I'll always do my best to keep you safe."

"I know you will." Sekhmet's arm circled his nape and pulled him down to her, offering him her lips and her tongue.

Ekon accepted both. They kissed—unrushed and with hands that explored.

Fingers kneaded his back, and hands gripped her ass. Thighs rubbed against each other and pert nipples teased brawny chest. Tongues danced and muscles flexed.

Blindly, Ekon reached for and found Sekhmet's wet washcloth and a bottle of bodywash. He'd smelled the scent on her before, a sweet and fruity fragrance he liked.

He lathered the washcloth with the gel, his mouth still fused to hers. Her hands had shifted to his chest, fingers toying with nipples as hard as her own. Ekon groaned into her mouth before pulling away. "I want to wash you."

From the look and smell of her, she'd already showered. He must've stressed over this moment in her bedroom much longer than ten minutes. That was fine. His desire to cover her in scented soap hadn't changed. If anything, seeing her sleek body supple and near, increased the urge to touch her everywhere before making love to her.

He shifted her away from the spray of water and then pressed her against the shower wall behind him. Smiling down into her golden-brown eyes, he touched her with the soapy cloth, rubbing slow, gentle circles over her breasts and nipples.

Sekhmet's eyes closed. Her mouth opened. Exhaled. A hand settled on his waist, the other fisted at her side. Her head fell against the tiled wall, and he glided the cloth over breasts, down stomach, up shoulders, and around neck.

Squirting more gel onto the cloth and wetting it, Ekon bent to a knee. Experimentally, he kissed Sekhmet's trimmed mound.

Her eyes fluttered open—dark and dangerous. "Do that again."

Ekon intended to, but first he wanted to finish washing his sekhem. Hands skated up and down sexy legs, paying extra attention to the spots that left her moaning. He kissed her center over and again, not staying too long or pressing hard enough.

A rumble started in Sekhmet's belly, so he kissed her there too, laving her belly button with a firmness he avoided applying to her clit.

"Toy with me at your own risk."

"Will the warrior goddess devour me whole, if I don't give you what you crave?"

"Come up here and find out."

Ekon did, wasting no time getting to his feet and accepting Sekhmet's hungry kiss. Spinning her around, he held her under the water. Pink soap ran down her body, circling the drain before disappearing within.

Then he had her pressed to the back wall again, fingers skating down her stomach and to her center. Gently, he massaged up and down her moist lips, sliding his fingers between them. With each downward motion, he slipped his finger in deeper, stopping when she'd taken him in fully.

It would take a lot to hurt a felidae female, even a virgin and in this sensitive area, but care should still be taken, proper respect extended to both her body and mind.

"Is this okay?"

Eyes closed, she nodded.

Ekon kissed her forehead. "Say the words, Asha." He shouldn't have called her that, but she would always be Asha to him, the girl who'd stolen his heart before he'd known it was missing.

She opened her eyes again, rolled her hips experimentally, and moaned at the effect. "You have my permission to touch me . . . to make love to me. I assume you grant me the same permissions."

Taking hold of her hand, he filled it with a part of him that would soon fill her. "You have my permission for both."

Sekhmet didn't hesitate, not the way Ekon had. She stroked him, her hand slick yet firm. He was already hard for her, but she wasn't yet wet enough for him. Ekon withdrew his finger then pushed it back in-side—steady thrusts that had Sekhmet's hand faltering on his dick.

Her first then me.

Ekon added a second finger, stretching her, preparing her, making her moan into the mouth that kissed hers.

Sekhmet clutched at his shoulders, rising on tiptoe and getting even closer.

In and out. He crooked his first two fingers, used his thumb to stroke her sensitive nub, and bent to take a nipple into his mouth—sucking hard and in rhythm with his strokes.

She clenched around his fingers, drawing him in deeper. His entire body ached to join them physically, but the moment was about her pleasure. So, Ekon gave Sekhmet what she needed—fast, hard pene-tration with his fingers and a mouth that bit and nipped every part of her he could reach, adding to her tactile sensations.

Ekon wanted to overload her system. He desired nothing more than to bask in the heady glow of an orgasm he helped her reach.

"Ekon. Ekon. Oh, ohhhh."

Sekhmet's walls clenched spasmodically, and warm liquid coated his fingers. He used the extra lubrication to add a third finger. The heel of his hand rubbed her clit, his fingers in deep, her orgasm a rolling wave of mutual pleasure.

Shit, Ekon was as hard as granodiorite.

Sekhmet grabbed his dick, tugging it as she came, and damn near pulled him into the orgasmic depths with her.

"Condom," she gasped. "We need a condom. Now!"

They did, and Ekon was on it. He sat on the built-in shower bench, snatched the condom from beside him, and tore open the wrapper. Green and glowing, he held it up to Sekhmet whose eyes had turned dark brown. "Do you want to do the honors?"

She licked her lips, and he remembered the pornos she'd watched their first night at Sanctum Hotel. Had the videos given her ideas? They certainly had given him a few.

Sekhmet shook her head. "I'm too nervous and wired to do it properly." She raised hands. Her fingernails had lengthened to small points. He thought he'd felt pinpricks on his back, when Sekhmet came. Small shifts were typical for felidae during the throes of passion.

Ekon rolled the condom on and gestured for Sekhmet. Between her orgasms and her body's natural ability to transmutate, being penetrated by a man for the first time would be all pleasure.

"You can face me or have your back to me. Your choice."

She straddled his hips, her feet planted on either side of him, one hand on his shoulder, the other on the wall behind him.

Yes, the best choice. I want to see your gorgeous face when we make love. Is that why you chose this position, so you could see what you do to me, while I watch what I do to you?

Sinking down, not all at once but by slow, toe-curling degrees, she took him all in, bottoming out, her ass on his thighs.

Ekon swore. *You feel incredible—tight and wet and all mine.* But, *ohh*, she moved, up and down his length and *shit*, he couldn't help but be enraptured by the way her sex swallowed his glowing dick.

Hands gripped her waist, not to slow her down but to speed her up.

Sekhmet obliged. She could transmutate into a lioness; going fast and chasing prey was what she did best. That rumble in her belly came again, but it didn't stay there. It roared out of her, a primal response he shared and matched.

She sank onto him over and over, unrepentant in the taking of her pleasure.

Ekon smacked her ass, and Sekhmet bit his lip. He pulled her hair, and she pinched his nipples.

His right partner. His—Ekon came, hips slamming upward and arms holding Sekhmet still and against him. He came, face buried in the crook of her neck, her arms holding him with a fierceness that had him grunting and spilling himself into the condom.

Gulping breaths and laughter weren't a good mix, but Ekon did both, embarrassed at his enthusiastic outburst.

Sekhmet caressed his jaw and kissed his cheek. "I can't believe how long you made me wait to have you like this."

Ekon laughed again. "Listen at you. Twenty minutes ago you were a virgin, now you're speaking as if you have years of experience."

"Years of experience? Hmm, sounds wonderful." Using his shoulders to steady herself, she climbed off him, taking her warmth and softness with her. "Will you be the one giving me those years of experience?"

"I better be." Ekon struggled to his feet, his dick still hard and, from the way Sekhmet's eyes drifted downward, she wasn't yet done either.

She left the en suite, and he made quick work of the condom.

By the time he followed, only a nightstand lamp was on in the bedroom and she under the duvet. For how quickly she'd turned off the lights and gotten into bed, she'd remembered the condoms. She'd placed several on the nightstand and within convenient reach.

Ekon crawled on the bed, a lion stalking his luscious prey. "Four condoms. Ambitious for a newly deflowered virgin."

"Or a challenge to my new lover."

Ekon pulled back the duvet and slipped into bed with Sekhmet. Propping himself on an elbow, he grinned down at her, reveling in the new phase of their relationship. "Lover. I like that title."

"I thought you would."

There was another title he craved more but patience had been a good friend to him. He could wait for them to become mates, adding the title of husband to the others she had already granted him.

She pulled him down for a long kiss and opened her legs to him when he rolled atop her. Nudging at her opening but not entering, he reawakened her clit, bringing it to a hard, unsheathed erection.

The second time Ekon put a condom on, Sekhmet helped him. She'd giggled, and he'd kissed her, not stopping until she'd wrenched her mouth away, needing air. By the time they'd finished, five open condom wrappers littered the nightstand and two sweaty, sated bodies were curled around each other.

"You called me Asha, the last two times you came."

"I know." Spooned front to back, Ekon buried his face in her wild mane of hair. "I'm sorry. I'll work on calling you Sekhmet."

"I don't mind when it's just us. But to Shona, to the world, I must be Sekhmet. But with you, Ekon, I'll always be Asha."

"The First Evolution Union Party is scrambling to secure their political standing and, after last week's bloodbath, the people of Vumaris are divided over who to blame."

Seated in an office and behind a desk she would always think of as Zarina's, Sekhmet held the phone to her ear, listening intently to Mi Sun Choi.

"More than two dozen soldiers were killed over the course of three days, including former Deputy Chief Frank London. There are reports of a lion-headed woman spotted at the scene of two of those murders. Sounds impossible, doesn't it?"

"Which part?"

"Take your pick, Sekhem Asha."

"Sekhmet."

"Excuse me?"

"You may refer to me as Sekhem Sekhmet, and nothing you've said is impossible."

"So, you admit the Shona were involved?"

"You sound as if you aren't sure whether you should feel shock or fear. Or perhaps you are reconsidering forming an alliance with my kingdom."

In the space of Ms. Choi's long pause, Mafdet knocked on the ajar office door and peeked her head inside. Noticing Sekhmet on the phone, Mafdet started to back away but she waved her inside. In the time it had taken Mafdet to sit on the couch on the opposite side of the room, Ms. Choi had gathered her thoughts.

"I don't want to place my party in a position to have the lion-headed woman come after them."

Sekhmet had no intention of repeating the invocation, no more than she planned on adopting vengeance as a political stance. But her intentions and people's perceptions did not have to align.

"The Shona are an honorable people, Ms. Choi. We treat our allies well and our friends better."

"And your enemies?"

"Are we enemies, Ms. Choi?"

Laughter rippled through the line—neither forced nor mocking. "You are your parents' daughter. Your mother asked me the same when we first spoke of a possible alliance. I assume you confess to nothing concerning the deaths of London and the soldiers."

"No more than you'll confess to seeking an alliance with a foreign government to secure your party's rise to power."

More laughter from a woman who, if their trees bore fruit, would become the next Chief of the Republic of Vumaris. But no fruit would grow from seeds not yet planted.

"Whether we become allies or not, I am grateful for your assistance in garnering my freedom from the Rogueshade. For that act of kindness, you have a friend in this felidae."

"I was raised to believe that friends are harder to come by than allies of convenience."

"My parents believed the same."

"Have you ever had a human as a friend, Sekhem Sekhmet?"

"I have not. Do I now?"

Whatever humor that had Ms. Choi laughing no longer lingered in the voice that said, "I liked and respected your parents. Their murders saddened and angered me. We weren't yet friends, but we were building that bridge. I would like to continue the construction of the work they began. Yes, Sekhem, I accept your friendship and extend to you mine."

Bridges and trees. They would build one while planting the other. Both analogies fit the work they would perform together.

"I'll have my secretary arrange our next phone conference. In the interim . . ."

Quickly, Sekhmet outlined what she would require from Ms. Choi before they spoke again. She'd intended on discussing a couple of specific points during this phone call but, with Mafdet having sought her out, her presence reminded her of an important conversation they needed to have.

"Yes, we'll speak again soon. Thank you. You have a good weekend, as well." Sekhmet ended the phone call and hung up the receiver.

"You didn't have to shorten your call on my account." Closing the book Mafdet held in her hand, she placed it on the cushion beside her.

Sekhmet couldn't see the cover, but she doubted Mafdet found a book to her liking. Mafdet's and Zarina's tastes in literature were as dissimilar from each other's as Mi Sun Choi's Common Peace Coalition Party was from Royster's First Evolution Union Party.

"Pretending to read."

"Not pretending. Practicing patience." Frowning down at the book, she added, "I must admit, ten minutes of reading about the politics of international relations had my mind wandering and my eyes glazing over. No wonder you avoided some of your lessons."

Sekhmet would give anything to sit through one of her parents' boring lessons. But those days were in her past, while their relevance was her present and would be her future.

Tempted to join Mafdet on the couch, her head on her shoulder and seeking the parental assurance she still wanted but needed to learn how to do without, she remained seated and nodded to one of two chairs in front of the desk. "Come and sit, Mafdet."

"Of course, my sekhem." Mafdet joined Sekhmet, her expression one of feigned openness. "I came to discuss security for your upcoming visit to the southern part of the kingdom. Have you had an opportunity to review Tamani's suggestions for rebuilding the alpha Shieldmane team, now that you've fully embraced your role?"

"I have. I know, with me resuming my travels, even if only for right now within our borders, I require a fully staffed Shieldmane team. Tamani recommended Ekon to serve as my Second Shieldmane. Unsurprising and a recommendation I will accept. Where I should've seen Mafdet Rastaff recommended as my First Shieldmane, there was another name instead. In fact, your name was mysteriously absent from Tamani's document." Lifting her chin but narrowing her eyes, she waited for Mafdet to explain.

"I don't like the way you're looking at me." Mafdet's sigh cut through the unvoiced tension between them. "You're growing up way too fast."

"I don't have much choice."

"You're nineteen."

"I'm sekhem of a kingdom of two hundred thirty million people. I can't afford to be nineteen."

"Yet you are."

Rising, Sekhmet walked around the desk and claimed the chair beside Mafdet. "Yet I am. Are you leaving?"

"I . . ."

"I know Mom asked you to train Ekon to take your place as my First Shieldmane when I ascended to the position of sekhem. We both know she thought that would be years into the future. I should've asked her why you wouldn't be the one serving me in that critical capacity, but my thoughts were more on being given an opportunity to spend more time with Ekon than on the reason behind her decision. Will you explain?"

Mafdet wasn't one to appear uncomfortable in her own skin. Sekhmet certainly had never seen her bothered by anyone in a position of authority. Yet Sekhmet's three-word question had Mafdet pausing and looking away from her and to the sliding glass doors in front of them.

"When I arrived in Shona, your parents gave me sanctuary. In return, I pledged my loyalty, promising to protect their child until that child could protect herself." Dark eyes returned to Sekhmet, unspoken sadness in their depths. "True, you've become sekhem sooner than your parents and I thought you would, but my promise remains the same. You're sekhem now and have the blessing and protection of a goddess. In comparison, I have little to offer."

Temper tantrums hadn't worked when Sekhmet had been a child, and one wouldn't alter Mafdet's stance now. It had taken a year and countless Rogueshade deaths for her anger and guilt to run their ugly, painful course. Mafdet had omitted decades of details from her seemingly simple statement. Sekhmet didn't require such facts, however, to understand her mother's gentle manipulation and overriding hope.

"Mom and Dad gave you more than a sanctuary. They gave you a home, a family, and a renewed purpose for life—protecting their only child. They had options—Panthera Leo options—but they chose you, an outsider. It's clear you do not want me to know your past, and that is your right. But don't you dare sit there and lie to me. I need you as much as you need me." Sekhmet rose, determined not to waver or whine. "Just as Mom accepted your decision, I will do the same. I will not keep you where you do not want to be. But know, just as you told me that I was not alone, the same is true for you. Whether you stay or leave, we're still family. I'll never turn my back on you."

"You think I'm turning my back on you?"

The question lacked all the emotion Sekhmet saw in Mafdet's eyes.

Leaning down, she kissed her on her cheek. "You're turning your back on your own heart. Either Mom didn't tell you or you didn't believe her when she did."

Mafdet's gaze shifted to the sliding glass doors again. Sekhmet understood because she had done the same dozens of times.

The Temple of Sekhmet. How many times has she visited the temple now that Mom and Dad are enshrined there? Every day, like me?

"Tell me what?"

Sekhmet glanced to the sword at Mafdet's hip—a Shona-designed weapon that no one else in the kingdom carried. Mafdet followed her gaze and then their eyes met. Sekhmet didn't hold it long. She'd promised Ekon they would have lunch together before her council meeting. According to the desk clock, Sekhmet would be late for her date in two minutes.

She straightened.

"You're valued and loved as a person, Mafdet. You've always had much to offer this kingdom as a Shieldmane. But, for the Leothos family, you being Shieldmane, just as you being named as my godmother, was Mom's strategic way of getting around your pride and dealing with whatever guilt that held you hostage then and, apparently, holds you hostage now. You've added Mom's and Dad's deaths to your list of the reasons you don't deserve happiness."

More needed to be said, but enough had been stated for one day. No good would come from pushing, so Sekhmet kissed Mafdet's cheek again. "Join Ekon and me for lunch?"

"Thank you, but no. Do try to remember there are household staff on duty."

"One time, Mafdet."

"You were caught having sex with Ekon in your pool."

"By you and at midnight." Sekhmet caught herself from rolling her eyes. "That's old news. I can't believe you're still bringing that up."

"Old news? Still? I caught the two of you only yesterday." Mafdet tsk-tsked. "As I said, you're nineteen."

Sekhmet wouldn't argue further, especially since they both knew Mafdet was correct. And, well, inviting Mafdet to join Ekon and her for lunch had been a sincere offer but one she hadn't minded Mafdet rejecting. Sex before, during, or after lunch hadn't been far from her thoughts. Although Sekhmet didn't appreciate Mafdet's assumption.

"You remind me so much of her. She—"

Images of Zarina and Bambara came to mind, and she rushed to interrupt. Sekhmet did not need or want to know how, in this area, she also favored Zarina. "Mafdet, please don't tell me stories about times you caught Mom and Da—"

"Not your mother . . . my daughter. You remind me of my eldest daughter—Zendaya."

Eldest daughter, as in Mafdet had more than one. The unexpected revelation had Sekhmet returning to the chair beside Mafdet and reaching for her hand—squeezing. Lunch with Ekon could wait. The opening of a closed door into Mafdet's past could not.

"I'm listening."

"I was almost as young as you are when Hondo and I pledged ourselves to each other. Our minds were filled with dreams and our hearts full of innocence. We thought we could conquer the world and right wrongs. Even as a young woman, I knew the world could be cruel but, until I came face-to-face with its lethal claws, I had no idea how much. Life takes, as you already know, but not always equally and hardly ever painlessly. I first learned that gut-wrenching lesson when . . ."

The story of Mafdet's life before Shona flowed from her. With each graphic disclosure, so too did her tears.

"In the end, I couldn't save any of them. I barely saved myself . . ."

Sekhmet hugged Mafdet. Kissed her cheeks. And uttered the most potent truths between them. "We are family. You are not alone."

Chapter 18: She Whose Opportunity Escapeth Her Not

2000
Fourteen Years Later
The Republic of Vumaris
Batari County, Minra
The Kingdom of Shona Embassy

Tau opened the limousine door for Sekhmet. She knew this day would come, and she'd prepared for its arrival. Yet, as Sekhmet stared out of the vehicle and at the building that used to be Sanctum Hotel, she realized her preparations hadn't been adequate.

"Give me a minute."

Tau, her Second Shieldmane, nodded. She thought he would leave the limousine door open. Instead, he granted her the dignity of her lapse into painful memories and closed the vehicle's door. Through tinted, bulletproof windows, Sekhmet could still see the hotel from her old nightmares. Most of the renovations she had approved had been of the interior. The exterior, however, looked much the same as it had fifteen years earlier—stately with ornate, steeply pitched roofs, dormers with parapets, and a stone exterior. But the crash-bollards and perimeter security gate were new.

Neither addition made Sekhmet feel safer. She no longer harbored the fears of the girl she'd once been, no more than she did the anger. Pushing open the door, she accepted Tau's sturdy hand of assistance from the limousine.

Ocean blue eyes smiled down at her, and full lips lifted in a feral smile. "No one would dare."

"Of course not. Your wife has Shieldmanes stationed everywhere." Some were in black suits and boots like Tau, while others were undercover and dressed as embassy staffers. "Tamani is . . ." Sekhmet had been about to say *overprotective* but walking through the doors of the building where her parents had been murdered, she understood not only Tamani's caution but the unvoiced pledge of the Shieldmanes.

None of them were to blame for what had happened to Zarina and Bambara, not even the alpha Shieldmane team of fifteen years ago. But the Shieldmanes had taken the deaths of their leaders and her kidnapping as a personal failure. Sekhmet didn't require the words of *never again* to know they carried the sentiment in their hearts.

"There is no more secure world leader than the Sekhem of the Kingdom of Shona."

Obviously pleased with Sekhmet's compliment, Tau's shoulders relaxed but nothing else about the man softened.

The people in the embassy lobby had gone silent when they saw Sekhmet enter the building. Felidae and humans alike gawked at her, a phenomenon she didn't enjoy but had long since accepted. To many, Sekhmet was the "Mortal hand of the Shona gods." She disliked the title, but it had served her kingdom well. But fear was a shortsighted plan that despots viewed as a long-term political strategy. It was not.

Three Shieldmanes joined Tau, surrounding Sekhmet and ready to escort her through the throng of embassy staffers and onto an elevator. During her stay, her team would have many opportunities to serve as her physical shields. Now, however, she neither wanted nor needed shadows during her tour of a building that, when first purchased, she had intended on razing to the ground. A waste of money, but she had wanted no physical reminders of her pain, including a building a country away.

Sekhmet laid a hand on Tau's forearm. "Tamani has vetted everyone granted access to the embassy."

She hadn't posed a question, but Tau nodded, confirming her statement as a fact.

"I am free to take in our new embassy alone." Sekhmet's headshake silenced the rebuttal she saw in Tau's eyes and sensed in the other three members of her alpha security team—two women and one man. All trained by Mafdet. "I'll be fine."

Sekhmet wouldn't add that she could take care of herself. From personal experience, she knew quite well that even a highly skilled fighter could be defeated. So, she smiled at each of her Shieldmanes in turn, hoping to reassure them but also firm in her position.

"Meet me in my suite an hour before my press conference with Ms. Choi."

"Until then?" Tau asked.

"You have your suite assignments but check in with Tamani before you go up to your rooms."

"She's probably in the security office."

Sekhmet agreed with Tau. In four hours, the embassy's lobby would be filled with politicians and news reporters. She could see the podium from there, the flags of the Kingdom of Shona and the Republic of Vumaris on the wall behind the sound lectern.

She felt her Shieldmanes' eyes on her when she walked away from them and not to the elevators but the stairwell. Opening the door, the same one her parents had gone through the last time she had seen them alive, she questioned the sanity of taking such a walk down an unpleasant memory lane. But walk she did, up flights of stairs, stopping when she reached the thirteenth floor. Humans may have considered thirteen an unlucky number. If she were a superstitious person, she wouldn't have converted the Sanctum Hotel into the Shona embassy in Vumaris.

Sekhmet strolled down the hallway, recalling the last time she'd been on this floor, with whom, and why. The memory, still fresh but less potent, squeezed her heart—leaving her reflective and melancholic but not breathless and angry. The murder of her parents wasn't an experience to "get over," no more than her sorrow was an emotion to "conquer."

As much as Sekhmet was an alpha and sekhem, a queen by human standards, she was first and foremost a woman . . . a person. *I hurt. I laugh. I cry. I love. I'm imperfect. And I accept all of me.*

Mind on thoughts more important than the reason for Sekhmet's visit to Vumaris, she walked down the steps and onto another floor, oblivious to her surroundings.

A door opened to her right. A hand shot out, grabbed her arm and tugged her inside a room. The door slammed shut and she was pushed against it.

Sekhmet didn't snarl or fight. Two reasons kept her from doing either or even both. One, there was a mouth fused to hers. Two, the mouth belonged to her husband.

She returned his kiss with building enthusiasm but, when he pulled away and dropped to his knees, her reply whine was unbecoming of an alpha. Gentle hands glided from shaking knees to trembling thighs and then up to quivering sex, compelling a moan from a mouth gone dry. Who knew two months without her husband's touch would produce such carnal need?

Ekon's head, like his hands, disappeared under her dress.

"You feel so good." Voice muffled against the mouth Ekon had pressed to Sekhmet's center, he kissed her there, and she thought her legs would melt like ice cream on a sultry day. "You sound even better. I've always loved the way you say my name when I do this."

He kissed her center again, pressing his lips and lingering through the long length of her moan.

Sekhmet's head fell against the door, and her mouth hung open.

"I've been dreaming of having you in this way for weeks."

"We're going to do this right here and now?" Not that Sekhmet knew what room Ekon had pulled her into—likely his office since that was the location for their agreed-upon reunion.

They shouldn't indulge, but she had never been one to deny her sexual urges. The fact that they often coincided with Ekon's made her submission that much sweeter.

Ekon stood, his tall, brawny frame as delicious as the lips that had teased and tempted. Sekhmet's eyes drifted to said lips. She wanted them on her again, so she went on tiptoe and took them. *So soft.*

She got lost in the taste of him and the glorious sensation of touching her husband after a necessary but annoying separation. It hadn't been the first time government business had taken one of them away from the other, but they had never been apart for such an uninterrupted stretch of time. While Sekhmet traveled as much as she once had with her parents, she had limited her visits to Vumaris to the essential and unavoidable.

"Shit, that's good."

Sekhmet had cupped Ekon through his dress pants, his erection a bulging temptation she wanted inside of her. With a firm gentleness, she caressed him the way he liked.

Lowering his head to her shoulder, his breathy groans tickled the warm flesh of her neck.

"I feel as if I've loved you forever." Ekon's head rose, and his earnest brown eyes, combined with what he'd said, stilled her hand. "I loved you when I watched you from afar, a book in your hand and your mind in the clouds. I loved you when you placed your faith in a young Shieldmane. I loved you when you left me in the restaurant walk-in freezer." He stole a quick kiss. "I was mad as hell, but also full of love. I loved you when you buried your parents. No stoicism but a daughter's unashamed grief. I loved you when you awoke in my arms and told me that was the first time you'd slept through the night since your return to Shona. It also saddened me, but I was happy you found comfort with me beside you."

Sekhmet tucked herself against Ekon's chest. Her husband—at thirty-six—was taller and broader than he'd been when they'd first met. She'd changed too. At thirty-three, Sekhmet was still young by felidae standards, but she had grown much over the past fifteen years—in body and in mind.

Ekon cradled her face in his hands, the same way he had when she'd returned from Vumaris, wearing a lion's head and smelling of divine retribution, blood, and death. "And I love you now. My Asha but also my Sekhmet."

"What am I to say to such sweet declarations?"

Ekon nuzzled her neck, treating it to worshipful kisses. "A proverb, perhaps. A sexy one, preferably." Raising his head, he grinned down at her. "If there's such a thing as a sexy proverb." His mouth returned to her neck, which made thinking of a quality response a challenge.

Sekhmet excelled at challenges, but no sexy proverbs came to mind, but ones about love did. She stroked his cheek, the way she did upon waking each morning and before falling asleep every night, happy with the person she'd become and grateful for the people in her life. "Let your love be like misty rain, coming softly but flooding the river."

Ekon lifted his head again. "I like that one." Deliberately . . . teasingly, he glided his hand up her thigh, stopping at her waist and circling until he held her bottom in the palm of his hand. "It had coming and flooding in it. Tell me another."

Sekhmet was tempted not to, but a decade of marriage made her vulnerable to Ekon's playful charms. He'd worked hard to turn Sanctum Hotel into Shona's first embassy. The embassy hadn't been part of her parents' plan with Ms. Choi. But an embassy dedicated to healing wounds and building bridges would better serve her people than a million-dollar building decimated to rubble.

She nipped his jaw. "The best part of happiness lies in the secret heart of a lover."

"I like that one too. A third, please."

Sekhmet thought about the life she once had with her parents, and the life she now had with Ekon—different yet the same in the ways that mattered the most. "Where there is love there is no darkness."

"I think that one is my favorite." Ekon lowered to his knees again and, before she knew it, he'd removed her panties.

"Ekon . . ."

"You know it will be good." He ducked his head under her dress and big, possessive hands parted her thighs.

Being with Ekon was always better than good, but she could hear people in the hallway, entering and exiting rooms. Neither Sekhmet nor Ekon had locked the door and . . . soft, probing lips kissed her, bringing an abrupt halt to her wayward thoughts of being caught. He kissed her again and again, no hesitancy in the way his mouth moved up and down her slick folds.

Sekhmet couldn't help it, her eyelids slid closed.

Intense kisses turned into purposeful licks. Ekon's tongue slipped between her lips, compelling her to widen her stance. Hands clamped onto hips and pulled her against his ravenous mouth.

"Ekon . . . E-Ekon . . ." Sekhmet's voice cracked, and her knees threatened to buckle.

Gripping her bottom and laving her flesh, he gave her the best Panthera Leo kiss. He hoisted her right leg onto his shoulder, and she nearly came from the change in angle. His tongue slipped inside, and she could've sworn she saw stars.

She rocked into his mouth, but the position wasn't ideal for equal participation or good balance.

As perceptive as ever, Ekon stopped. "What's wrong?"

"I'm going to fall on my face if you don't let me down."

"Face, hmm? That gives me an idea." He popped out from under her dress. "Let's get this off you."

With a few deft movements, Ekon had rid Sekhmet of her clothing. "You're gorgeous. Sexy. I want to devour every inch of you, and then do it over and again. But first, you mentioned something about a face."

Pulling Sekhmet to her knees, Ekon situated himself on his back, the crown of his head a few feet from the door of what she could now see was indeed his office. Her mindless wandering had taken her to his office. Sekhmet had found Ekon . . . or rather he had scented her outside of his office door.

"All aboard the Ekon Ptah Express."

"Excuse me?"

"Face, remember?" Ekon pointed to his lips. "Right here. We've done this before."

They had but . . . Sekhmet pushed away her trepidation of making love to her husband in a place where only a wooden door separated them from everyone else in the embassy.

Sekhmet climbed on the Ekon Ptah Express. Any awkwardness she felt drained away the second he sucked her clit into his mouth. She swallowed a scream and slammed shut her eyes.

The position made it easier on Sekhmet's legs. Her knees were on either side of his head and her palms on the closed office door. Sekhmet rocked against Ekon's mouth, tongue, and nose, careful not to smother him but taking all the pleasure he offered.

Ekon's tongue was a steady, delicious piston, a reminder of all the ways she'd missed her husband.

Belly tightened. Sex throbbed.

One finger then two breached her sex. His mouth found her unsheathed clit again and sucked with such intensity she muffled her scream with her hand. Her orgasm was right there.

Yes. Yes. So close. So clos—

The door pushed in, hitting Ekon on the head. At the same time, Sekhmet's palms slammed back on the door, closing it the few inches it had opened.

"What's going on? Is something wrong, Ekon?"

"Yes, yes," she gritted out, chasing her orgasm.

"Sekhmet. Good. I saw your team with Tamani. I hoped you had come here."

"Don't. Don't."

"I'm not stopping," Ekon whispered at the same time Mafdet asked, "You don't want me to come in? Why? What's going on?"

Sekhmet couldn't stop. All she could do was keep her hands pressed against the door and ride her husband's fingers and mouth until the end of the line—the Ekon Ptah Express a five-star travel experience.

"Mafdet, if you open the door before I'm finished, I *will* kill you."

How Sekhmet managed to gasp out that hollow threat through her roiling orgasm, she would never know, but Mafdet said nothing more and the pressure on the door ceased.

Wave after wave of pleasure smashed into and over Sekhmet, drowning out apologies running through her mind. She would owe Mafdet many. But not now. Later, when Ekon's masterful fingers weren't buried deep in her, and his mouth wasn't holding her clitoris as a willing hostage.

Ekon laughed, and even that felt good against her sensitive skin.

Sekhmet collapsed on Ekon's chest, languid but far from sated.

Loving arms wrapped around her. "I missed you."

"I missed you too."

"Unless you've forgotten," Mafdet said, her voice that same exasperated tone she'd taken when she'd caught them having sex before their wedding reception, after a council meeting and . . . well, too many times, "you have a press conference in less than four hours. It wouldn't do if the sekhem and khalid of Shona arrive to greet Chief Choi smelling of sex. Shower and be on time."

Mafdet retreated, and Sekhmet knew she would order everyone to steer clear of Ekon's office.

"I think we upset her."

Sekhmet rolled off her husband but didn't stand. Instead, she reclined on her back beside him, naked and gloriously happy. "Our sex life tends to have that effect on Mafdet. She'll either feel better or worse, once I tell her our news."

"What news?" Ekon shifted to his side, propping his head in his hand. "What news?"

Taking hold of his free hand, she placed his palm on her stomach . . . and waited. It didn't take long. They'd ceased using birth control nine months ago. Ekon wanted a big family—five or six children. Sekhmet would be content with two or three.

"I'm partial to the names Zarina and Bambara."

Eyes sparkled and his grin delighted. Ekon leaned over and kissed her stomach. "I'm partial to the name Asha." He truly was her Adorable One. "It has a nice ring to it, wouldn't you agree?"

Their mouths met, his hand on the stomach that carried their first child. She'd visited the Temple of Sekhmet before boarding the plane for Vumaris. Sekhmet had sat with her parents, sharing her good fortune with them and the goddess. A breeze had entered the temple, stroked her cheek and kissed her forehead.

She'd cried happy tears for her future, present, and past selves.

Hafsa Sekhem Asha—Overcomer of All Enemies.

Sekhem Sekhmet—Lady of Jubilation.

Kingdom of Shona

Epilogue: Swiftborne

Batari County, Minra
The Kingdom of Shona Embassy

Looking at what used to be Sanctum Hotel, no one would know horrible crimes had been committed within its elegant walls, that innocent felidae had been killed by cruel humans. She once believed all humans were cruel. Little in her life had challenged that belief. But where most humans were heartless toward felidae, some felidae betrayed their own kind, choosing to side with humans and do their bidding.

She stared down at the clipped newspaper article in her hand. "The Shona Queen Returns to Vumaris: New Embassy Opens Next Month."

"A rag newspaper. You couldn't even get the sekhem's title correct. But the photographer is excellent. I finally know where you've been and where to find you."

Crushing the article in her hand, she tossed it into the back seat of her parked car.

The international community knew where Shona's sekhem and khalid would be today. If the rest of the article was correct, the couple would be in residence at the embassy for a week.

She climbed out of her car, grabbed her suit jacket from the back of the seat and slipped it on. *Play the part. Get in. Seven days. That's all the time I have before she returns to Shona.*

Reaching inside the car, she retrieved her pocketbook from the front passenger seat. She wasn't a member of the press nor had a legitimate reason to be admitted into the embassy. But she had an identification, an insider's name, and one hell of a sparkling smile. Neither her real ID or fake smile would get her past the security checkpoint and into the embassy, but a single name would.

I hope.

Looking both ways, she crossed the street and joined the line of people seeking entrance into the Shona embassy.

You should be dead. But I found you. And I'll make you pay for betraying me. For betraying us all.

Upper West Minra

Mafdet never understood the point of furnishing a kitchen with a television, no more than she comprehended humans' affinity for working lunches. Combining one with the other diluted both.

"Turn it up. I don't want to miss the grand opening of the embassy."

The man on the barstool beside her pushed the volume button on the remote control. Considering she sat directly in front of the television and had enhanced hearing, the request wasn't necessary. But Mafdet had waited fifteen years for this moment, so who could blame her for wanting to play with her prey?

Mafdet smiled. *A working lunch. I understand now. On occasion, humans have made positive contributions to the world. Not the human male beside me but others like Mi Sun Choi and members of her political party.*

"What do you think of Sekhmet's dress?"

The orange and red of the sleeveless wrap dress complemented her eye color, as well as the golden flecks in her hair. The necklace she wore, a beaded gold choker, belonged to Zarina, as did the three-tone brass and copper cuff bracelets and gold knuckle ring with a ruby center. Sekhmet rarely wore extravagant jewelry, but her visit to Vumaris was a special occasion. Not as special as Mafdet's side visit to the Blue Spruce gated community in Upper West Minra, though.

She removed the remote from the man's trembling hand. "When you last saw her, she was Hafsa Sekhem Asha Leothos. Back then, Sekhmet was so young—barely a woman." Mafdet slid her blade from its sheath and placed it between herself and the man who'd lived fifteen years too long.

"So, former Chief Royster, do you like my sekhem's dress?" Tapping the television screen with her knuckle, she asked another question meant to entertain her but annoy him. "What do you think of Choi's repeal of the anti-transmutation policy?" Mafdet pointed to the two lions who flanked Sekhmet. "The Shieldmane to her right is Khalid Ekon. He snarls every time he thinks someone has moved too close to his wife. The lion on Sekhmet's left is Tau, General Volt's husband. Trust me, his roar is not worse than his bite. Between the two of them, they'll keep my sekhem safe while we have our chat."

"A chat? That's what you call breaking into my home and threatening me?"

"It's more warning than your Rogueshades gave us fifteen years ago."

Despite the intervening years and the restructuring of the new embassy, when Mafdet had entered the renovated building, she was transported back to Sanctum Hotel and the soul-crushing sight of her beloved friends' corpses. Mafdet's failure to save them still haunted her.

Sekhmet had bestowed Mafdet with the title of Great Cat of the Nation of Swiftborne. The kindness had touched her more than words could ever express. She hadn't been referred to by that name in over a century. For just as long, she hadn't felt worthy of the title. Some days, she still didn't.

"I didn't mean for anyone to get hurt, especially not a kid."

"Perhaps not but people did, including a young adult not yet ready to be on her own. Sekhmet was raised well, and she's always been far older than her years. But," she twisted on the barstool to face the man who had helped ruin so many lives, "at the end of the day, Sekhmet . . . Asha, was thrust into the role of alpha at eighteen because greedy men's wants outweighed the value they placed on her parents' lives."

Royster's eyes darted to Mafdet's sword. The hand nearest her weapon twitched, and she smelled the fearfulness that wouldn't have the human risking the remaining minutes of his life on the unlikely probability that he could grab her blade and kill her.

Mafdet snatched her sword from the island. She despised Royster even more for his casual willingness to send others to commit atrocities that would benefit him while harboring the heart of a coward.

Lifting his eyes from her hand that held Zarina's gift of friendship and trust, he turned off the television. "Choi and the Common Peace Coalition Party came out of nowhere."

Standing from the island counter, Royster walked away from Mafdet but not out of the kitchen. She permitted the distance. Fear would keep him compliant while self-pity had prematurely aged him. Royster had gained forty pounds but lost his political standing, respectability, friends, and family. He'd even lost most of his hair, the horseshoe-like ring around the sides and back of his head was all that was left of what had once been a full head of hair.

"Billings and Aguilar never had a chance, did they? Shona bankrolled Choi. That's how a nothing party swept national, state, and local elections."

Using the spikes on the knuckle guard handle of her blade, she spun the weapon. "Sekhmet helped fund the campaigns of *all* Vumarian parties, including the one you used to lead. The Common Peace Coalition Party more than the others, of course, because Choi is a valued friend to the kingdom and sekhem."

Zarina and Bambara had initiated negotiations between Shona and Choi's party. But it had been Sekhmet who had expanded her parents' vision to include political and economic negotiations that resulted in the building of Shona embassies in select felidae and human countries. It was Ekon, however, who oversaw the erection and management of each political residence. Together, Sekhmet and Ekon ruled as well as but differently from Zarina and Bambara.

Mafdet smiled. The love Sekhmet and Ekon had for each other mirrored that of Sekhmet's parents. In that vein, the alphas were very much alike.

The sword stopped spinning. The sharp end of the blade pointed past Mafdet's arm and toward a frowning Royster.

She stood. Time to conclude her working lunch. "Would you like to call your daughter and say goodbye?"

Royster stumbled backward, tripping over his cat's food dish and falling against a sink filled with soapy water and dirty dishes, reminding Mafdet of what he had been doing before he'd sensed her standing behind him.

Royster's wide eyes darted around the sunny kitchen. They settled on a knife butcher block at the end of the counter near the sink.

Mafdet retrieved her sword and slid it into its sheath. As much as she loved Zarina's gift—Mafdet's Claws—the weapon couldn't replace what humans like Silas Royster had taken from her and the felidae of the Nation of Swiftborne.

She nodded to the butcher block. "Let's see who's faster. If you beat me to it, I'll leave and never return. If you don't, I'll slit your throat after you call your daughter to let her know you love her. That's more than the Rogueshade gave Sekhmet before they took her parents from her."

"If, umm . . . if I win, you'll let me go?" Royster licked pink lips over which a faint sheen of sweat had formed. "You'll keep your word and let me go?" Eyes skidded to the knife butcher block then back to her, the calculation clear in his eyes.

Mafdet was across the room from the rack of knives while Royster stood a mere ten feet away. Probability was on his side, wasn't it?

Royster must've thought so because, with a speed impressive for a human male of his age and weight, he ran for the butcher block. His arm stretched, so too did his fingers, both long—longer than Mafdet's.

She watched him run for his life—gritted teeth and flushed skin.

Royster lunged, his hand an inch away from extending his lifespan.

Mafdet smacked the butcher block off the counter. Knives flew from the slots and the wooden block crashed to the floor.

Royster's hand froze in midair, his eyes on the spot where the knife butcher block had been. "H-how? I am right here. R-right here." Like dead weight, his hand dropped to his side. "You didn't move. You . . . you didn't move."

"Swiftborne," she snarled into his ear. "Now call your daughter."

Royster cried.

Mafdet handed him his phone.

Fifteen minutes later, it was done.

Ball cap low and collar of her sports jacket pulled high, Mafdet walked away from the quiet house and up the street. Sword hidden under her jacket, not a speck of Royster's blood remained on the blade. *It's finally over.*

The phone in her sweatpants pocket vibrated. She dug it out and—

"Where are you?"

"What have I told you about snapping questions at me? I—"

"Is he dead?" Tamani asked.

Scanning the surrounding area, Mafdet made sure to keep her head down but ears and eyes alert. She couldn't prevent someone in the community from seeing her, but she could minimize the probability of them getting an unobstructed view.

"I'm Sekhmet's First Shieldmane, of course Royster is dead."

"Good. We should've killed the bastard fifteen years ago. But the sekhem didn't sanction Royster's murder—then or now."

No, Sekhmet hadn't. Without such a sanction, Mafdet couldn't expect her sekhem to shield her from potential legal repercussions. Mafdet expected nothing from Sekhmet, not even her forgiveness for acting on her own but in her name.

"Look, I didn't call to discuss Royster. We will, though, because no one, not even you, Mafdet, has the right to take action, especially of this magnitude, without consent from our alphas."

"Any blowback will fall on me."

"You're too damn old to be that naïve, and I don't have time to chew your ass out the way you deserve. Sekhmet is here as a political ally to the new Vumaris chief. How do you think it will appear when Royster turns up dead?"

Exiting through the metal security gate that hadn't been able to keep Mafdet out, she escaped onto a quiet suburban street. She'd parked her rental truck a mile away. If she jogged, she could reach it in ten minutes.

She stopped. "Maybe I should return and dispose of Royster's body."

Tamani's half sigh, half snarl annoyed Mafdet because, in her long life, only a handful of people had the ability to get under her skin when she'd made a poor choice. Of those rare few, Tamani was the only one still alive to remind Mafdet that her actions bore consequences for others.

"It's too late. Leave it. We'll handle any potential backlash. The entire world saw Sekhmet on television while you were with Royster. At least there is that. That, and I know you are too skilled to have been seen or left evidence capable of being traced back to us. So, bring your ass back to the embassy."

Cell phone clutched securely in her hand, she ran down the street, careful to maintain a human-level speed. "If you didn't call about Royster, why did you call?"

"A woman came to the embassy's security checkpoint looking for you."

"A woman? Who?"

Mafdet couldn't hear anything other than Tamani on the other end. She wondered why she had left the security office to call her when that was a secure location.

"I thought you said you had no family."

"I don't. Not blood family."

"Either the woman being held in the security office is a liar or you have more family than you know. We've known each other for a long time, Mafdet, and you're many things but a liar isn't one of them. So, tell me why I have a felidae female not only asking to speak with you but claiming to be your daughter."

Mafdet skidded to a halt, winded but not from the short run. "My what?"

It had been so long since she'd seen her deceased girls, it took a few disorienting seconds to conjure images of them. But, once she had, the guilt that bloomed whenever she thought of her lost family felt like the knife wound she'd given Silas Royster. Instead of dying, however, as Royster had, Mafdet became angry.

"I don't know who that woman is in your security office, but she isn't my daughter. I no longer have children." *Nor a husband, or parents, or . . . Swiftborne Nation.*

Unlocking the door to the rental truck, Mafdet hopped inside. Tossing her ball cap onto the passenger seat beside her, she jammed the key into the ignition. She didn't know who in the hell the imposter was or why she'd decided to target her, but she would make her regret seeking her out.

"She says her name is Zendaya Rastaff."

Mafdet peeled away from the curb and straight into traffic. She ignored the warning blare of horns and headed for the Shona embassy.

"It's not her. Zen is dead. They're all dead."

"Hold on."

Mafdet barreled down streets, running red lights and exceeding driving limits.

"Are you still there?"

"Where else would I be?" Accelerating, Mafdet made a right turn faster than she should've. Her mind whirled and her heart pounded. Her girls were gone. Dead. Killed. And Mafdet had been powerless to protect them. Just as she had failed to protect Zarina, Bambara, and Asha.

"I'm now outside of the security office. I can put her on the phone or wait for you to get here. What is your ETA?"

"Twelve minutes."

"Not far. Your call, my friend."

Every self-preservation impulse screamed for Mafdet to put an end to the charade right there and now. But a stronger instinct—one she thought buried with her girls—maternal love, had Mafdet's fists tightening on the steering wheel and foot pushing down the pedal.

"It's not her." More, it had been so long, Mafdet wouldn't recognize Zendaya's voice if, miracle of miracles, the woman turned out to be her child. She tossed away that impossibility as a dream unbecoming of a woman of her years and experience. "I don't know what she wants but, whatever it is, she won't achieve her ends. Does Sekhmet know?"

"Not yet. She and Ekon are still meeting with Chief Choi, Deputy Chief DeGuzeman and the press. When they finish, I will report to them. So, I suggest you get here before I have to make my report without your input."

In record time, Mafdet arrived at the embassy and was out the truck and on the other side of the security office door—winded and anxious. But also afraid of what slimy creature had slithered its way out of her past and into her present.

Mafdet opened the door.

THE END

If you enjoyed the novel, the author invites you to leave a review.

Other Books by N. D. Jones

Winged Warriors Trilogy (Paranormal Romance)
Fire, Fury, Faith (Book 1)
Heat, Hunt, Hope (Book 2)
Lies, Lust, Love (Book 3)

Death and Destiny Trilogy (Paranormal Romance)
Of Fear and Faith (Book 1)
Of Beasts and Bonds (Book 2)
Of Deception and Divinity (Book 3)
Death and Destiny: The Complete Series

Forever Yours Series (Fantasy Romance)
Bound Souls (Book 1)
Fated Path (Book 2)

Dragon Shifter Romance (Standalone Novels)
Stones of Dracontias: The Bloodstone Dragon
Dragon Lore and Love: Isis and Osiris

The Styles of Love Trilogy (Contemporary Romance)
The Perks of Higher Ed (Book 1)
The Wish of Xmas Present (Book 2)
The Gift of Second Chances (Book 3)
Rhythm and Blue Skies: Malcolm and Sky's Complete Story
The Styles of Love Trilogy: The Complete Series

Sins of the Sister (Dark Fantasy Short Story)

Fairy Tale Fatale Series (Urban Fantasy)
Crimson Hunter: A Red Riding Hood Reimagining

Feline Nation Duology (Urban Fantasy)
A Queen's Pride (Book 1)
Mafdet's Claws (Book 2)

ABOUT

USA TODAY BESTSELLING AUTHOR
N.D. JONES

N. D. Jones, Ed.D. is a USA Today bestselling author who lives in Maryland with her husband and two children. In her desire to see more novels with positive, sexy, and three-dimensional African American characters as soul mates, friends, and lovers, she took on that challenge herself. Along with the fantasy romance series Forever Yours, and a contemporary romance trilogy, The Styles of Love, she has authored three paranormal romance series: Winged Warriors, Death and Destiny, and Dragon Shifter Romance.